Thalia had
and settled
come along

She wanted to
She had the fe
through her, through to her vulnerable heart.
That he knew exactly the unsettling effect he
had upon her. And were he to discover her
secret, what use might he make of that knowledge? She shivered. The possibility did not
bear thinking about.

Sarah Westleigh has enjoyed a varied life. Working as a local government officer in London, she qualified as a chartered quantity surveyor. She assisted her husband in his chartered accountancy practice, at the same time managing an employment agency. Moving to Devon, she finally found time to write, publishing short stories and articles, before discovering historical novels.

Recent titles by the same author:

SEAFIRE
THE OUTRAGEOUS DOWAGER
FELON'S FANCY

A HIGHLY IRREGULAR FOOTMAN

Sarah Westleigh

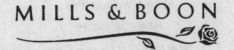

MILLS & BOON

*First published in Great Britain 1996
Harlequin Mills & Boon Limited,
Eton House, 18–24 Paradise Road, Richmond, Surrey TW9 1SR*

© Sarah Westleigh 1996

ISBN 0 263 80019 9

*Set in 10 on 12 pt Linotron Times
04-9702-77607*

*Typeset in Great Britain by CentraCet, Cambridge
Printed and bound in Great Britain
by BPC Paperbacks Limited, Aylesbury*

CHAPTER ONE

SEBASTIAN TOPE sat ensconced in an upright armchair in his overheated, over-stuffed bedroom. His bushy grey eyebrows drew together and his wrinkled lips pursed as he scrutinised the latest applicant for the vacant position of footman.

Thalia Marsh stood to one side, hands clasped at the waist of her sensible grey gown, a bunch of keys, symbol of her office, hanging at her hip. This was the third creature to answer her advertisement in the *Kentish Times* and, on the face of it, by far the most suitable.

'Think you can lift me, young man?' Mr Tope demanded abruptly of the strong, youthful figure standing deferentially before him.

'Aye, sir.'

'Then prove it. Help me up and over to the bed.'

Thalia watched the performance with critical eyes. Mr Tope's valet, Pringle, hovered anxiously about his master, his face sour. She knew how much he resented any intrusion into the cosy relationship he enjoyed with Mr Tope, but his puny frame could not cope with the disabilities of a heavy man crippled by a bad fall from a horse. Now that he was out of bed Mr Tope needed a sturdy arm to lean on. It had taken Pringle, Jenkins the elderly footman, Rose the parlour maid, and herself, to juggle Mr Tope into that chair.

'Told him he shouldn't've bin out riding, not at 'is

age,' Pringle muttered to no one in particular as he watched the young man heave Tope to his almost useless feet. Tope grunted and winced with pain, deepening the lines of suffering etched on his face; the fellow clasped him round the waist and half-carried him to the high bed where he sank down gratefully on its edge. The prospective footman gently lifted the crippled legs, turning the body so that Tope could lie back.

Stretched on the bed, his shoulders comfortably supported by several pillows, Sebastian Tope smiled for the first time.

'Began to think there weren't any respectable strong men left in England,' he muttered darkly. 'The only one I had here met up with a recruiting sergeant and got himself tricked into taking the King's shilling when he went into Sandwich on his day off. Thought I'd have to bring in one of the groundsmen, all yokels, the lot of 'em. What do they call you?'

'Jack 'amilton, sir.'

'Hamilton, eh? And what does a fine young fellow like you want with a job like this?'

Jack Hamilton shrugged his wide shoulders. 'I shall be fed, 'ave a roof over me 'ead, sir, live in a decent 'ousehold.'

This was the longest speech the fellow had made. Thalia frowned slightly. His gruff voice held an undertone of culture—the dropped aitches didn't quite fit.

'If you want food and somewhere to sleep, why not join the army, eh?'

'I did, sir, some years back. Discharged, I was, at the Peace. 'Ad enough of killin', sir, don't want to go back. But it ain't easy to make an honest livin', sir.'

'Hmm.' Tope, his shrewd old gaze fastened on the downcast eyes of Jack Hamilton, pursed his lips again. 'Can't say I blame you. Not a deserter, are you?' he suddenly barked.

'No, sir!' The cry was indignant.

Tope smiled again. 'Good. Where d'you come from?'

'North Kent, sir. Sevenoaks.'

'What's your age?'

'About six and twenty, if me ma's reckoning be right.'

He looked younger, though not much, for beneath his crop of fair curls his was the face of a man of hard experience.

'Very well. Fifteen pounds a year and all found. Wednesday and Sunday afternoons off, not tomorrow, though, won't have been here a day. You help me to move and attend me whenever I call, run errands on foot or on horseback—you can ride?' A nod from Hamilton satisfied him. 'And serve at table whenever I entertain, which ain't often. D'you want the job?'

'I'm very grateful, sir,' said Hamilton gravely.

Thalia, still watching, thought she saw some other emotion flick momentarily across the long face, undoubtedly handsome despite its aquiline nose and bushy, straw-coloured eyebrows. But when she met his eyes, all she saw was their peculiar colouring, amber next to the pupil, shading through blue and green and grey to a dark outer rim. They stared back at her guilelessly and she felt a strange reluctance to break off the contact.

'When can you start?'

He looked back to Tope. 'Immediately, sir, if that

would suit. Though I shall 'ave to collect me pack from the King's Arms in the village.'

Tope nodded. 'Put me back in my chair.'

With the manoeuvre executed with the minimum of fuss, Tope sighed his satisfaction. 'Aye, you'll do. Mrs Marsh'll look after you, she's in charge here, you'll obey her orders after mine. You do agree, Thalia, my dear?'

Thalia inclined her head, acutely conscious of the lack of a ring on her wedding finger. Mr Tope had used the courtesy title accorded to all housekeepers. 'Of course, Mr Tope.'

As she led the way from Sebastian Tope's room, with the new footman closing the door carefully behind them, Thalia firmed her lips, glad of the severity of her scraped-back hairstyle and of the white cap, plain but for the narrowest of frills, that she wore to cover her abundant brown hair.

Her outfit was one she thought necessary to her position in the house. It was difficult enough with the other servants but, to compensate for her lack of years, she would need all the added authority an austere appearance could afford her to keep this fellow in his place.

The impression was solidified when, on entering the housekeeper's office, she looked up to see irreverent humour dancing in his strange eyes.

'Not a bad old codger, is 'e?' he remarked confidentially.

Thalia stiffened. She held Sebastian Tope in some affection, which she knew was returned. The elderly bachelor had treated her with nothing but kindness and understanding and it was not on his orders that she kept so strictly to her position as housekeeper. She could so easily have slipped into the role of his daughter, mistress of the house, had her own sense of rectitude not prevented her taking advantage of his good nature.

'If you cannot show respect for your employer, you may take your leave, Hamilton. I have the power to dismiss you and shall not hesitate to use it.'

'I'm sorry, ma'am. No offence meant.' He gave her his most winning smile and all Thalia's hackles rose. Why did this indispensable young man have to remind her of that scoundrel Varley? It must be the fair curls, the air of irresponsibility, the irreverence that his remark had confirmed lay hidden beneath his outward show of deference when in the presence of Mr Tope. Varley had brought her to this; she needed no unpleasant reminders of his falsity to plague her every day.

But Mr Tope's needs must come before her own. While he required this fellow's strong arms she would put up with his presence in the house. But she'd see that he behaved. She sat behind her large desk and eyed the tall figure, neatly if poorly clad in rough brown breeches, woollen socks and a darker brown frock coat of indeterminate age.

'You'll need a uniform,' she told him. 'I might find one to fit. Otherwise, no doubt, Mr Tope will order one made for you.'

He inclined his head gravely. 'Yes, ma'am.'

'Jenkins, who has been with Mr Tope for years, will show you to the room in the servants' quarters that you will share with him, and explain the household routine,' she went on coldly. 'Then you may go and collect your things. Be back within the hour, if you please. Stonar village is a mere fifteen minutes walk.'

'Yes, ma'am, I know,' he answered deferentially. 'I walked here.'

Why did she think the deference assumed? She didn't know, she couldn't pin the reason down, for his face was deadpan, his voice subdued, yet something in his attitude told her he was not used to being in service. She supposed that, as part of the drunken scum which filled the ranks of the British army, he would not be. That gave her another idea.

'Mr Tope dines at four. You will be back in time to wheel him along to the dining-room in his invalid chair, and then you may help Rose and Jenkins to serve the meal.' That would tell her whether he had ever been a footman before. She rather doubted it, but he would quickly learn. He looked bright enough, too bright perhaps, not like drunken scum. But you couldn't tell what a man would be like once the drink got in him. She'd have to keep a sharp eye on Jack Hamilton.

She rang the bell and Jenkins presented himself. She introduced the two men and gave Jenkins his instructions.

'That will be all, Hamilton. I hope you will be happy here. By the way, try not to upset Pringle, Mr Tope's valet. He is devoted to his master.'

'I shall do me best, ma'am,' said Hamilton, bowing himself out of her presence, and Thalia thought that, whatever else he might or might not be, in that promise he was sincere.

* * *

With the lovely old Queen Anne mansion and its trim park behind him, Jack strode along the lane that led to the village, swinging a stout stick he had picked up, and whistling. Things couldn't have gone better, apart from the blunder he had made in trying to ingratiate himself with that tartar of a housekeeper.

He wondered how old she was. Not old enough to bear the responsibility of her job, he decided, which was why she was such a dry stick. Chits of girls, in his admittedly limited experience, left the running of their households to an older woman, but here was one of them trying to hold down a position which was too much for her. He'd have to tread carefully around the prickly Mrs Thalia Marsh if he wanted to keep his position and carry out his purpose.

She had dusky eyes, soft as velvet despite her attempts to harden them, and strands of silky brown hair had managed to escape her ridiculously prim cap. If she were to let it flow free and manage to smile, she would be quite passable-looking, he thought, grinning. When their eyes had met, hers had held dawning awareness. Mrs Thalia Marsh might be worth cultivating.

It had taken him ten minutes to follow the drive to the gates but only a further five to enter the village, where, at the far end, the sign of the King's Arms swung in the slight breeze coming from the sea. There'd been a view of the Channel from Stonar Hall but here in the village it was hidden, the coast some league away to the east.

He strolled down the street with lazy strides, ignoring the inquisitive stares of the older inhabitants, but smiling engagingly at a couple of young village maidens who blushed and giggled before retreating into the safety of a nearby cottage.

On entering the inn he called for two mugs of ale and went to join a man seated in a dark corner of the taproom. The man went to rise, but Jack waved him back into his seat.

''Ere's your ale.' The innkeeper plonked the brimming tankards on the table top, looking nervously at Jack's companion, whose dreadfully scarred face gave him a repulsive, evil look. 'Fair fit to scare the devil 'isself,' he muttered darkly as he held out his hand for Jack's silver.

'Isn't he,' agreed Jack as he paid, and his friend leered. 'So treat him kindly, landlord, or maybe the devil will get you.'

'I'm to stay 'ere, sir?' demanded the man once they were alone.

'Yes, Sidney, you are. I landed the job and I need you nearby.'

'Very well, sir,' muttered Barton gloomily. Then, suddenly, his distress burst from him. 'It's all right with them as I knows, sir, but strangers are that afeared o' me, it don't seem right.'

Jack pushed the man's mug closer. 'Drink up, Sidney. Ignore 'em. You got the wound fighting for the likes of them, the bastards, so don't let 'em see you care.'

'No, sir. You'll be going back, then, sir?'

'Aye, I've been given an hour,' said Jack with a rueful grin, then added, 'I'm to help serve dinner.'

Both men kept their voices low, although there was no one near enough to hear what they said.

Sidney Barton smiled, which twisted his poor face into an even more grotesque mask. 'I'd like to watch that, sir, that I would! What's the old man like?'

Jack hesitated. 'Not what I'd expected. He can't walk—injured himself riding.'

'Serve 'im right, then, don't it?'

'Maybe.' Jack frowned. 'But he seemed a decent fellow. Easy to please, I'd say. Not like the prim Mrs Marsh, the housekeeper. Proper tartar, she be.'

He'd slipped back into his rough speech and Barton grinned again. 'You'll manage her, sir, never known a lady you couldn't charm.'

Jack grinned. 'Thanks, my friend! Wearing my regimentals, perhaps!'

'Wish you still was, Major?'

'No, Sergeant, I do not! I have a different kind of battle to fight now,' said Jack rather grimly. 'And from now on you'd better remember to call me Jack or folks around here will begin to wonder. You've got my kit?'

'Aye, sir, right 'ere, sir.'

'Aye, Jack, right 'ere, Jack,' corrected Jack with a mock frown. 'Don't forget, Sid, or you'll give the game away. Have you booked a room yet?'

'Not yet.' Barton, finding himself unable to use Jack's name, called him nothing.

'Then do it the minute I'm gone, you've got the money. Frighten 'em into giving you one if necessary!'

'Aye. . Jack.' Barton grinned. 'Me looks can come in 'andy sometimes!'

'That's the spirit!' Jack stood up, drained his mug and stooped to collect his belongings from the corner behind Barton. 'I'll be in to see you on Wednesday afternoon, if not before. Being at everyone's beck and call, I may be sent into the village on an errand. Meanwhile, just keep your eyes and ears open.'

Barton nodded. 'Good luck. . .Jack.'

With an old army pack slung on his shoulder, Jack strode off to his new employment.

He arrived back in his shared room to find blue breeches and waistcoat, white stockings and frilled shirt, and a silver-grey frock coat with blue facings and silver lace and buttons, all laid out on the thin mattress of his iron bedstead. Beside them lay a grey, powdered wig. His hand-me-down uniform for formal occasions! Beside these splendid garments lay a more sombre black and grey uniform for normal wear. The question was, did they fit?

With a chuckle, he laid his pack aside, stripped off the serviceable garments bought from a pawnshop in Sevenoaks, and began to don those of his servitude. Since he was supposed to be waiting at table he'd better appear in full fig. The things fitted better than he'd thought they might—one of his predecessors must have been a large man, too. He combed his unruly crop of fair curls before covering them with the wig, grimacing slightly as he noticed its greasy lining.

No one would recognise him in this outfit, he thought, peering into the small tarnished mirror hung on the wall opposite the attic window. It reflected the light so that his image was little more than a dark silhouette. Unlikely as it was that Sebastian Tope would entertain anyone acquainted with him, one nevertheless never knew, and the unfamiliar sight of himself in the powdered wig was reassuring.

A gong reverberated through the house and he guessed that meant he should present himself down on the first floor, which held the master suite and all the other main rooms, the drawing-room, dining-room and library among them.

The housekeeper's and all other offices and service rooms, including the kitchen, were on the ground floor; as he descended from the attics by one of the two sets of service stairs—the one which debouched on the main landing by Tope's bedroom—he peered along the passageway of the second floor where nurseries—long disused—and guest rooms were located. The housekeeper had her private suite on this floor, too.

He tapped softly on Sebastian Tope's door, which was opened by Pringle.

'There you are!' said the valet irritably. 'You should've bin in the servants' hall, ready to answer the master's bell!'

'I was changing,' said Jack mildly, indicating his person, gorgeously arrayed in the once-splendid uniform.

'Quite right, too,' came Tope's voice from his chair. 'Let's have a look at you.'

Jack stepped into a room which, facing south and east, was lit by the slanting glow of a late July sun already beginning to sink round to the west.

'Hmm,' muttered Tope, his eyes remarkably bright beneath his beetling brows. 'Suits you. Does it fit?'

'Well enough, sir,' said Jack. 'The breeches and the shoulders of the coat are a little tight but they'll do.'

'They'll do for now, anyway. Help me into that damned contraption.'

The contraption was a wooden armchair to which wheels had been added. Pushing handles had been attached to the back and Jack used them to bring it near the other chair. Tope clung to Jack's shoulders as the young man reached out to lift him under his arms, and sighed his satisfaction as he settled in the wheelchair.

'You'll have to help Pringle get me up and put me to bed. Not the valeting bit,' he hastened to add, 'just to lift me about. I'm too much for him now. Hate it!' he suddenly muttered as Jack began to push him towards the door. 'Being dependent. Just pray you never lose the use of your legs, m'boy.'

'Yes, sir,' said Jack, thinking of the times he'd overcome the fear of death or mutilation and somehow escaped both.

To reach the dining-room, situated above the kitchens in the coolest corner of the house, Jack had to wheel the chair across the landing and through the music room and the drawing-room, both of which went from back to front of the house.

Entering the latter, two doors faced him, one to the library on the west face of the house and another to the dining-room on the east, both rooms projecting into a small wing back and front, as did the master suite at the other end of the house.

Sebastian Tope had lavished quite a sum of money on refurbishing the place, Jack noted as he passed through the rooms. He wondered who had been responsible for renovating with such good taste. No expense spared, Tope had probably employed a top architect to do the job, though it didn't look like Adam's work. Yet Tope did not go in for ostentation; he did not flaunt his wealth as did some of the City's *nouveaux-riches*—and most of the ancient nobility, he acknowledged to himself wryly.

Jack wheeled Sebastian Tope to the head of the table and placed the chock provided under the wheel of the chair to stop it from moving.

The dishes were already set upon the table: a tureen of soup for the remove, glazed ham, baked fish, a couple of jugged pigeons, a bowl of peas, another of fried sallary, and a bean pudding—far too much for one man to eat and there was the second course to follow!

Jack's mouth began to water. He had missed the dinner served to the servants, at noon, so Jenkins had informed him. The pie he had eaten at the King's Arms before setting out for his interview seemed remote. He was hungry. He wondered who would consume the remains of the master's meal.

Mrs Marsh was there, not to eat with the master but to supervise the serving of the meal. A parlour maid stood by her side. Now he had finished carrying in the dishes, Jenkins was standing back grinning, waiting for the new footman to make a fool of himself. Mrs Marsh's attention had been momentarily diverted by the need to flick a fly away from the decanters on the side table behind her. The maid was unashamedly eyeing him up and down. Jack winked. She blushed and giggled.

Thalia spun round but too late to see anything but a grave Hamilton ladling out a portion of soup for Mr Tope. She glanced grimly from his deferential back to the girl's pink face and seethed inwardly. The creature was up to something, even were it only the seduction of the parlour maid, and he looked likely to succeed. She decided to deal with the situation with a firm hand.

'Go to the kitchen, Rose. See if Cook is ready with the mutton. Wait there until you can report that she is, and I'll send Hamilton to fetch it.'

'Yes, ma'am. I could bring it myself—'

'I want to see how the new footman executes his duties. Just come back and tell me.'

'Yes, ma'am.'

Rose dipped a bob and disappeared through the door screening the service stairs leading to the kitchen. Hamilton, standing behind his master's chair as Sebastian Tope consumed his soup, stared impassively ahead, apparently gazing at a portrait on the wall above her head.

It had come with the house, Mr Tope had told her, and was of the previous owner's wife. Her husband's portrait hung over the mantel in the drawing room. Both had been painted in about 1770 by Thomas Gainsborough, and the style of the clothes confirmed the period. There must have been money in the Earl of Eardley's coffers at that time.

Tope emptied his glass of claret and Hamilton refilled it. Tope finished his soup and pushed his plate away. Thalia moved silently forward.

'Jenkins will deal with the tableware. Do you take the soup tureen back to the kitchen, Hamilton, and return with the mutton.'

'Yes, ma'am.'

Rose had not returned to say the dish was ready yet,

but it must be. The girl was probably gossiping with Mrs Gale, the cook, a woman in her mid-forties, no more wed than Thalia was herself.

Hamilton and a breathless Rose met in the doorway, Rose almost knocking the tureen from the footman's grasp as she sped back with her message.

'Take care!' snapped Thalia sharply, dreading the cascade of soup which would ruin both servants' clothes and leave a mess on the carpet.

'Whoops!' cried Hamilton with a laugh and by some miracle of dextrous juggling saved the soup and avoided disaster.

Jack gave Rose another wink, unseen by the house-keeper, and hurried downstairs to the kitchen. He had not yet met the cook.

''Amilton, new footman,' he introduced himself to Mrs Gale and sundry kitchen and scullery maids, a boot boy, and men he imagined must be stable and ground staff. Since they were gathering in the kitchen, perhaps there was a meal in the offing. The warmth in the room was almost overpowering, but through it all came the tempting aromas of cooking, that of roast mutton overwhelming the rest.

But he was devilish hungry! He flashed his winning smile at Mrs Gale, who had a huge platter before her on which rested a large, glistening shoulder of mutton and the baked suet pudding which had been cooked in its fat.

'Fair makes yer mouth water, don't it?' he said, nodding at the joint.

''Ungry, are you?' said the large woman, with a

comfortable chuckle. 'Supper's at six. 'Ere, 'ave one o' my cakes to keep you goin'.'

'Cook, you're an angel,' declared Jack, picking up a delicious fruit bun and eating it in two quick bites. 'Thank you.'

'I'm Mrs Gale,' the cook introduced herself. 'You'll meet the rest of these scoundrels at supper. You'd best hurry or you'll 'ave Mrs Marsh after you.'

Jack raised his eyes heavenwards. 'What a tartar!'

'She ain't so bad. Now, get along with you, you impudent devil!'

Cook's tone had cooled. Jack gave her a disarming smile as he picked up the hot platter and prepared to mount the stairs, cursing himself for another misjudgment of the relationships within this household. He'd best keep his tongue to himself, he decided, as he took the stairs two at a time. He emerged into the dining-room to walk in dignified majesty towards Mr Tope, who watched his approach with barely-concealed amusement.

He set the mutton down where the soup had been. Tope's plate was already filled with portions of other dishes on the table.

'Shall I carve the meat, sir?'

'Aye, do. I don't like the fat, except the crisp outside.'

'Very well, sir.'

Jack began to carve, thanking his stars that he'd learned to cut up a joint, with his sword if necessary, when on campaign.

He slipped the knife under the skin, peeled it off and removed the thick wedge of fat which lay beneath. Then he began to cut succulent slices of flesh and lay them on Tope's plate.

'That is not the way to carve a shoulder of mutton,' came an icy voice from behind him.

He straightened up. 'Really, ma'am? Is there some other way?'

'Cut towards the bone, Hamilton, not across the top of the meat—'

'Thalia, my dear, do not concern yourself with the niceties of correct carving. Hamilton has given me slices of meat I can eat without having to fiddle with the fat. Leave him be, Mrs Marsh.'

It was a mild reproof, but a reproof nevertheless. Thalia bridled and flushed but bowed her head in acceptance. 'Very well, Mr Tope.'

She'd known the creature would disrupt the household, try to usurp her place in Sebastian Tope's regard. She shared a fellow feeling with Pringle, who was wandering round wearing a hang-dog air.

'Thank you, Hamilton, that will be sufficient,' said Sebastian Tope as Jack placed another slice of meat on his plate. 'Just a little of the crisp skin, if you please, and I'll take a portion of the baked suet pudding.'

Dinner was by no means over. When Mr Tope had finished his first course, some of the dishes were taken away and others brought up to replace them. This time there was potted venison, whole salmon in pastry, fried celery and a selection of tartlets, both sweet and savoury. There was a fruit syllabub, a spectacular pink blancmange covered in some glistening fruit sauce, and a jam roly-poly. Sebastian Tope, who liked his puddings, finished with the roly-poly.

'Excellent, my dear,' he told Thalia as the footmen and Rose cleared the table, drew the cloth and set fresh decanters of wine and spirits and bowls of fruit on the polished mahogany. 'Congratulate Mrs Gale for me.'

'Certainly, sir.'

'And Hamilton did quite well, don't you think?'

'Quite well, sir, but I doubt he's ever waited at table before.'

'Of course he hasn't! I'm not a fool, my dear. But he's just what I need and he learns fast. He'll do.'

'Yes, Mr Tope,' said Thalia reluctantly. She couldn't voice her unease to Mr Tope, she had no reason for it. Yet for some reason she could not explain, Jack Hamilton seemed to pose a threat to both her peace of mind and to Sebastian Tope's well-being.

Jack, coming back to attend Mr Tope in case he should be needed, saw Mrs Marsh leave by the other door.

She'd suffered a defeat and it served her right. She didn't like him, and Jack was not used to being disliked. Her icy indifference ignited a response deep inside him. He vowed that, come what may, Mrs Thalia Marsh, who hid a delectable body beneath her frightful gown, would eventually lie in his bed.

CHAPTER TWO

SEEING Hamilton return, Thalia retreated from the
dining-room as speedily as possible without surrender-
ing her dignity. Mr Tope had not meant to humiliate
her, she felt certain, but that did not reduce her
mortification at the way he had championed the new
footman.

She normally had no trouble at all with servants; she
had been brought up to accept their presence in the
household and to keep them in their places. Her father
was a stickler for that and, for all her loathing of him,
his training, moderated by her own judgement, had
stood her in good stead so far. Mr Tope had never
criticised her direction of his minions before.

But she had never before felt the need to keep a
footman in his place. As she ate a lonely supper of Mr
Tope's leftovers in the privacy of her sitting-room, she
wondered why it was that, from the very first sight of
him, she had wanted to keep Hamilton out of the house.

He had an unsettling effect upon her, partly, she
supposed, because he reminded her a little of Lord
Varley, but it was more than that. His very presence in
a room made her nerves twitch. She supposed this
strange reaction would go away in time, once she was
used to his proximity and had imposed her authority,
but meanwhile it irked her dreadfully.

She wondered how he was fitting into the servants'

hall, a room off the kitchen where the indoor staff
gathered to wait for orders and where all but the
married outdoor employees with estate cottages and
families to return to, ate their meals and socialised.

She could imagine them sitting round the long deal
table that ran down the centre of the dark, plainly
furnished room where Cook and Jenkins presided. She
could have taken her meals with the rest of them, sitting
at the head of the table, but preferred to eat apart, not
to be drawn into intimacy with the under-staff. Not
because she felt it beneath her dignity, but because she
feared their discovering her secret.

Pringle, too, ate alone, but Cook, a gregarious
woman, liked the company. Hamilton, judging from his
effect upon Rose, should have no trouble ingratiating
himself. Unless, of course, he made some of the male
staff jealous of his success with the maids. She just knew
he was going to disturb the even tenor of the household.
How she wished him at Jericho!

The sudden vexation which swept over her at thought
of him laughing, joking and flirting with them all, made
her reach down for her bunch of keys. Lifting the white
cloth which covered its inlaid surface, she unlocked a
drawer in the Pembroke table, took out a silver-framed
miniature and set it amongst her supper dishes.

Her eyes misted as she studied the likeness of the
child thus revealed. It might not be a particularly good
painting, but having it eased Thalia's loneliness. She
put out a finger and lightly touched the yellow rep-
resenting fair ringlets surrounding the child's face. Miss
Wright had caught the mischievous expression which so

often lit Fanny's features even if the nose was too snub and the chin too pointed.

Not for the first time she wondered whether she had been fair to Fanny when she'd chosen to make her own way in the world rather than wed a man she loathed. Had she married Lord Stimson, she would have been mistress of a lavish establishment and Fanny surrounded by luxury. But the earl had offered for her because he assumed her pregnancy would result in a boy child, an heir, while, in fact, she had produced an unwanted daughter.

She would, she supposed, have been expected to conduct a discreet *affaire* and become pregnant again by some other man, since Stimson had never managed to sire even an illegitimate child himself. He would not have cared how many lovers she had, who the father was, as long as she remained careful of her reputation, for he needed an heir to carry on his tarnished name and inherit all his estates and riches.

Thalia had known she could not do it. Her one experience of intimacy, although enjoyed outside the bonds of marriage, had been a fraught, painful episode, unsatisfactory. And as for Lord Stimson—a shudder shook her even now at the thought. In theory, she need never have occupied her husband's bed. In fact, she guessed he would have insisted on exercising his marital rights simply to dominate her. And by what she'd heard of his tastes, she would by now have been petrified for Fanny's sake.

Her father had refused to countenance any of her arguments for declining to wed Stimson rather than bear the ignominy of giving birth to a bastard. He had thrown her out rather than have his name dishonoured.

'You have a choice, miss!' Sir Gilbert had thundered. 'You may go abroad, bear the child, have it adopted and return here and hope to find a husband you find more congenial, or you may wed Lord Stimson—the only earl, I fancy, who would stoop to wed a mere baronet's daughter. What chance would I stand of being elevated to the peerage with a disgraced daughter in the house and a bastard grandchild under my feet?'

Thalia remembered the panic which had threatened to overwhelm her. His choices were both impossible! 'I could not abandon my child,' she had protested.

'Then you will wed Lord Stimson!'

'No, Papa, I cannot. Would you truly condemn me to a life with that...that gross, slobbering roué? Please, Papa, I was foolish, I admit, to trust Lord Varley, but he had your approval—'

'As a suitor, miss, not as a lover! You should have kept your maidenhead!'

Thalia stirred uncomfortably at memory of her father's crudity. She had pleaded desperately with Lord Varley to wait, at least until their engagement had been officially announced, but he had continued to press her to prove her love and in the end her resistance had crumbled. She recognised afterwards how cleverly he had planned the encounter, presenting himself at a time when he knew both her parents would be out and bribing a footman to bring him straight up to her room.

Her hand had been on the bell-pull to summon her maid when he'd grasped her wrist.

'We are soon to be betrothed, Thalia!' he'd protested,

mocking her prudery. 'You surely do not think it unseemly for us to spend a few moments alone together?'

Smiling his disarming smile, he had removed her hand from the tasselled velvet and led her to sit with him on her day bed.

It had not quite been rape, for he had roused her with his practised tricks, but his taking of her had definitely been against her true will and she had never regretted anything so much as making that reluctant surrender.

And then Patrick had disappeared. A hot flush flooded through her at the memory of her humiliation, her shame, as she had come to realise that he had sampled what she had to offer and found her wanting.

With her father, for the first time in her life, she had stood her ground, determined never to be weak again now she had something to fight for. 'I will not give up my child and I will not wed Lord Stimson!' she had declared vehemently.

'Then you may leave my house, miss! You are no longer a daughter of mine. You need not look to me for your support.'

Her mother, always terrified of her husband's temper, had been helpless against his wrath and her brother, Arthur, had been away at Oxford. Not that he would have been much help—he was too much under his father's thumb and had ignored her since. She had not known what to do, who to turn to, until she remembered Miss Wright, her old governess.

She had gathered together as many of her possessions as she could pack into a trunk and an overnight bag, begged her mother for money for her fare, and taken the stage to Canterbury. From there she had travelled by carter's dray to Asham.

Emily Wright, living in the village in genteel retirement, had taken her in without a word of reproof and had looked after both her and the baby until Thalia had felt strong enough to seek work. The vacancy at the beautiful old Stonar Hall, advertised eighteen months after Fanny's birth, had appeared providential.

Mr Tope had taken to her at once. Although she had confessed her true situation and despite her youth and lack of experience, he had taken her on as his housekeeper. He'd been glad to have a young lady of her consequence to run his household, Thalia wryly acknowledged. But the position suited her. The number of indoor staff required to look after one elderly gentleman was not large and she had quickly gained in confidence.

She returned the miniature to the drawer and locked it away. One of the housemaids would come to bring her tea-tray and clear her table before long, and must not see it. Thalia guarded her secret fiercely. The rest of the staff would lose all respect for her if they ever discovered that she had a bastard child.

Thalia padded across the carpet to the damask-draped window. A comfortable armchair faced east through the long window. Sitting there, she could see in the distance the pale gleam of golden sand, the shimmer of the sea, colours muted now that the sun had died. Tomorrow afternoon, it being Sunday, she would be seeing Fanny again. Her heart lifted at the thought. She would enjoy the ten-mile walk, five miles there and five back again.

Her mother, having begun by bestowing the money for her fare, had afterwards sent money from her own allowance to help Thalia provide for Fanny, doing it through the kind offices of a dear friend, Lady Wharton.

Lady Marsh sometimes sent a letter and Thalia wrote back care of the same friend, for Sir Gilbert read all the correspondence arriving at the house for his wife, who was petrified of his discovering her deceit. So, although a little news was exchanged, they could never meet. Grateful as she was to her mother for her continued concern and support, Fanny and Emily Wright were her family now.

Almost all the staff were free on Sunday afternoons after attending the church service in the village in the morning. Mr Tope, a regular worshipper himself, took note of any absentees. Going to church was the one thing he was unbendingly insistent upon.

'Country's becoming ungodly,' he'd explained his inflexibility to Thalia. 'Can't have it. Got to counter all this Jacobin nonsense. See that everyone attends church regular. Mr Wyndham will put some sense into their heads!'

Thalia only wished the vicar would, but his sermons were so long-winded and erudite that those of his congregation who did not drop off to sleep chatted and giggled amongst themselves in the back pews. Better him, she supposed, than someone who preached hellfire and damnation and frightened them all to death. But a nice, sensible sermon that everyone could understand would have been preferable.

After this week Hamilton would have Sunday afternoons off, like the rest of them. Pringle, Jenkins and a
senior kitchen maid were the only servants left in
attendance on Sebastian Tope on the Lord's day. Thalia
wondered how Hamilton would enjoy attending church
with Mr Tope and what he would do during his time
off. Dally with one or other of the maids, she guessed
sourly. Or go into Stonar village and get drunk in the
company of a groom or groundsman. Maybe both.

Even as the thoughts passed through her head, she
knew she was being unfair. Hamilton was undoubtedly
a flirt, but he did not have the look of a man sunk in
depravity. Neither did he have the look of a man used
to servitude, she reminded herself. He, she knew
instinctively, could not be bribed as her father's footman had been.

Damn the man! She had better things to do than
worry about the creature simply because his presence
annoyed her. He would turn out to be harmless enough,
she assured herself, and welcomed the diversion caused
by a housemaid bringing in her tea-tray.

On the way to Church next day, Hamilton sat up on the
box of Mr Tope's elderly coach beside Ben Treddle, the
coachman, while Thalia rode inside with Mr Tope. The
new footman had handed her into the carriage with
grave attention and then turned back to lift Tope into
the seat beside her. Even for him that had been a
struggle and Jenkins had helped to heave his master
into the vehicle before mounting the step to stand up
behind.

Both footmen wore their black and grey uniforms

with tall black silk hats. Hamilton's suited him excep-
tionally well, perhaps because he wore it at such a
rakish angle.

At the church, as he pushed Tope in his chair and she
walked beside it, she glanced up at him.

'You need to straighten your hat, Hamilton.'

His strange eyes gleamed down, seeking hers under
the brim of her chip bonnet. 'Do I, Mrs Marsh? I'll see
to it in a moment.'

Whenever she dared to turn and take a surreptitious
look during the service his face looked grave; he
appeared to be attending to the sermon. He sang the
hymns in a strong tenor voice that floated forward from
several rows behind, on the other side of the aisle, to
drown her own rather weak soprano and Sebastian
Tope's breathless baritone. The fact that he was so
obviously enjoying the singing annoyed her.

In the porch afterwards, Sebastian Tope, against all
the rules of polite society, introduced Hamilton to the
vicar. But then, much as she admired her employer,
Thalia recognised that he had not been born a gentleman. Usually, the easy relationship he enjoyed with his
staff endeared him to her, however unsuitable his
attitude might be considered in first circles. But for
some reason, at that moment, it did not.

'This is Jack Hamilton, Vicar, new member of my
staff and of your flock.' Tope chuckled. 'Lifts me about
like a baby!'

Hamilton gave a deprecating smile and touched his
hat, now sitting severely straight across his brow. 'Mr
Tope is a fine man to work for, sir.'

The Reverend Wyndham seemed unperturbed by the

irregular introduction. 'Glad you're happy at Stonar Hall, my boy, glad you're happy! Welcome to the village. Anything I can do. . .'

'Thank you, sir,' said Hamilton hastily. 'I'll be sure to ask if I need help or guidance.'

Hypocrite! thought Thalia, almost laughing. She could not imagine Hamilton needing the withered Mr Wyndham's assistance under any circumstances! Meanwhile, Mrs Wyndham was demanding her attention on some question to do with the village fête, due to be held in mid-August.

As they left the churchyard Hamilton held open the coach door for her.

'Thank you, Hamilton, but I shall not be returning to Stonar Hall. I have the afternoon off, like almost everyone else.'

'Of course, ma'am, but I thought you'd be taking dinner first? Like almost everyone else?'

Thalia shook her head, ignoring the impertinence implied by the fellow's last remark. 'I eat with the friend I visit. Do you wish for assistance with the master?'

'Jenkins is 'ere, ma'am. 'E'll help if necessary.'

He'd remembered to drop his aitches this time. Thalia smiled thinly. 'Then I'll leave you to your duties, Hamilton. I'll just collect my basket from the coach first.'

'Yes, ma'am,' he said gravely. She wished she hadn't noticed the mocking expression in his eyes.

'Mama! Mama!' Fanny rushed at her mother and clasped her round the knees, burying her bright head in the folds of Thalia's sprigged muslin gown.

'Hello, my love. Let me put my basket down.'

Fanny reluctantly backed off, hopping with excitement, watched while Thalia set the basket of food down on the brick path and then, with her mother's arms freed, held out her own to be picked up.

She would soon be too heavy to be lifted, thought Thalia, as, Fanny's sturdy legs splayed round her hips, she held her daughter close and received her smothering kisses. But until she was, she would continue to enjoy Fanny's version of an exuberant, loving welcome.

Emily Wright, a slender, still upright figure in pale blue, emerged from the front door to walk between riotous, lavender-edged beds of forget-me-nots, gillyflowers, Sweet William, clarkia, stocks and cornflowers, to pick up Thalia's basket. Behind her, roses, wisteria and clematis climbed the cottage's whitewashed walls.

She smiled, her eyes bright, her grey head nodding slightly. 'How are you, my dear?'

Thalia put Fanny down and kissed her old governess. 'I'm fine, dear Emily.' Thalia's need and Emily's instant acceptance of her into her home had broken down the barriers of formality between them and made them friends. 'And you look to be in full bloom, like so many of your flowers! I would never have guessed, when you had me penned in the schoolroom all those years ago, that you would have such a talent for gardening!'

Emily smiled again. 'All I lacked was the opportunity, my dear Thalia. I'm glad you like it.'

'I helped weed!' cried Fanny, 'Didn't I, Aunt Wright?'

'You were a great help, Fanny. And now, you'd

better come inside and see what Mama has brought for us today!'

'Oh, yes! Is there any cake, Mama?'

'Let's have a look.'

Mr Tope had given orders that Mrs Marsh was to be allowed to take any spare food to her friend when she visited. Mrs Gale was glad enough to supply a basket of leftovers twice a week, knowing it was going to a good home, as she put it. She did not know that Fanny existed, so there was nothing special for a small girl. But Emily was an excellent cook herself and Fanny did not lack for treats.

Today, Cook had packed the remains of the ham, an opened pot of venison, several tartlets and half a fruit cake. Tucked in amongst it all were four freshly baked rolls.

'This can go to the birds,' remarked Emily of a stale crust of bread. 'Run along and feed them, Fanny.'

'Can I have a slice of cake?'

'Later, after you've fed the birds and we have eaten our dinner. When I make the tea.'

Fanny, disappointed but resigned, ran out into the back garden and Thalia watched as her daughter broke up the bread and threw it on the tiny patch of grass. Any birds kept a judicious distance.

'She's growing up so fast,' she sighed.

'Yes, dear, children do. This will help the budget,' remarked Emily as she put the ham and potted venison in the meat safe and closed the mesh door.

'Are you short?' Thalia turned from watching Fanny to ask anxiously. 'Mama hasn't sent me an allowance just recently, but I have a little saved. I can let you have some extra—'

Agitated, Emily flushed. 'My dear girl, I was only joking! What a thoughtless remark for me to make! I can manage very well on my savings and what you give me for Fanny's keep—never think otherwise! But there's no denying that I could not afford most of the more expensive things that you bring with you when you come!'

'But you will let me know if you are ever in need? Promise?'

'I promise, Thalia. But I manage very nicely, and I can afford to keep Peggy to help me.' Emily's face, remarkably free of wrinkles, wreathed into a wry smile. 'I confess that Fanny can be a handful at times. I am very glad of Peggy's assistance.'

'She'll be back to put Fanny to bed?' asked Thalia wistfully. She would have to leave long before her child's bedtime, for even at a brisk pace it took her a good hour and a half to walk back to Stonar Hall. It was the thing she missed most, the tending of her daughter. Yet she had much to be grateful for. She saw her twice a week, could watch her grow, knew the child was happy and cared for by good, loving hands.

She always left in time to be home in daylight, even in the winter, when the early onset of darkness made her visits brief. But, unless it was raining, snowing or blowing a gale, she always came.

That day she did leave it rather late, but the sun had sunk in a warm glow which left the sky brighter than usual, so it was still quite light when she reached Stonar village and began the final stretch to the Hall, looking forward to a late supper despite the satisfying meal she had eaten earlier. The walk always made her hungry.

The King's Arms was doing good business, she noted as she approached, sounds of cheerful shouting and laughter coming from the taproom. The doorway darkened and two men emerged, one of whom she recognised on the instant.

Hamilton! Wearing the clothes he'd arrived in. What was he doing in the village this evening? And who was that villainous-looking creature he was conversing with so earnestly? They looked thick as thieves and Thalia instinctively slowed her steps. What was Hamilton up to, consorting with a man who looked as though he should be hanging in chains at the nearest crossroads? It could not be anything good, on that she'd take her oath.

She did not wish to meet him so she slipped into the inn's yard and tapped on the back door. She was acquainted with the landlady, Mrs Cracker, who supplied the Hall with eggs, as her husband supplied it with ale.

'Why, Mrs Marsh!' cried Mrs Cracker on opening the door. 'What a surprise. Come you inside fer a minnit. 'Tisn't often you come around 'ere of a Sunday!'

'I was passing, Mrs Cracker, and we're a little short of eggs. Have you a dozen I could take in my basket?'

'Aye, that I 'ave, ma'am. Give it 'ere.' The landlady went to a crock in the corner of a kitchen overheated by the necessary cooking fires, picked out the eggs and handed the basket back to Thalia.

'Thank you. Mrs Cracker, I just saw an evil-looking

creature leave the taproom. I've not seen him about before. Who is he?'

'I hasn't been in there just recent, but I 'spects you means a fellow called Barton. He's staying 'ere awhiles. 'Is looks fair puts the fear of the Lord into you, doesn't they?'

'He gives me the creeps! He looks like a murderer at the very least!'

'Well, he ain't done nuffink wrong so far. Quiet sort of chap, for all 'is 'orrible looks. 'Ere, if he's the fellow I fink you means, he's friendly with that chap as you took on up at the 'all. Arrived together, they did.'

'Really? Well, thanks for the eggs, Mrs Cracker. Put them on the account.'

'That I will, ma'am. Is the old gentleman well?'

'He's still in pain, but otherwise he is.'

Thalia took her leave and emerged cautiously into the street. The two men had gone and she hoped Hamilton would be far enough ahead—he must be going back to Stonar Hall—for her to avoid running into him.

She peered through the small taproom window as she passed, but could see nothing clearly, just a crowd of unidentifiable heads. There was no sign of Hamilton ahead of her on the road. She breathed a sigh of relief. He could not have lingered talking for long.

As she passed the end of the building a figure stepped out and began to walk beside her. Her heart skipped a beat, then began to race.

'Evenin', Mrs Marsh, ma'am.' Hamilton touched the brim of his battered hat. No shining black silk tonight. 'Thought as 'ow I saw you going into the yard, ma'am, and wondered if I could escort you 'ome. 'Tis getting mortal dark.'

It was dusk, but she'd be home before true darkness fell.

'Thank you, Hamilton, but I shall be perfectly all right. You will no doubt wish to walk faster than me.'

She began to move on. His voice came after her.

'Not at all, ma'am. It'll be my pleasure to keep a few paces be'ind you, ma'am.'

She'd have to be really rude to shake the fellow off. And his stalwart presence behind did give a surprising sense of security. As her heartbeat slowed she strode on at a steady pace, all too aware of the firm footsteps following.

Before long the silence stretching between them began to irk her. Annoyance grew into uneasiness and uneasiness into alarm. There were only the two of them on an otherwise deserted road. The sense of security vanished. It was years since she'd walked the dangerous London streets with a footman in attendance, a trusted footman who had been with the family for years. She did not know Hamilton. Something about him continued to cause her grave disquiet.

She'd feel safer with him beside her, where he couldn't jump her from behind. She stopped, turned, and waved him forward.

'There's no need for you to follow behind me, Hamilton. I'm only the housekeeper, not your mistress.'

'If you say so, ma'am.'

Thalia caught the suppressed laughter in his voice and realised her mistake. Her colour rose. Trust the abominable creature to find a *double entendre* where none had been intended!

Ignoring her faux pas, she resumed her progress and Hamilton obediently walked at her side, adjusting his steps to hers. As her agitation subsided, Thalia decided to question him about the scarred man, but not directly. She would be more subtle.

'I assume Mr Tope gave you permission to leave Stonar Hall?'

'Aye, ma'am. He said as 'ow he wouldn't be needing me again until 'is bedtime, ma'am.'

'You missed supper?'

'I 'ad something at the King's 'ead. And Mrs Gale'll rush something up at bedtime.'

'I see.' She could not quite eliminate all the sarcasm from her voice. 'You've learnt her ways quickly, Hamilton.'

'Me name's Jack, ma'am. Couldn't you call me Jack, when I'm off duty, like?'

'No, Hamilton, I could not! No more nonsense, now! I may not be your employer—' how she wished she'd used that word earlier '—but I am your superior. You've not been here much more than a day and already you're taking advantage.'

He gave her a disarming smile which softened his features and took years off his age. She felt her heart lurch and mentally shook herself. The creature was using his undoubted charm to bamboozle her.

'Sorry, Mrs Marsh, I didn't mean to. I just like to be friendly.'

Thalia had only one defence against that charm. Her

authority. 'You must learn to keep your place,' she told him severely.

'Yes, ma'am.'

He did not sound as subdued as his words implied. She waited a few moments, regaining her ruffled composure, before asking, 'Did you find the villagers friendly?'

'Some were, some weren't,' said Jack neutrally.

'But you found someone to talk to?'

'Oh yes, ma'am. Lots of people like to chat.'

Thalia lifted her fine arching brows. 'To gossip, you mean!'

He grinned. 'Well, yes, I suppose you would call it gossip, ma'am!'

'And did you learn anything of interest?'

'Not as I could tell *you*, ma'am.'

Impudent devil! 'No enlivening *on-dits*?' she enquired sweetly.

He glanced at her strangely. 'Er...I don't know, ma'am.' He shrugged. 'I don't know what an "ondee" is.'

'Scandal, Hamilton, scandal. But I forgot, you've been in the army, not in service, where you might hear your betters speak of such things.'

'Very true, ma'am.'

In the half-light she couldn't be certain, but she suspected he was amused by her condescension. He was not only impudent, but a devious devil. She'd tried to probe and he'd turned the tables on her. She had revealed a knowledge of society she would have done better to keep hidden.

* * *

Sebastian Tope was delighted with his new footman.

'Superior fellow, my dear,' he informed Thalia when she presented herself to read to him a few days later. Mr Tope's eyesight was not what it had been and besides, as he told her frequently, he preferred to have things read to him, provided the reader was proficient and put meaning into the words. She, apparently, read extremely well.

He had the London papers sent down. Thalia had learned much of what went on in the world whilst reading them to Mr Tope. They arrived out of date, but any important item of news, of victory or defeat, of peace or war, was relayed by the mail coaches and spread quickly across the countryside. The Peace Treaty with France had been signed at Amiens, on the first day of October in 1801. The Peace of Amiens had lasted just over eighteen months. When war was renewed on the eighteenth day of May in 1803, the news had reached them within four and twenty hours.

'Yes.' Thalia had to agree with Mr Tope's judgment of Hamilton. 'Too superior,' she added forcibly. 'It won't be long before he gets above himself.'

Sebastian Tope regarded her with amused eyes. 'You don't like the fellow, Thalia?'

'Not much. He's too forward for my liking.'

'I can't fault the way he does his job. Can you?'

'No,' admitted Thalia reluctantly. 'He does everything asked of him quickly and well. He makes an excellent footman. But he isn't one.'

'Well, neither are any of 'em before they start!'

'At home,' said Thalia, 'they started off as bootboys, rose to be doorboys and were then trained up to become under-footmen. Either that, or they came with references from another employer. Hamilton had no references.'

'You think I shouldn't have taken him on?'

'Not exactly. You needed a strong man. But be careful, Mr Tope. You are too trusting.'

'I've been used to judging people all my life, my dear. I agree with you up to a point. Hamilton is not all he seems. But he's honest, on that I'd take my oath. So, whatever his reason for taking this job, I still trust him.'

Thalia relaxed and smiled. 'As long as you're happy, sir, and are aware of the dangers. I'd forgotten how used you were to dealing with all kinds of people in your days as a banker in the City.'

'If I hadn't been a good judge of character and up to all the tricks of the dishonest, I wouldn't be the rich man I am, my dear. Now, read me that piece about the new regiments of redcoats being sent to guard our coast against invasion.'

Thalia obliged. As she finished, she shivered. 'I do hope an invasion will not succeed!'

'Not a chance!' said Tope breezily. 'With the Channel fleet in action no armies will ever get across.'

'I hope you are right,' murmured Thalia, fearful for Fanny and Emily Wright.

At that moment the echoes of a great commotion floated up to them and almost at the same time a flustered Rose, forgetting to knock, came bursting into the room.

'Oh, sir! Somethin' dreadful's happened! The kitchen's on fire! Oh, ma'am, can you come at once?'

Thalia was already on her feet. The house was large,

the kitchen attached to the other wing. Her employer could be in no immediate danger.

'Don't worry, sir! I'll deal with it,' she said as she hastily followed Rose from the room.

She arrived at the kitchen breathless and flung open the door. One glance inside told her that, despite Rose's panic, everything was under control. Hamilton had taken charge.

CHAPTER THREE

'GET out and shut that door!' Hamilton roared as the through-draught caught the flames, made them leap and swirled the smoke.

Thalia did not get out but she did shut the door, leaving Rose on the other side. The blaze was confined to the area around the fireplace at one end of the vast room. Hamilton, in his shirt sleeves, was flinging buckets of water at it, raising steam and hissing noises to add to the crackling sound of burning and the smoke.

Mrs Gale stood in the yard just outside the open door wringing her hands, with the kitchen maids gathered about her. Jenkins and Treddle the coachman were helping Hamilton, throwing the water where told, while the bootboy and several of the outside staff filled the buckets at the yard pump and handed them back in a chain. Everyone in the kitchen was coughing, even Hamilton, despite wet handkerchiefs tied over their noses and mouths.

Thalia began to struggle for breath as she gazed in helpless awe at the speed with which the flames raced along the no-doubt greasy beams overhanging the fireplace. Dripping, charred rags still hung suspended over the recess.

She pressed her handkerchief to her face, wishing it was wet but there was no water near her. Streams of the stuff went winging upwards at the other end of the kitchen, dousing the racing flames. Jenkins, at a gesture from Hamilton, spread another bucketful over the smouldering remnants of the fire and whatever had been cooking on it.

'All right,' called Hamilton to the chain of men passing in the water. 'That's enough. The fire is out.' He ripped the handkerchief from his face and immediately coughed. Then, looking at Mrs Gale, 'You can come in and open the windows now, to clear the smoke. And someone take these outside,' he added, indicating a couple of charred stools which had been standing before the range.

Thalia stepped forward, treading carefully across the swimming floor. 'Thank you,' she said, rather breathlessly, for although the kitchen was single storey and attached to the house by one wall only, she had been fearful of the fire spreading. The sight of the new footman's ruined waistcoat and equally scorched and damp shirt, which clung to his broad shoulders like a second skin, showed how close he had been to the fire. Jenkins and Treddle still wore their coats and they, too, had suffered, though more by smoke and water.

'That was most resourceful of you.' She addressed all those who had been involved in fighting the fire and had now crowded into the kitchen and were busy opening windows. 'You have saved the house. Mr Tope will no doubt be glad to show his gratitude.'

'Thank you, ma'am,' said Ben Treddle, who had come running across from the stables to help. 'But Hamilton almost 'ad the fire under control afore we arrived.'

'That he did, ma'am,' put in Mrs Gale eagerly. 'Flung

'is coat over that blazing pot o' fat which young Tilly here left on the hob and wot started it all.'

Tilly, a scrawny youngster who could not be above ten years old, stood sobbing quietly by Cook. 'I'm that sorry, ma'am,' she choked. 'I didn't know as 'ow it would catch alight like that. Please, ma'am, don't turn me off!'

'It's only what you deserve, Tilly! Your carelessness could have caused the house to burn down!'

Thalia hardened her heart against Tilly's wail of despair. The child must be punished, though not sent away to starve. But before she could formulate a suitable penance, an acid voice cut across her thoughts.

'Tilly does not deserve to lose her job for a moment's inattention! Particularly if she had not been warned of the danger!'

As all eyes turned on him in surprise, Hamilton seemed to recall himself. He smiled apologetically at Thalia. 'Forgive me, ma'am, but it weren't Tilly's fault them cloths was 'anging above the fire, ma'am, and it was them as caught fire, ma'am.'

'He's right, Mrs Marsh,' acknowledged Mrs Gale heavily, her normally rosy face positively crimson with embarrassment. ''Twere my fault for hangin' 'em there to dry. But o' course, I didn't expect as 'ow Tilly would forget to watch the fat heat up. The drying's usually safe enough.'

Thalia glared at Hamilton. She had not been going to dismiss Tilly and now it would look as though she had given in to his entreaties! Bother the man!

'Very well, since you have taken responsibility, Mrs Gale, I will leave Tilly's punishment to you. And now I suggest you all begin to clear up this abominable mess. Everything will need scrubbing and any exposed food is probably ruined, so throw it away. Hamilton, Jenkins, you too, Treddle, please come with me. You will all need new clothes.'

Hamilton reached over and picked up the sodden mess of his black coat, which had been badly burnt by the blazing fat. He shook it out and pulled a rueful face.

'Beyond repair, I'm afraid, ma'am, but it did put out the worst of the flames.'

'Saved the 'ole place from goin' hup in my opinion,' put in Jenkins admiringly. 'As 'ead footman, ma'am, I'd like to recommend 'amilton for special reward, ma'am.'

Thalia nodded. 'Very well. We are all very grateful to you, Hamilton. Rose, go and reassure the master that all is well. You others come with me.'

'My coat's all right, ma'am. Just needs airing to get rid of the smoke. It's only me old one,' said Ben Treddle.

'Very well, Coachman. And thank you again.'

Treddle left for the stables. Hamilton and Jenkins dutifully followed her to the room where spare uniforms were stored. It proved easy to fit Jenkins up with working coat and breeches to wear while his own were cleaned. Hamilton, needing permanent replacements, posed a difficulty. He'd ruined the only outfit in the store which had fitted him.

'I'll have to order another coat and waistcoat,' Thalia told him. 'You'll be without for several days.'

'And me. . .er. . .?'

He delicately indicated where the flames had scorched his grey breeches almost through to the skin.

'Those too,' acknowledged Thalia. 'At least we have another shirt which will fit you, but you'll have to wear your formal uniform meanwhile.'

'Unless I wore me own things?' suggested Hamilton.

'Well, yes, that might be preferable.'

'More comfortable, ma'am.'

Thalia was gazing at his hands. 'You need something on those burns. Come to the still-room with me. Are you hurt, Jenkins?'

'No, ma'am.'

'Then you may return to your duties.'

In the room where fruit was preserved, jam made and creams, lotions and tinctures mixed, brewed and distilled, Thalia chose a small pot of ointment with which to treat his burns. They were not severe, but painful.

Jack sat with clenched teeth while she cleansed his hands, dabbing the scrapes and blisters with a rag dipped in clean water. As she applied the soothing cream and bound his hands with strips of linen he relaxed, reflecting that, since he'd not be able to do much with his hands for a few days, he'd be spared any part in the clearing-up operations.

He did not speak while she worked, her bent head only inches from his face. Her delicate fragrance filled his nostrils. Her touch was gentle, her expression concerned, intent. She was, he decided, like a sweetmeat with a hard shell and a soft inside.

Her ministrations made him realise just how much of a woman she was. He felt a stir in his loins and crushed it down, for he could not afford to have Mrs Marsh aware of the desire she roused in him at this stage of his campaign. She'd be frightened to death. Besides, he'd been at Stonar Hall barely a week, so far without accomplishing anything useful to his cause.

She was looking down at his singed breeches now and he prayed she would not notice anything amiss. Perhaps she'd fail to realise the significance of the slight movement he could not prevent. She looked virginal— he was certain she'd never been wed despite her housekeeper's honorary title—and if she went on the way she was going she'd end up a crabbed old tabby. He would, he thought wickedly, take much pleasure in saving her from that fate.

Luckily her gaze was concentrated on the scorches on his thigh.

'Would you like some cream to put on any other burns?' she asked, blushing slightly.

Ladies did not regard gentlemen's thighs or mention unmentionables. He had already decided that, despite her employment, she had been born a gentlewoman. 'Thank you, Mrs Marsh. My shoulders do sting a little,' he informed her diplomatically.

'Put this on when you change your shirt, then. You'd better go and do it straight away.'

He stood up, glad to be moving. 'Yes, ma'am. Thank you, ma'am.'

Left alone, Thalia washed her hands. She dried them and then held them out in front of her, daring them to tremble. No, steady as a rock. Yet she'd felt the tremors in her nerves as she touched Hamilton.

She knew what it was. Her slight experience with Varley had taught her that touching a man could have that sort of consequence. It meant nothing. Provided she kept him at arm's length in future she need not worry, though it was annoying, the effect he had on her. She'd been enjoying a calm and settled life before he'd come along to upset it.

She wanted to despise him, but she couldn't. No man who could act so decisively to avert a disaster deserved that. Although the ease with which he commanded the obedience of his fellow servants, even her, vexed her deeply. Hadn't she had to force herself not to obey his order to get out of the kitchen? In his position he should not be able to throw orders about like that and take it for granted that they'd be obeyed. It was highly irregular.

Her life had become increasingly difficult. She had the feeling that he could see right through her, through to her vulnerable heart. That he knew exactly the unsettling effect he had upon her. And were he to discover her secret, what use might he make of that knowledge? She shivered. The possibility did not bear thinking about.

A week later, an unexpected squad of soldiers arrived at Stonar Hall. After a short discussion with their youthful lieutenant, Sebastian Tope ordered the staff to gather on the lawn at the back of the house.

With Mr Tope settled, Hamilton joined Jenkins near the women and boys of the indoor staff. The bailiff, Harry Shepherd, had his groundsmen gathered about him. Ben Treddle and his stable hands stood in a separate group.

From her stance beside Sebastian Tope's chair,

Thalia viewed the assembled staff and their families with critical eyes. Everyone looked reasonably respectable. The few wives and children of the bailiff and other married men were neatly dressed, even if their clothes were of poor quality. A tribute, she thought, to Mr Tope's care of his servants.

Her eyes focused on the two footmen. Jenkins's new coat did little for his puny figure. In contrast, cut to fit, the black coat and grey waistcoat and breeches, highlighted by a pristine white shirt and stock, emphasised Hamilton's already superior appearance. They suited him to perfection.

Thalia found it difficult to remove her considering eyes from him. Apart from the poor quality of the rough material, which distance disguised, he could have passed for a fashionable man about town. He stood with easy elegance, un-selfconscious, assured. Footman or no, he stirred her blood in a way she'd never experienced before, there was no denying it. Just who was he?

Lieutenant the Honourable Timothy Oldham cleared his throat, creating a welcome diversion.

'As you know, we expect an invasion of England will be attempted, possibly in the autumn,' he began. His clipped, precise voice and rigid stance were the result of nervousness, Thalia guessed, eyeing his immaculate and splendid regimentals admiringly.

He had arrived on horseback with an escort of trudging redcoats. The men, standing at ease behind him, still looked hot and tired, although they'd only come from Sandwich and had been given mugs of ale from the kitchen. Oldham appeared completely unaffected by the heat. But then, he hadn't had to walk here.

'You are therefore advised to organise a defence of this house, sufficient to hold it, if necessary, until help arrives,' Oldham went on ominously. 'You will need someone to command you. Mr Sebastian Tope is unfortunately incapacitated and cannot take on the task.' He looked round expectantly. 'May I have a volunteer?'

Silence. Then Ben Treddle spoke up.

'I propose Jack Hamilton,' he said. 'He's bin in the army. He should know what's what.'

Hamilton shook his head, but Tope added his voice to Treddle's. 'An excellent suggestion, Coachman. Do you all agree?'

'Aye,' came a chorus of relieved voices. No one wanted to be blamed if an invasion came and the place was taken. Some might envy Hamilton the prestige and resent him for lording it over them, but no one wanted to undertake the responsibility. Even the bailiff, who could be expected to think that he should lead what would mostly be his own outdoor staff, made no demur.

Tope's shrewd gaze rested upon him. 'You've no objection, Mr Shepherd?' he enquired.

'None, sir. I've no knowledge of military matters so if Hamilton is willing. . .'

Tope nodded. 'Good.'

'Hamilton? Which of you is Hamilton?' demanded Oldham.

Hamilton shrugged, accepting the inevitable. 'I am, sir.'

'Hmm. What rank did you hold in the army?'

The footman appeared to hesitate. Then, 'I was just a soldier, sir,' he said.

'Why aren't you serving your country now, eh?'

'I was discharged, sir, at the Peace.'

'Well, you can make yourself useful here instead. Come with me. The rest of you, dismiss!'

Thalia would have given much to be able to listen in to the ensuing conference between Tope, Oldham and Hamilton. But she had no excuse to remain. She went to cut some flowers for the hall.

'A damned nuisance,' grumbled Jack. 'I had no wish to get involved in anything like that. I shall not be there long enough to do any good and then I'll have to leave 'em in the lurch.'

'You'll have the men organised, though, and taught to fire a musket—'

'Some of the groundsmen can fire a gun already, they shoot vermin and game. Oldham left four muskets to supplement the guns already on the estate, one each for me, Jenkins, Pringle and Treddle. Pringle won't touch his and Jenkins almost broke his shoulder with the recoil. Treddle will be all right once he's got the hang of it.'

Sidney Barton grinned. 'I remember learning to fire a musket, sir. . .Jack,' he corrected himself, seeing his companion shaking his head. 'Wasn't no fun, but like all the rest I got real fast at loading, ramming and firing. And then, as sergeant, I had to teach the recruits.'

'It's the drill that does it, Sidney. I wish I could hand 'em over to you! But I can't drill the fellows at Stonar Hall as though they were recruits to a line regiment! They're willing, but slow and fumbling and, apart from

Shepherd and his gamekeepers, can't hit a target to save their lives! It's a waste of time.'

'But a few shots from the house might surprise invading troops and bring 'em up short. Not that I expects 'em ever to land, o' course.'

'Neither do I, that's why I think it's a waste of time. But I'm trying to ensure that Shepherd is ready to take over when I go. Thinking they're being defended gives Tope and the women a sense of security.'

'Will that be soon, s. . .Jack? You leaving?'

'I don't know. I can't discover a damned thing against Sebastian Tope apart from the fact that he employs a most unsuitable young woman as his housekeeper. Anyone less like a housekeeper I've never encountered. If I were a suspicious person, I'd say she was probably his love-child but, on the other hand, she has quality he lacks. I don't know, Sid, but Mrs Marsh intrigues me. There is a mystery there.'

'But not the one you went there to solve,' pointed out Sidney with the liberty of one who has served his master long and devotedly. 'Still—' he gave his frightening grin '—if I knows you, s. . .Jack, that's the one you're really longing to solve, ain't it?'

Jack's irrepressible grin broke out. 'You could be right, Sid. But I'll not lose sight of the other one—too much depends upon it. I wish I knew how Tope came to own Stonar Hall!'

'You'll find out.' A pause. 'Why don't you ask 'im?'

'Sidney, you do have the most incredible ideas! A footman, asking his employer a question like that?'

'Well, if he seems a decent cove, you could tell 'im who you really are—'

'Quite impossible, Sidney. He'd simply tell me to mind my own business and show me the door. Then I'd never have a chance of finding out. No, I'll continue as I am for the moment. I'm quite enjoying myself, if the truth be told. Though I shall be expected to do a bit more work now my hands are healed.'

'Which is more than I be doing,' muttered Sid.

'What, you're not enjoying drinking ale with all the villagers and tempting 'em to gossip?'

'They don't 'ave much to say about 'im up at the big house, just that he's a devout and charitable gentleman, a good landlord. Better than the Earl of Eardley, they do say,' Sidney added reluctantly, avoiding Jack's eyes. ''Twas no surprise to them when his lordship shot hisself. Too far up River Tick 'e was, they say, never a penny to bless 'imself with, nought to spare for repairs and the like.'

Jack looked sour. 'He had an extravagant heir,' he muttered, emptied his mug of ale and shouted to the landlord for another.

It came. He drank it down and thumped the tankard back on the table. 'I'll see what I can do this evening before all the other servants return,' he said, rising abruptly to his feet. 'Tope will be glad to see me back early—he's always ready to be put to bed. Then I'll see what I can find. I do at least know where to look, now.'

'Be careful,' warned Barton, seeing the reckless expression on his employer's face.

Jack's grin was wolfish. 'It's my house,' he declared softly. 'I'll do what I damned well like in the place.'

* * *

Thalia kept a sharp lookout as she walked through Stonar village, but Hamilton was not anywhere to be seen. He'd not repeated his trick of waylaying her to escort her home and she was not sure whether to be glad or disgruntled. He would know by now that she always visited the same friend on her afternoons off; Cook would tell him if no one else did. So presumably he had no further interest in her company. Or had other fish to fry.

She had set him down rather severely for impudence, she remembered, so small wonder he did not wish to repeat his self-imposed service. His subsequent lack of chivalry was probably her own fault and if so she was glad. The creature was too attractive by half and probably as dishonourable as Varley. She would find it difficult to trust any man again, and particularly one as dubious in his origins as Hamilton.

He behaved with extreme rectitude in her presence now, but she was aware all the time that those strange eyes were watching her. Interested, slightly amused, puzzled.

Why she should puzzle him she could not imagine. That he puzzled her was a quite different matter. She was who she said she was, housekeeper to Sebastian Tope. Any claim she may have had to a superior position in society had died the moment she departed her father's house. There was no mystery about who she was and, except—admittedly a big except—for the existence of Fanny, she had nothing to hide. Hamilton, she instinctively felt, had plenty. He was pretending to be a footman.

He seldom spoke of his past life, passing off any enquiries by his employer or fellow workers with an easy, evasive answer. Sometimes he'd describe life in the army, but only when pressed. He'd never married, he'd told a delighted Rose, who'd passed the information on with significant blushes.

But Thalia knew Rose stood not the smallest chance of shackling the charming but elusive footman. He flirted with her, but that was all. He flirted with any passably good-looking woman, he'd even tried it with her. But he wouldn't wed Rose. Or anyone else, probably.

She was back a little early today. Without maids and footmen moving about attending to their duties the house seemed empty, abandoned, as she entered by the service door and climbed the stairs to her quarters.

Reaching the main floor, she decided to go along and see that Mr Tope had everything he needed. He would be waiting for Hamilton to return to put him to bed, for Pringle could not manage the task on his own. He would be impatient, for he liked to retire early and lie at ease in bed. He might like her to read to him.

Since she was using the service stairs, she must walk through the main rooms to the other landing to reach Tope's suite. Removing her chip bonnet as she went, she passed through the dining-room into the drawing-room. She was about to carry on across it when she heard a noise coming from the library. Its door was pushed to, though not closed. No one should have any business in there at this time, unless Mr Tope had sent Pringle on an errand. She turned back.

Jack did not hear her silent approach. He did, however, hear the slight squeak of the hinge as she pushed the door back. By the time Thalia could see his broad, brown-clad back, he was taking a book from a shelf near the writing table Mr Tope used for his correspondence.

Thalia knew that Tope had used it that morning. He kept the drawers locked, the same key fitted all three and he kept it with him. Yet now it protruded from one of the locks.

She eyed Hamilton suspiciously. He smiled back with bland indifference.

'What are you doing in here?' she demanded.

She stepped forward, her bonnet swinging from her hand by its ribbons, and removed the key, checking to make sure the drawer was locked.

'Choosing a book.'

'You can read?'

'And write,' said Hamilton proudly, ignoring any irony he may have detected in her voice. 'I can sign me name and a bit more.'

Much more, thought Thalia grimly.

'Is the book for Mr Tope?'

'No, Mrs Marsh, it be for me.'

Thalia eyed the slim volume with disbelieving eyes. 'You like poetry?'

The fellow's eyes dropped to the book in his hand. The faintest of wry smiles touched his lips.

'Oh, yes, ma'am. I'm trying to improve meself. And I do have Mr Tope's permission.'

'No doubt. I was just on my way to see him.' She held up the key, meeting his eyes with her own. 'I'll return this to him.'

It wasn't like Tope to leave it in the lock and she

wondered... But Hamilton met her gaze without a trace of guilt.

'Yes. He must've forgotten it. My fault, I should've noticed and reminded 'im. You'll find him in bed.' He gave a mischievous grin. 'That's where I'm off to, ma'am.' He flourished the book, his eyes resting on her shining hair and passing down suggestively to the sprigged muslin of her summer dress. The same one she'd been wearing when he'd escorted her from Stonar village. 'With only John Donne's love poems to keep me company,' he added with an exaggerated sigh.

The frisson of undoubted excitement his innuendo provoked frightened Thalia. She took refuge in anger.

'Mind your place!' she snapped.

Hamilton's eyes widened. 'But, ma'am, what did I say?'

He hadn't said anything to make her react so. His guileless words—except that she knew they had been far from guileless—had roused unexpected and unwelcome longings from deep in her own subconscious. And as for his show of injured innocence—she'd see him in Hades before she'd back down!

'It is not what you said, Hamilton! It is what you meant that vexed me. If you desire a woman in your bed do not seek to satisfy your lusts under this roof or you will soon find yourself seeking other employment!'

Her brown eyes held a sparkle of undisguised excitement, red flags of emotion coloured her cheeks. An answering spark made the amber in his eyes flare, the rest darken to slate grey, giving an impression of burning coals.

For a moment they stared at each other. Then Hamilton reached out and pulled her towards him.

'So dismiss me,' he challenged as his lips burnt down on hers.

Taken by surprise, for an enervating moment Thalia did nothing except enjoy the shock of pleasure his kiss sent shivering right down to her toes. Then her position, his position, his impudence, her suspicions of him, came crowding back to wipe away delight and replace it with mortification and new anger.

He wasn't expecting it. As she tore her lips free, her palm delivered a stinging blow across his cheek.

His shock showed now. He'd been lost in that kiss, she realised, unable to hide the desire she stirred in him, for her body had been pressed against his. The strong thrill of satisfaction the knowledge brought surprised her. After Varley, she'd not dared hope for such a response to or from any man. But why this man? Why, why, why?

He'd recovered quickly. His smile mocked. He bowed slightly. 'I'll be gone by morning.'

'No.' She could not deprive Mr Tope of this creature's aid. She drew a breath, said, 'The master needs your services. But step out of line once more, Hamilton, and I shall be forced to tell Mr Tope precisely why I wish you to go.'

Hamilton's face had now become inscrutable. 'I may not wish to stay.'

Thalia twisted the ribbons of her bonnet in hot fingers, not noticing how she was crushing them. 'I leave that to your conscience. At least remain until we can replace you.'

That had not quite been a plea, but too nearly so for her liking. She did not wish to be beholden to this arrogant, annoying creature who insisted on behaving with an assurance far above his station.

'How long will it take you to find someone else?' he demanded.

Thalia quailed at the thought of going through the rigmarole of interviewing dozens of quite unsuitable men again. 'It may be longer than I'd wish,' she told him grimly.

After a moment's pause, 'I will remain for Mr Tope's sake,' he informed her, bowed slightly again and walked from the room.

Thalia stared after him. He had not waited for her dismissal. Had walked off as though he owned the place. Only then did she look down to discover the mess she'd made of her ribbons.

CHAPTER FOUR

JACK cursed himself for a fool as he made his way up to
the small attic room he shared with Jenkins, who
fortunately had not yet retired. He poked the volume
of poems, picked at random from the library shelf,
under his pillow, flung off his coat and stretched out on
the hard mattress of his bed. It was as well, he thought
as he sought comfort, that he'd been inured to hardship
in the army.

With his hands clasped behind his head on the lumpy
pillow, he contemplated the cracked ceiling above his
head. He'd had the perfect excuse for leaving in the
morning, but had thrown it away for the sake of a pair
of brown eyes and the promise of passion latent in her
amazing response to his kiss.

He'd just discovered all he needed to know. His
masquerade as a footman at Stonar Hall was no longer
necessary. He had no further reason to stay—except
that Sidney Barton had been right. The mystery of Mrs
Thalia Marsh had him caught fast in its coils and he
couldn't force himself to leave before he'd solved it.
Especially now he had tasted the pleasure that intimacy
with her could give. And discovered another reason for
pursuing his interest in her.

Surprisingly, he also found himself reluctant to leave
Sebastian Tope in the lurch. He'd grown fond of the
man, had admired his courage and had been relieved

beyond measure to discover earlier that Tope was not the despicable cause of all his troubles, but an honest man of business enjoying what should have been a happy and trouble-free retirement.

So two things now held him at Stonar Hall despite the fact that, in order to pursue his own interests, he should go to London.

Mayhap he could salve his conscience when he left by finding a suitable replacement. . .

But not just yet. Retribution in London could wait while he discovered Thalia Marsh's secrets. And if during that time he could charm her into surrender, so much the better. Thalia Marsh would make a most satisfactory conquest. She'd posed a challenge from their first moment of meeting.

He knew now that she was not wholly indifferent to him, although she thought him infinitely her inferior in station—which made him wonder once more what exactly her station might in truth be. A poor relation of a family on the fringes of polite society, he guessed. She had undoubtedly been gently reared.

He sat up slowly, wrestling with the uncomfortable thought that perhaps she was not fair game for a conquest. Swinging his feet off the bed, he began to strip off his clothes. Fair game or not, he was determined to have her. She had tempted him too much, had heaped too much scorn on his head to escape him so easily. And besides, her regard for him might prove to be the only ultimate solution to his problems.

As he hung his jacket on the back of a chair he eyed with some disfavour the wig he would be forced to wear the following day. Sebastian Tope had invited several of his neighbours and friends to dinner. Jack had been ordered to don his dress uniform for the occasion and to help Jenkins and Rose to wait at table. He was not looking forward to it. Not that he knew any of the expected guests, thank the Lord, but he did not wish to make a cake of himself and was all too afraid that he might.

Thalia stepped out of the wooden tub and took the large towel handed to her by an eager Tilly, who had been moved from the kitchen to the house and been delighted beyond measure to be chosen to wait upon Mrs Marsh.

As she helped Thalia to don her chemise she eyed the rippling ivory silk spread over the bed.

'Oh, ma'am,' she sighed, 'you'll look lovely in that!'

The creation, trimmed with the gold and silver ribbon braiding Thalia had sewn on around the hem and neck in place of the original fussy decoration of bows and flowers, was caught in a shaft of sunlight.

Like all her other gowns, this one had been made for her come-out six years earlier. Her favourite, and the most costly one she had brought with her, it had been too elaborate for a quiet country dinner party. But it was the one gown she had not worn previously when acting as Sebastian Tope's hostess. None of the guests would have seen it before, so she had re-trimmed it for the occasion.

She was on easy terms with most of Mr Tope's friends and acquaintances now, and was looking forward to the dinner. He had invited Lieutenant Oldham to attend, and the soldier was bringing his superior officer with him. She had placed the two officers opposite each other near Mr Tope's end of the table.

She hoped Hamilton would behave himself. Her cheeks burned at the memory of their encounter the previous evening. He had reacted as though he did not care whether she dismissed him or not.

She wondered whether he had intended leaving anyway, with the contents of the strong-box in which Mr Tope kept his money and a few valuable items of jewellery. If so, he'd stolen the wrong key from Mr Tope's pocket. Mr Tope kept only papers in the drawers of his writing table. How disappointed Hamilton must have been, thought Thalia grimly, if her suspicions were true and he had been intent on robbing his employer.

Yet... She couldn't quite believe that. He'd been in the library with Tope and should have known which key he needed. Perhaps, like all servants, he'd only been curious, wanted to discover Tope's business—but then he should have pretended not to know how to read. Except that he'd moved instinctively when she'd come upon him and reached for the nearest excuse for being where he was, a book.

She had no proof, of course, and his presence might have been as innocent as he'd protested. Mr Tope had looked slightly surprised when she'd returned the key, had frowned and had said in a wondering voice that he could have sworn he had not left it behind. But he hadn't questioned the matter further, merely remarking that he was glad Hamilton was taking his advice and trying to better himself.

She slipped the gown over her head and Tilly fumbled with the hooks at her back. The neckline was a little revealing, the puffed sleeves short. She had no jewellery to relieve the bareness of her neck so used a length of cream velvet ribbon fixed with hook and eye at her nape. Although she was acting as hostess she did not wish to look matronly, so she had sewn more ribbon into a rosette with trailing ends which she fixed with pins above her chignon.

Instead of scraping her hair back she'd arranged ringlets to fall about her face and this seemed to soften her features. She looked more like the young girl who had so enjoyed her London Season all those years ago: but older, more mature, less ready to trust. The staff were used to this transformation by now and took it for granted, the metamorphosis of housekeeper into poised hostess for a few hours.

Hamilton, although he had seen her in informal dress on her afternoons off, had not seen her attired like this. Her breasts, made the more evident by the cut of her corsets and the waist of her dress pulled in just beneath them, heaved conspicuously as she took a sudden breath.

But why should she care what Hamilton thought of her? With a defiant toss of her head, she picked up her skirt and descended to join Sebastian Tope in the drawing-room, where he awaited his guests beneath the portrait of the bewigged former owner of Stonar Hall.

They arrived. First came a local squire and his wife with their two daughters, the youngest only just out in society—they would no doubt appreciate being seated next to the two red-coated officers. Next, an elderly couple living in a large mansion built almost on the sands of Sandwich Bay, closely followed by a former hunting crony of Sebastian Tope's, a widower. Last of all came the two military men.

Hamilton, in full fig, was announcing the guests as they arrived. A little squeal of excitement escaped an otherwise demure young lady's mouth at the sight of the officers' regimentals in the doorway.

'Captain the Lord Varley and Lieutenant the Honourable Timothy Oldham,' Hamilton intoned with impeccable formality.

Thalia's heart thumped; the blood fled from her face. A roaring filled her ears and the room darkened. She knew she was about to swoon.

Then he was standing before her, bowing, a surprised, faintly amused expression on his face. Not a trace of shame at the way he had abandoned her, had disappeared from London, before he could be called to account for withdrawing his suit. She'd always supposed he'd been hiding away in Ireland, on his mother's estates. She had never dreamt of seeing him here.

Things came back into focus as she pulled herself together. Wasn't this what she'd always wanted, to meet the creature again, to tell him exactly what she thought of him?

He had changed. Gone were the fair good looks, the slender figure she had admired. He had gone to seed, had Patrick Tolley, Viscount Varley. His blue eyes were set in puffy folds; the cut of his uniform could not disguise his corpulence. Even his smile was different, the charm of it quite lost as far as she was concerned in the slackness of dissipation. Now she could only wonder at herself for finding him in the least glamorous.

Years of training in good conduct sustained her. She

held out her hand for his greeting. The contact sent a shudder of distaste through her. The hand jerked.

'We were expecting Captain Frost,' she uttered.

The fair brows lifted, the smile became almost a sneer. 'I took over his company only yesterday. I did not expect to find you here, Thalia.'

His impudent familiarity incensed her: her nerves steadied. 'Nor I you, my lord.'

He glanced from her to Tope, his eyes insolently speculative. Tope, a look of sharp interest on his face, greeted Varley as Thalia, drawing on all her reserves of composure, exchanged the necessary courtesies with Lieutenant Oldham.

'You are acquainted with Mrs Marsh, my house-keeper, Lord Varley?' Tope enquired.

Turning from Oldham, Thalia answered before Varley could speak.

'We met years ago in London, sir. I have not seen his lordship this six years past.'

The chill in her voice indicated that she was not inclined to renew the acquaintance unless obliged.

'You have changed little, my dear,' murmured Varley.

'I cannot say the same for you, my lord,' retorted Thalia, her colour rising high, then draining away again in waves. 'When did you join the army?'

'I bought my commission during the Peace. Now, of course, my services have become invaluable. I,' he stated grandly, 'am here to defend the coast against invasion.'

'So we have been given to understand,' interjected

Tope drily. 'Tell me, my lord, do you believe an invasion imminent?'

'It is expected in the autumn, sir, and we must be prepared. Bonaparte is assembling his forces now; he has inspected troops and barges at Boulogne. But we shall not lack for defenders. So many have come forward to join the Volunteers.'

Thalia breathed a sigh of relief. Varley's attention had been diverted.

After nodding a greeting to Lieutenant Oldham, Tope engaged both officers in conversation and Varley expanded on the preparations to repulse invasion already in hand.

Hamilton presented himself nearby carrying a small tray of glasses filled with pre-dinner drinks. 'Help yourself,' Tope invited the Captain. 'You too, Lieutenant Oldham. Do find yourself a seat.'

The Lieutenant, grateful to be relieved of the necessity to listen to his Captain taking credit for the things others had done before his arrival, accepted a drink and went to sit in one of the few chairs available. It happened to be near the young ladies and their mother, who eagerly drew him into conversation.

To Thalia's relief Varley moved on too, standing alone to gaze with supreme disdain at the rest of the company, well aware that all those present were of inferior station to himself.

Hamilton still hovered.

'A sherry, ma'am?' he enquired, proffering the tray.

It was just what she needed. She gave Hamilton a grateful smile, little realising how much the strain showed on her face. A few sips of the alcoholic beverage brought a little steady colour back to her cheeks and stilled the tremble in her hand. But she still must endure dinner in Varley's presence.

She had already decided that nothing on earth would make her reveal Fanny's existence. But he must wonder why she was working as Sebastian Tope's housekeeper. If he asked, what could she say? A frown settled between her eyes.

Jack realised that Lord Varley's presence had upset her. He had overheard most of the exchange between them so it took little imagination on his part to know that she must, at one time, have moved in Society. He himself had been presented with a pair of ensign's colours at an early age and had seldom visited London, which held few attractions for him.

He did not know Varley, but took an instant dislike of the fellow. A typical, hard-living, useless officer who would send all his men to their deaths because he did not understand the first thing about war. But, thank God, that was not his worry any longer.

His concern now was to discover exactly what lay between Varley and Mrs Thalia Marsh. He had thought her about to faint when he announced the officers. Varley's attitude had been one of surprise, followed by cruel amusement. There must be some scandal attached to their acquaintance. He would not have heard, but his mother might know the gossip; she corresponded with friends in London.

But he quickly rejected the idea of asking her.

There was an easier way to find out. Ask Mrs Thalia Marsh herself. Except that she'd never tell him.

With her tough shell shattered and not yet fully back

in place, her vulnerability showed. Yet this was the woman he had dubbed a tartar! Clad as she was in shimmering ivory silk, her hair softly dressed, her brown eyes dazed, she looked almost beautiful. Defenceless, beautiful and in some deep trouble.

Now, not only his curiosity and desire were aroused, but his male instinct to protect, too. Damnation take it, her problems were none of his business! He had enough troubles of his own, without shouldering hers as well. He should have left Stonar Hall last night.

But he was glad he had not.

To his immense relief, Jack made no catastrophic errors during the meal, despite the fact that his attention so often strayed to the end of the table where Mrs Marsh so ably and charmingly executed her duties as hostess.

No one else seemed to notice it but he sensed her nervousness. She had, however, recovered enough to cover it up, drawing on reserves of experience she had gained in some other time and place. But her eyes kept fastening on Varley in the same way that they might have been drawn to a coiled cobra.

The evening dragged on. At last the guests began to take their leave. Varley bent over Thalia's hand with exaggerated courtesy and said something which caused her to shake her head vehemently.

'No, my lord,' Jack heard her say fiercely, 'I have no wish to renew our acquaintance. We have nothing more to say to each other.'

'Really, my dear?' Varley drawled. 'I think otherwise. I wish to know what you are doing here. I hereby engage to seek you out in the very near future.'

Bastard! thought Jack as he hurried forward to present the officer with his sword, shako and whip. It would be appropriate to keep a close watch on Thalia Marsh, even at the expense of neglecting his other duties. Curiosity about her was, after all, the main thing keeping him at Stonar Hall. Varley was not the only one who wanted to know what she was doing here.

Thalia's equilibrium had been badly upset by the reappearance of Lord Varley in her life. His threat that they would meet again haunted her. He wanted to know what she was doing here and she could not tell him the truth. She'd tell him a half-truth: that she'd left her father's house rather than be forced to wed Lord Stimson. That should be explanation enough. Then perhaps he'd go away and leave her alone.

She set off for Asham after church on Sunday as usual. She could not disappoint Fanny simply because Varley's presence in the neighbourhood made her nervous. Friday and Saturday had passed without his appearing to trouble her and, if she were not at Stonar Hall, he could scarcely bother her today.

As she chatted to the vicar's wife, she saw Hamilton hoist Sebastian Tope into his carriage before he joined his evil-looking companion and retired in the direction of the King's Arms. She supposed he would spend the day drinking in the taproom. But that was his business, provided he did not report back for duty drunk. It took her a long time to extricate herself but ten minutes later she set out for Asham.

There'd been rain overnight and it was a little cooler than it had been, with a fresh breeze blowing in off the sea, and she was glad of the pelisse she had donned over her muslin gown.

The crops growing on either side of the lane would benefit from the water, she thought, eying the turnips on one side and the oats already beginning to ripen beyond the verge, luxuriant with cow parsley and other wild flowers, and the ditch. But it meant she had to tread carefully around the muddy puddles which had collected in the ruts and potholes of the surface.

Thalia stepped out, anxious to reach Asham and reassure herself that her daughter was thriving. Miss Wright would send a boy to let her know if Fanny became seriously ill, but wouldn't bother for a childish cold, even for a chill or fall, so she always set out with a slight feeling of apprehension.

Scattered trees and bushes and some lengths of low hedges dotted an otherwise rather flat landscape. She was walking away from the sea and, as she progressed, the hedges became more profuse.

She'd just rounded a curve and was approaching the old chestnut tree and the thicket of hawthorn and hazelnut bushes which marked the cross roads where she turned for Asham, when the sound of hooves behind her made her glance over her shoulder. In this narrow lane she'd have to step to one side to allow the horseman to pass.

She immediately saw the red coat of a mounted officer. Then, as he came fully into view, her heart began to hammer as she recognised the lone rider.

Lord Varley!

She stood on the verge, willing him to pass by with no more than a greeting, but knew as soon as the thought entered her head that the hope was doomed. Of course, he had followed her, intending to catch her alone. Perhaps, she thought in renewed panic, intending to find out where she was bound!

He touched his shako with his riding crop. 'Good day, Thalia. I trust you are well?'

Thalia inclined her head, resenting again his familiarity. He had never called her Thalia before he'd seduced her, any more than she had called him Patrick. She determined to set him down.

'I do not remember giving you permission to call me by my given name, Lord Varley.'

Varley grinned unpleasantly. 'At least you are entitled to be addressed as Thalia, my dear. I do not believe the same can be said for your adoption of the title of a married woman?'

The observation almost undid her. Did he suspect that she had a reason for pretending to be wed? She must deny it immediately! He must never be allowed to discover that he had fathered a child!

He had stopped a little short of her. Thalia stepped off the rough, overgrown verge, afraid that a sudden movement might precipitate her into the ditch. She needed to feel more secure.

'You know very well, Lord Varley, that cooks and housekeepers are given the title as a courtesy. I am employed as Mr Tope's housekeeper. I need no other excuse.'

He had not dismounted. He looked down at her, the unpleasant smile still on his face.

'Housekeeper?' He guffawed with laughter. 'Why did you leave home, my dear? Was it from shame because your expectations had been so rudely shattered? Could you not face the scandal? Or manage to lure another into parson's mousetrap? Or did others refuse to leg-shackle themselves to soiled merchandise?'

As Thalia stared at him, stunned by the vulgarity of his attack, he laughed again.

'Housekeeper, you say? When you act as his hostess, my dear? Who do you think you are bamming? I taught you well, did I not? And if you are prepared to be mistress to that old cripple, you should welcome the attentions of a man in his prime, like me. I enjoyed the chase, but was never prepared to be caught in parson's mousetrap, y'know. But come, my dear, mount up before me and I will take you somewhere where we may enjoy ourselves as we did before.'

Thalia took a step backwards. 'You are out of your wits, Lord Varley!' It was beneath her dignity to directly deny being Mr Tope's mistress or to answer his other cruel innuendos.

'You mistake my situation. I left home because I quarrelled with my father.' She must tell him that much, or he would be left to wonder. 'I am employed by Mr Tope and am at the moment on my way to visit an old friend. She will become anxious if I am late. I most certainly do not wish to repeat an experience which I remember only with loathing! Good day to you, my lord.'

She turned on her heel and, on shaking legs, began to walk on towards the crossroads, hoping Varley would accept her dismissal and return the way he had come. It did not to prove so easy to repulse him, however.

She heard the hooves behind her and felt the horse's

hot breath on her neck. At walking pace there was just room for them both on the road. Thalia marched on.

The tossing head passed her shoulder. She was tempted to grasp the creature's headstall, to circumvent Varley's intention of drawing fully alongside. But even as she thought of the idea it was too late. At Varley's bidding the chestnut surged forward and then stopped, leaving Varley in the ideal position to lean over and grasp her arm.

'Not so fast, my sweet,' he sneered as he forced her to a halt. 'You remember our intimacy with loathing, eh? Then I must teach you to like it better! You will not escape me so easily.' He reached down further to haul her up into the saddle before him.

Thalia's basket went flying as she fought him off. She managed to wrench her arm from his grasp and fled, stumbling, along the lane. She knew, with a sinking sense of helplessness, that her flight was useless, for Varley could catch her wherever she chose to run — taking to the fields would serve no purpose. Her only faint hope lay in reaching the thicket by the crossroads and taking refuge there until someone passed and help arrived.

Varley, taken by surprise and put off balance by her spirited defence, was slow in spurring after her. He had never excelled as a horseman. Even so she realised that her hope of reaching cover was doomed. He was almost on her again as she panted despairingly towards the bushes ahead. Then her pumping heart almost stopped before galloping on.

A figure detached itself from the undergrowth. It

raced towards her, brandishing a heavy stick torn from a dead branch and uttering a fearsome cry.

Instinctively, she moved aside, leapt the ditch and stood among the oats, chest heaving, gazing incredulously at Hamilton as he drove on to put himself between her and Varley.

Varley, seeing what looked suspiciously like a madman charging him and his frightened stallion, drew his sword. Thalia caught her breath. Hamilton could not hope to challenge an armed, mounted man! He'd be struck aside and she'd be at Varley's mercy again.

But Jack had been a foot soldier long enough to know the best way to fight cavalry, and Varley was no cavalry officer. As he charged, swinging his sword intending to slap Jack aside with its flat, Jack stepped to one side and drove his stick into the horse's mouth.

The animal reared, shaking its head, as Jack forced his improvised weapon home. Varley struggled to keep his seat, his sword arm flailing wildly. Jack dodged round to bring his heavy stick down with bone-cracking force and wrenched the weapon from his opponent's nerveless hand.

The stallion, scared out of its wits, neighed and reared. Varley fell to the ground. Free at last, his mount snorted and cantered off, shaking its head, but it was not badly hurt; since nothing was chasing it, it soon slowed and stopped.

Jack stood over Varley, both hands on the sword's hilt, its point on the ground. Varley failed to recognise the deferential footman in the fearsome creature who had deprived him of his amusement and, more to the point, his sword.

Cautiously, for Jack looked formidable, he rose to his feet. Jack did not move. Encouraged, Varley resorted to the authority of his rank.

'Give me my sword and be on your way, fellow,' he snarled with forced bravado. 'I am an officer and a gentleman and have unfinished business with the lady, business you had no call to interrupt.'

He held out an imperious hand, at the same time whistling his horse, which, recovered from its fright, obediently trotted back to his side.

Jack merely smiled. 'The lady did not appear to wish to do business with you, Captain.'

Varley caught his mount's reins and hauled himself into his saddle. From his new vantage point he eyed his adversary.

Jack stood, steady as a rock, between Varley and Thalia, whose mind was in such turmoil that she did not even think of running for cover. Had she tried, her legs would not have carried her.

His tone casual, but holding an undercurrent of authority which Varley could not ignore, 'I suggest you be on your way back to your billet, Captain,' said Jack. 'I will see that your sword is returned to you in due course. You will scarcely need it in the immediate future.' He lifted the point and weighed the weapon in his hand, made a few scything passes with the blade. 'Of course, should you wish to challenge my right to protect Mrs Marsh, I shall be happy to meet you at any place and time your seconds should care to name.'

Varley stared at Jack in blank astonishment and then addressed Thalia.

'You know this impudent fellow?'

Thalia, rooted to the spot, watching Jack Hamilton's display of mesmerising superiority, closed her open mouth. Her emotions were in such chaos that all she could do was to nod.

Lord Varley looked back to Jack, disdain in every inch of his bearing. 'I am surprised that you acknowledge such a ruffian, Thalia, but then, you have come down in the world since last we met, have you not? And as for you, fellow, if you think a man of my consequence would deign to agree to a meeting with such as yourself, your wits must be addled.'

Jack laughed. 'Consider yourself superior if you must. But I warn you, Varley, that should you attempt to molest Mrs Marsh again you will answer to me. And I doubt you would survive the experience.'

The threat was spoken quietly, without overt menace, yet Thalia shivered, and saw Varley blanch.

He wheeled his horse. 'Neither of you will escape my vengeance for this,' he snarled, and spurred his mount back towards Stonar Village.

Jack watched him go. When he was no more than a head bobbing in the distance, he turned to Thalia, who had begun to shake with reaction. He held out his free hand to help her back across the ditch.

'Are you all right? He did not hurt you?'

Thalia took the hand he offered. It was strong, warm, comforting. When she was once more on the road and he let go she missed his touch.

'Thank you,' she murmured, realising they were the first words she had spoken since Hamilton had erupted on the scene. 'It was fortunate you were nearby.'

He had, in fact, been intending to follow her from

the crossroads. But he could scarcely admit that! 'I had taken a walk across the fields,' he said easily, then grimaced as he looked down at his muddy boots. 'None too wise after the rain, but just as well I did. Are you certain you are not hurt in any way?'

'My wrist is bruised,' admitted Thalia, pushing down her glove and rubbing at the red marks which would probably turn blue. 'He was trying to force me up in front of him.'

'And his plans were not those of a gentleman, that I'll warrant!'

'No,' admitted Thalia. Some kind of explanation seemed necessary. 'We met years ago, before he joined the army. He—he. . .' She found she could not go on.

'Never mind,' said Jack softly. 'But I collect that your working for Mr Sebastian Tope is as a direct result of his influence on your life?'

Mute, Thalia nodded.

Jack decided not to press her further for the moment. 'You dropped your basket,' he observed prosaically. 'Wait here.'

He stuck Varley's sword point into the mud and left it there while he walked back to where the basket and its scattered contents lay strewn over the verge. Some of the items, well wrapped by Mrs Gale, still appeared to be edible. But one or two things which had rolled into the wet ditch had to be abandoned. His curiosity over the destination of the luxury foods grew.

He took the refilled basket back to Thalia and handed it to her, explaining, 'The napkin on top is only a little soiled, but I'm afraid the bread rolls and a couple of pasties fell into the ditch. The rest should be fit to eat.'

Thalia, who had watched him gather together her precious offerings with such mixed emotions that she could not name one of them, nodded, accepted the basket and peered under the cover. She had recovered most of her equilibrium, but her hands still shook.

'Mrs Gale usually wraps the food well, thank goodness.' She looked up at Jack, her eyes showing open curiosity as well as admiration and all those unknown, mixed feelings the sight of him roused. But she had command of her voice and addressed him in her housekeeper's manner. 'You dealt with Lord Varley in a masterly fashion, Hamilton. I cannot believe that you were always merely in the ranks?'

'Well, ma'am, I did gain some promotion.' That was no lie. He'd risen from ensign to major, at first by purchase, but later through his ability in the field. 'But Captain Varley is not a true soldier,' he went on as he picked up Varley's sword and put it gingerly under his arm for lack of a better way of carrying it, 'simply a spoilt sprig of the nobility who fancies himself in a red coat.'

His voice held such dismissive disdain that Thalia was forced to smile. 'In that, I believe, you speak the truth. But—' and now she dropped the formal manner of housekeeper to footman, finding it impossible to maintain what she suspected to be a charade '—I beg to doubt whether much else you have told us is true. You are no ordinary footman,' she declared with such certainty that Jack knew he had failed dismally in his attempt at deception.

Yet he was not ready to confide the truth. He had too much interest in her and her past to be content to gain her confidence merely because he was who he was. He wanted her to confide in Hamilton the footman.

'Well, ma'am,' he said with his most winning smile, 'I badly wanted the job and so I did keep a few things to myself. I know you have been suspicious of my motives for working at Stonar Hall, but there is really no need.'

'Then why not tell Mr Tope the truth? What harm could it do?'

Jack considered. 'I had no way of telling whether the truth would be welcome. But I can assure you that I have grown to admire and respect Mr Tope and have no desire other than to help him. I wish him no harm. Just as I wish you no harm, Thalia.'

His voice had deepened. The intimate use of her given name did not irritate Thalia as much as it should have done. In fact she liked the sound of it on his tongue. But all the same. . .

'Do not presume, Hamilton,' she scolded, attempting to infuse some censure into her voice. But somehow, her smile would not be suppressed.

'No, ma'am,' returned Jack gravely. 'May I escort you wherever it is you are going? You really should not be walking these lanes alone.' He held out a hand. 'Let me carry your basket.'

Thalia froze. She could not allow him to go with her to Asham. Once he knew where she went he would quickly discover Fanny's existence.

'No,' she said abruptly. 'No, I shall be quite safe now.'

'I think not. You heard Lord Varley's threat. And he is not the only soldier roaming in the area now. Some of the men in the ranks can be very rough. Allow me to escort you, please?'

Thalia looked deep into those strange, changeable eyes and saw nothing to frighten her. She knew she should fear Varley—and Jack Hamilton had proved himself in her defence. He had offered his help so humbly. It was just that she could not quite bring herself to trust him with her secret.

'I shall not be coming straight back,' she prevaricated. 'You will not wish to wait for me.'

'Why not?' He shrugged. 'I have my afternoon off and I expect there is an inn near wherever you are going?' At Thalia's reluctant nod he smiled. 'I can wait there.'

CHAPTER FIVE

THALIA could think of no further reason to refuse his escort. Besides, Varley's attempted abduction had frightened her more than she liked to admit. She bowed to the inevitable.

'Very well.' She passed the basket for him to carry. 'I am going to Asham to visit a friend. I warn you, it is about five miles from the Hall.'

'I believe I can manage the distance,' responded Jack drily, a smile taking any sting from his words.

Her austere front had been broached once again and Jack determined, as he adjusted Varley's sword under his arm, to try his luck and endeavour to reach the real person hidden behind it. From the glimpses he'd had, he knew that Thalia Marsh was not the tartar he had at first thought her. She was as vulnerable as the next woman, perhaps more so than most, though she hid the fact most successfully. She intrigued him. And, more than ever, he wanted her.

He broadened his smile. 'May we not be comfortable together, Mrs Marsh? I should be greatly honoured if you would allow me to call you Thalia. I think it a lovely name. And I asked you once before to call me Jack. Off duty, of course.'

How could she possibly refuse such a request from a man who had just saved her from Varley? She had reluctantly given herself to Varley's younger version but nothing would induce her to submit to him willingly now.

It had been as good as rape then—she had been persuaded under pressure. The Varley she had met today would truly rape her. He would have no compunction were she to refuse her consent. Though why he should wish to, given her failure to properly satisfy him before, she could not imagine. How well he had hidden his vicious nature all those years ago!

She glanced sideways at the lithe, strong figure of the man striding along beside her, the man who had saved her from such a fate. His proximity had always had a strange effect upon her, but it had taken that kiss the other night to make her admit it as physical attraction— something she had never expected to feel for any man, especially after the debacle of Varley's assault on her. Equally surprisingly, Hamilton seemed attracted to her.

At this point in her musing, the memory of Varley's possession acted on her like a douche of cold water. She had not liked his pawing hands, his hot lips, his harsh grunts as he pinned her under him. At first responsive, she had soon panicked. He had found her unsatisfactory. So would any other man.

If she relaxed and accepted Hamilton's modest request to call her by her first name, would he take advantage of it to try to seduce her? She could not be certain what her reactions might be were he to make advances as Varley had done.

Hamilton could undoubtedly charm the birds from the trees if he troubled to exert himself. He had charmed her, and she had considered herself beyond any such thing. She had enjoyed his kiss, and known unmistakably that he had wanted her. And then she had panicked, just as she had before. But from the same cause?

The answer to that question remained unclear. Unlike Varley—how strange to be comparing Tope's servant with a viscount!—Hamilton was a strong character, a man to trust, one who, if not exactly a gentleman, gave a fair imitation when he was not pretending to be a footman. Despite that kiss—perhaps because of it—she knew she had no need to fear rape or undue pressure from him.

But what of her own reaction? Could she trust herself to resist her impulse to respond? And how far would the impulse take her? Would she panic again?

She had not wanted to make love with Lord Varley. She'd been uncertain, frightened and eventually repulsed. Yet were she to be honest, she had to admit that she found the idea of making love with Jack Hamilton wildly exciting. She did not understand herself. But a heady temptation to agree, to allow a friendship to develop between them, consumed her. Might he not be induced to confide in her? Tell her why he had come to Stonar Hall in the guise of a footman?

She returned his smile. But wariness had returned to dampen her initial leap of pleasure at his request. She did not know Hamilton—her trust was founded on nothing more than instinct. She had been wrong about Varley. She could be equally wrong about Hamilton.

So her voice remained cool as she said, 'Since you have just saved me from the unwelcome attentions of Lord Varley I can scarcely refuse such a modest request. . .Jack.'

Inadvertently, her tone had softened as she spoke his name. Jack's pulses leapt. She had been so long answering him he had felt certain she would refuse. He must be making headway.

'You do me great honour, Thalia,' he murmured.

'Do I? Can you not, in return, tell me who you really are, Jack?'

He had already rehearsed his reasons for refusing her request. But he did not offer them. Instead he decided to make his next words comparable to a throw of the dice. 'A bargain, Thalia. You tell me who you really are and what you are doing at Stonar Hall and I will do the same.'

Thalia gaped at him, eyes wide, while her heart did a flip before settling down into a steady, hammering beat. How could he guess that she had something to hide? 'You know who I am. I am Thalia Marsh. Miss Marsh, to be absolutely exact. And I am housekeeping for Sebastian Tope.'

So she was no more ready to confide in him than he in her. Jack smiled again. 'And I am Jack Hamilton, personal servant and footman to Sebastian Tope.'

'Is that truly your name?' murmured Thalia, not quite believing him.

'It is.'

She looked down. 'Oh.'

He wished he could see her face but it was hidden by the brim of her bonnet. 'You thought I had taken the job under a false name?' he enquired, making his tone severe. 'How could you misjudge me so?'

Since they were supposed to be improving the terms between them, Thalia ignored the mocking tone of his voice and answered honestly. 'I do not believe that you normally work as a servant.'

'I was in the army, Thalia,' he said mildly.

She nodded and lifted her head to look at him again. 'That I can believe after your recent demonstration. But not, I think, in the ranks. You spoke to Varley as though you might be his superior officer. And your rough accent has quite disappeared.'

Jack threw back his head and laughed. '*Touché*, ma'am! I make a poor actor. But I do assure you that my name is Jack Hamilton.'

'But who are you and what are you doing at Stonar Hall?'

'My business is personal. At the moment it is to escort a beautiful young lady to Asham. What more pleasant task could any man ask?'

So he refused to be drawn. Yet she had little choice but to confide in him herself, at least in part. Everyone in Asham knew that Fanny's mother came to visit her. They did not know, however, exactly who her mother was, except that she was a respectable lady living at some distance.

Most had no dealings outside the village and those who did shopped and traded in Canterbury, off in the opposite direction. Occasionally, she supposed, someone would visit Ramsgate, Deal or even Dover, but no one had any call to go near Stonar.

She had been lucky so far that her jealously guarded secret had remained undiscovered; no hint of her connection with a child in Asham had filtered through to Stonar. She knew it could not last forever, but she wanted the inevitable disclosure delayed for as long as humanly possible.

However, if Jack went to the inn in Asham, he had only to make the most casual of enquiries to discover that Fanny Marsh's mother visited her twice a week from somewhere over Sandwich way.

Painful as it would be, she must tell him she had a daughter and trust him to keep her secret. But that did not mean she had to confess to being the daughter of a baronet—of a baron soon, if her mother's latest information about her father's hopes bore fruit—or that, because her mother had married beneath her, in rank if not in fortune, she was distantly connected to an earl.

Of course, he could always discover the truth from Varley, but she did not think he would stoop to enquire from that quarter. She did not stop, at that moment, to ask herself why it seemed so important to keep the truth from him.

So, 'You may not think it so pleasant an enterprise when you know why I am going there,' was all she said.

She was looking at the ground again, her face once more shielded by the brim of her infernal bonnet. Her voice had been low, uncertain, as though she were on the verge of tears. Jack stopped, turned her to him and forced her chin up with his free hand.

'Why not, Thalia?' Her lids were lowered, the fan of brown lashes almost brushing her cheeks. Perhaps he was near to solving the puzzle of Thalia Marsh at last. 'My dear,' he said softly, 'please trust me.'

'If you are to accompany me to Asham I have no choice,' admitted Thalia miserably, and at last lifted her gaze to meet his. She saw nothing but puzzlement in the depths of his eyes, now almost entirely a green-blue, the amber extinguished by concern.

The fingers under her chin did not move, but his thumb brushed lightly over her lips. 'Tell me, Thalia. Unless you would rather I left you here and returned to Stonar?'

That had been exactly what she had wanted once; but now, suddenly, she changed her mind. His company was pleasurable, reassuring. Her emotions were in such turmoil after Varley's assault that she needed his steadying influence. The only thing was that by telling him she would forfeit his regard. Something which, to her amazement, had become precious to her. He would be shocked, disgusted, would probably turn back whether she wanted him to or not.

Yet he was a man of experience, whatever his origins, and probably nothing could shock him. Looking steadily into his eyes she thought he might be decidedly less disapproving than those members of Society, represented by her father, who would condemn her and cast her out because she refused to conform.

Jack tried to help her. 'It has to do with Varley?' he asked.

She nodded. He let go of her chin, settled the basket more comfortably on his arm, adjusted the sword again and turned to proceed along the lane. Thalia automatically walked beside him, glad not to have to meet his eyes as she confessed to her predicament.

'Lord Varley. . .' she began, and then found she could not go on.

'Raped you?' demanded Jack grimly.

'N-not quite.' Her voice trembled. She must be

honest in this. 'S-seduced me would be a more accurate description of what happened. You see, he'd given me to understand that he wished to wed me.'

'But he didn't.'

'No.' It was easier than she'd thought to confide in Jack Hamilton. He showed no surprise, no disgust, nothing but a grim anger which made her glad that Varley was by now miles away and swordless. 'He went away and refused to answer any of my father's letters. I was pregnant, my father furious. I would not abandon the baby or marry another and Papa turned me out.'

She heard Jack stifle an oath. 'What did you do?'

'Sought refuge with a friend. She lives in Asham. My daughter was born there and lives there still. It is Emily Wright and Fanny I am on my way to visit.'

They plodded on in silence for a few paces. Jack seemed bereft of words. Thalia risked another glance at his face and shivered slightly at the expression he wore.

'Who,' he suddenly demanded, 'is your father?'

For his own sake she did not want him exposing himself to her father's wrath, for Sir Gilbert Marsh, extremely wealthy, was a powerful man in his own sphere. And only now did it occur to her that she did not wish Hamilton to consider her above his reach. 'His name is Marsh. You have no need to know more.' There must be thousands of men called Marsh in London. Jack would never trace him.

'If he is of the nobility—?'

'He is not,' interrupted Thalia with perfect truth. Not yet, at least. But he suspected she was well-born and this dismayed her.

Now it was his turn to look sideways. Her face was

towards him; he could see the fright in her eyes. Fright of her father, who had treated her so shamefully?

Her next words corrected his misapprehension. 'But he does have influence in certain quarters and I would not have you suffer on my behalf.'

A certain chilliness crept into his voice. 'You need not fear for me.'

'Perhaps not, but you cannot conceive of the devious means he might employ to do you damage. He is not worth the risk, Jack. And it would hurt my mother, who is not to blame in any way except that she fears him so much she is unable to stand up to him openly. But she keeps in touch.'

Jack relaxed, his first dreadful wrath subsiding in the face of Thalia's reasoning. Though it amused him to know that she imagined her father, whoever he was, could do him harm.

'Very well. But I cannot answer for my actions should Varley cross my path again.'

She placed a restraining hand on his arm. 'Jack, please, do not risk your neck over this. I have survived, I am happy, Fanny is well cared for. Varley is a troublesome nuisance and I do fear him, but he is not worth hanging for.'

'Oh,' said Jack softly, thrilled by the touch of her hand, drowning in the depths of soft brown eyes, 'I shall not kill him, Thalia. But he will wish he had never been born.'

He tucked the hand beneath his elbow and Thalia did not remove it. She walked on in silence, wondering what she should do once they reached Asham. Should she send Jack Hamilton to the inn, or take him to meet Emily Wright and Fanny?

In a perverse way, now he knew of the child's existence and did not seem to condemn her for it, she wanted to show her daughter off. It would be the first time she had had occasion to do so to a stranger and Fanny was such a beautiful, lively child, full of mischief and fun yet, because of Miss Wright's influence, well-behaved and knowledgeable for her age.

In the end she had little choice, for they came to the cottage first and Fanny was in the garden waiting for her.

Fanny, overwhelmed by the presence of the tall, impressive stranger her mother introduced as someone who also worked where she did, turned shy. She was not used to meeting men other than the villagers she had known all her life. She clung to her mother's skirts but, urged on by Emily Wright, who had already greeted Jack with the respectful bob he seemed to demand, let go for long enough to make a creditable curtsy. Jack responded with a sweeping bow.

'Delighted to make your acquaintance, ma'am.'

Clinging once again to Thalia's skirt, Fanny smiled her mischievous smile. 'Your boots are all dirty,' she observed.

Jack looked down at the mud gathered during his trudge across the fields, and grinned. 'So they are. But you see, it rained last night and that made the earth wet.'

'Then you should have watched where you walked,'

reprimanded Fanny severely. 'Mama's boots are not nearly so dirty.'

Thalia lifted her eyes to heaven and removed Fanny's hand from her gown. 'Mr Hamilton is not a small child, Fanny. He is allowed to get his boots mired if he wishes to.'

Fanny pouted. 'That's not fair!'

'You will learn that many things are not fair, Fanny,' put in Emily sternly. 'You will apologise to Mr Hamilton for your rudeness.'

Fanny, aware of Jack's eyes twinkling down at her, was not to be abashed. 'I'm sorry, sir,' she said in her most dulcet tones, her blue eyes laughing back at him.

Fanny's cotton bonnet hung from its strings down her back. Unable to resist the impulse, Jack reached out to ruffle the golden curls thus revealed. 'So I should think,' he responded severely.

'And why isn't your sword in its sheath?' demanded the irrepressible Fanny. 'May I touch it?'

'Because it is not mine, and no, miss, you may not touch it, it is too sharp!' said Jack warningly. Thalia had taken the basket from him and now he hefted the sword, which Varley had fortunately neglected to have sharpened recently, watched intently by Fanny.

'Whose is it?' she demanded. 'How did you get it?'

'You ask too many questions, my child! I must find somewhere safe to stand it.'

'In the kitchen, I 'spect,' said Fanny, taking his hand and beginning to pull him towards the front door.

Thalia watched the exchange with new, strange emotions tugging at her heart. She could see that Jack Hamilton was all set to charm Fanny and even Emily, who was treating him with a respect and amiability quite at odds with all Thalia had told her of Mr Tope's new footman.

She resented the easy way he had captivated her daughter, yet she knew that the thing Fanny most lacked was the influence of a man in her life. Seeing her with Hamilton brought the deficiency to her notice, painfully, for it made her realise her own need.

She had convinced herself that she could manage alone, that she did not miss a man who would make demands and have the right to run her life for her. Perhaps she had been right in that. But she was beginning to think that she did need one to bring companionship, affection, even love into her barren existence. And, if she did not wed, she would never bear another child. If anything happened to Fanny. . .

Her thoughts were interrupted by Emily, who had ushered them all indoors, shown Jack where to park the sword in safety and then waved him to the most comfortable seat in the room, her own rocking chair. Emily should have shown some reserve, if not exactly suspicion, but was handling him like royalty, thought Thalia sourly, and he was accepting it all as though it were his right.

Perhaps it was. She still had no idea who he really was. But she was now fairly certain that he was no drunken lecher and that his influence on Fanny could not be harmful.

So, while she spoke with Emily and helped her prepare the tea, she watched Jack making friends with her daughter. Fanny had shown him all her most precious possessions and now they were engaged in a game of spillikins.

Fanny was playing with great concentration, her tongue held between her small white teeth. Jack's hand was steady as a rock and he removed the sticks with an expertise which looked to be born of long practice. Nevertheless, he made sure not to win every time, provoking squeals of delight from the child when the sticks moved at his touch.

Emily watched them too, and noted Thalia's reaction with a secret, knowing smile.

'He is good for her,' she remarked so that only Thalia could hear. 'I've not known her enjoy herself so much for years.'

'He'd soon tire of entertaining her if he saw her often,' muttered Thalia ungraciously.

'Do you still dislike him, my love? If so, why did you bring him with you today?'

'No,' admitted Thalia, 'I no longer dislike him.' And watched the smile with which Emily greeted this admission with exasperation. 'But I would not have brought him with me had it not been forced upon me.'

She gave a brief account of Varley's return into her life, his attempt to molest her and Hamilton's sudden appearance to rescue her.

'So, you see, I had no choice. He refuses to tell me anything about himself, but I've had to tell him about Fanny. And I expect he will offer to escort me in the future, at least until Lord Varley has left the district. And I do need his protection,' she admitted as a resentful afterthought.

'So we shall see him again. I am glad, Thalia my dear. His company will be good for both of you.'

'You need not think anything will come of it, Emily. I still do not know who he is or what his background is, apart from the army.'

'He certainly makes a very superior footman,' observed her friend drily. 'He does not come from the gutter, Thalia, or if he does then he is much to be admired for the way he has bettered himself.'

'He admitted he'd received some promotion in the army. I'm inclined to think he knows how to use a sword.'

'If he was commissioned from the ranks he must have shown exceptional ability and courage. You could do worse than look to him as a husband, provided he has the means to keep you and Fanny in reasonable comfort.'

Thalia stared at her erstwhile governess in shock. Had she run mad? Suggesting that Sir Gilbert and Lady Marsh's daughter should wed an unknown adventurer? 'Does he look as though he has?' she demanded, equally drily. But she could not prevent the blush which suffused her face.

'But if he is incognito—?'

'Oh, don't be silly, Emily! I did not realise you were a romantic dreamer!'

Emily merely smiled. 'We must wait and see,' she said, and added loudly, 'Dinner is ready.'

As Thalia took a fond farewell of her daughter, Jack seized the opportunity to have a private word with Miss Wright. Thalia saw her frown, nod and then smile. She said something Thalia could not catch. Then all their goodbyes were done and she was walking back towards Stonar Hall, Jack carrying the empty basket and the sword.

'Who will you ask to return Lord Varley's weapon?' she asked to break a rather long silence.

'A lad from the King's Arms. He'll do it for a shilling.'

'Have you—?'

'Yes, ma'am, I have a shilling to spare,' retorted Jack before she could finish her enquiry.

'I'm sorry,' said Thalia stiffly. 'But you are doing it on my behalf. I should bear the cost.'

'There you mistake, Mrs Marsh. I took a dislike to Captain Varley the other evening. Whatever I may do is because he annoyed me by persecuting you. You will owe me nothing. You have suffered enough at that scoundrel's hands.'

Her heart warmed towards him. It seemed she had a champion. 'You were not shocked by what I told you?' she asked shyly.

'Shocked? No. I know Varley's type. A young girl, like you must have been then, would stand no chance against him. If I am certain of one thing, it is that you were not to blame. I think it scandalous that your family treated you as it did.'

'You are in a minority. Almost everyone I knew would have judged me wanton. I was ruined.'

'But you made a new life for yourself. That took courage, Thalia.'

She remembered the terrible panic which had gripped her, the fears that had beset her on her journey to Asham. 'I did not feel very courageous.'

'True courage is in overcoming fear.'

'Is that something you learned in the army?'

'That and many other things.'

'I do wish you could confide in me, Jack.'

Her wistful tone almost undid him. But he knew it would not do to announce his true identity yet, even without his ulterior motive in not wishing Thalia to know. Besides, he enjoyed teasing her with the mystery. She had, most definitely, warmed towards him. Having to introduce him to her daughter had broken down a number of barriers.

'So do I,' he said untruthfully. 'But I'm glad I know about Fanny. She is the most delightful child I have ever met. I shall look forward to seeing her again. You will allow me to escort you on Wednesday?'

She had known it to be inevitable. 'Of course,' she replied, 'but please be careful not to let slip where we go. Others at the Hall would not be so understanding of my circumstances as you.'

'My lips are sealed.' Jack smiled. 'I assume Mr Tope knows all about you?'

'Yes. Unlike you, I did not feel that I could take a job under false pretences.'

'Oh, dear! What a set down!'

But he was laughing, and Thalia joined in as the crossroads came into sight. They looked at each other, suddenly serious.

'I am so very glad you came along when you did,' she murmured, and the choke in her voice made him stop, drop his burdens and take her into his arms.

The kiss was gentle, comforting, bore no resemblance to the assault on her mouth in the library. Yet it had the same devastating effect on Thalia. She clung to his strength and wished she knew who he was.

'I am so frightened for Fanny,' she whispered at last.

He scrutinised her lovely face, saw the fear lurking in her dark eyes, squeezed her reassuringly and smiled. 'Then we must make quite certain that both she and Miss Wright are safe.'

Reluctantly, she removed herself from his arms and turned to resume the journey. 'But how?'

He gathered up the basket and sword. Her face was hidden from him again. 'Trust me,' he said.

Now she turned her head to look at him. 'What can you do?' She sounded sceptical.

'When we reach the village I want you to come with me to meet someone. Then I'll explain.'

She could draw no more from him. He insisted on talking first of Fanny and Miss Wright, saying how much he had enjoyed the visit. After that he kept her amused by relating some of his trials as footman to Sebastian Tope, rattling on, trying to take her mind off her fears.

To an extent he succeeded, for he managed to make her laugh without in any way blaming anyone but himself for his misadventures. She supposed afterwards that, as housekeeper and his superior, she should have stopped him, but at the time their relative stations in the hierarchy of the household did not seem important.

It was not too far to the village and Thalia was glad when the first cottages came into sight.

'I believe you are acquainted with the excellent Mrs Cracker,' he remarked as they approached the inn.

Thalia nodded. 'I know her quite well.'

'Would she allow you the use of a private room for half an hour?'

'I'm sure she would. Why, do you wish me to go with you to the King's Arms?'

'Aye. I have to deal with Varley's sword, and I would like you to meet a friend of mine.'

Could he mean that villainous-looking creature she had seen him with before? Thalia did not much wish to meet the fellow, but if Jack Hamilton called him friend perhaps his looks belied his character. Or perhaps he meant someone else entirely.

'We can go in by the kitchen,' she suggested, wondering what Mrs Cracker would think of her consorting with her employer's footman. But the events of the afternoon had been so traumatic she was almost past caring.

Mrs Cracker willingly ushered them into a private parlour and, at Jack's request, called her stable boy.

'Ev'nin', Mr 'amilton,' said the lad, giving Jack a cheeky grin. 'Somefink I can do fer yer?'

'Aye. I want you to take this sword back to the regiment stationed in Sandwich. It belongs to one of the captains but take it to the commanding officer, a Colonel Pink. Say you were instructed to give it to the Colonel himself because his officers shouldn't leave their swords lying about.'

'To Colonel Pink hisself, and his officers shouldn't leave nasty dangerous swords lying about.'

'Good lad, that'll do,' said Jack, grinning. 'Here you are.' A shilling changed hands. 'Don't flash the weapon about. Here, bind the hilt in this and be careful not to hurt yourself.' He tossed over a large, fairly clean handkerchief.

'I suggest you avoid every officer in sight until you get to the Colonel's billet. One of 'em might recognise it and try to take it from you.' Varley's crest was on the hilt. 'Oh, and ask Mr Barton to come in here as you pass through the taproom. I expect you'll find him there.' Jack knew Sidney would be waiting for him to return.

'Good as done, mister,' grinned the boy, admiring the elaborate hilt and guard as he wound the linen round it with grimy hands.

Thalia had stood in the dimmest of the corners while this exchange took place. As the door closed on the boy she stepped into the light cast from the small window which overlooked the yard, and gazed out.

'How will he get there?'

'Walk, I dare say. It's not far. They might let him borrow a nag.'

'Lord Varley will not like his sword being returned to his Colonel.'

'He should not be so careless as to lose it.'

She turned troubled eyes on him. 'Be careful, Jack. He hates you already. This will make him vicious.'

Jack grinned. 'I know.'

'I believe you are enjoying yourself!' accused Thalia.

'Perhaps I am. Life can be a trifle dull at Stonar Hall.'

How right he was! Yet there was safety in being dull. She had reckoned that she'd had enough excitement to last her a lifetime when she'd been turned off from her home, that a quiet existence, unencumbered by the emotional traumas Varley had caused, would be what she wanted for the rest of her life.

Sidney Barton knocked before she could come to terms with the changes that had suddenly intruded into her comfortable, if boring, view of the future.

'The boy has just started out on foot,' she said as she turned to greet the newcomer. She could not subdue a slight shudder as his face leered at her in the dim light. But Jack did not seem aware of his friend's disfigurement as he introduced them and Sidney made a deferential bow.

'I am pleased to meet any friend of Mr Hamilton's,' she said, trying to sound as though she meant it.

'Thank you, ma'am. Jack 'as often spoke of you.'

'I wanted you to meet Sidney because I am about to ask him to do us both a favour. The two ladies we left this afternoon need protection. You agree?'

Thalia suddenly went cold. She had expressed concern, but had not fully faced the fact that Varley might discover her secret, yet he well might—after all, he had only to follow her. It would not be easy on a horse— she'd see him from a distance over the low hedges—but on foot he'd largely be hidden. As she thought about it a suspicion entered her head. How come Jack Hamilton had been waiting at the crossroads? Had he intended to follow her? Well, he'd been saved the trouble. And, truth to tell, she wasn't sorry.

CHAPTER SIX

'I SUGGEST,' said Jack when they had all sat down and he had told Barton where he had been and why, 'that Sidney goes to Asham and stays there instead of here.'

He did not explain what Barton had been doing in Stonar in the first place and Thalia did not ask. Whatever she was told, it would not be the entire truth.

'Sid and I were together in the army,' Jack went on. 'His face was slashed by a sabre and he almost died. So you must forgive his looks. But I can assure you he is a useful man in a fight.'

'I'm sorry,' murmured Thalia and, as she met the man's grey eyes, his disfigurement suddenly diminished in importance.

He was, she supposed, around forty, shorter than Jack, more solidly built, clean, decently and neatly dressed and, although she could smell ale on his breath, he showed no sign of over-indulgence. The idea of his guarding Fanny did not offend her. She only hoped that her daughter would not be frightened by the sight of his wound. He had been lucky not to lose an eye.

'We stuck together when we both left the army during the Peace,' Jack continued. 'Sid had nothing else to do so he came here with me.'

That was some sort of explanation of his presence, she supposed. But staying at the King's Arms would cost money. The more she tried to figure things out, the more confused she became. And the more curious.

'That will have two advantages,' went on Jack. 'It will save money, because Miss Wright has offered to accommodate him in her outhouse, and he will be right on hand in case Varley puts two and two together, discovers Fanny's existence and whereabouts, and tries anything.'

Thalia remembered his conversation with Emily while she had been taking leave of Fanny. She tried not to sound offended. 'You asked Miss Wright before we left? You did not consult me?'

'I did not imagine you would have any objection and I wanted to ask Miss Wright out of Fanny's hearing. There is no point in alarming the child unnecessarily.'

'No.' He could have mentioned it on the way home. 'Well, it seems you have it all arranged, and I must be grateful for your help, Mr Barton.'

'I'll go tomorrow, ma'am. Perhaps you'd give us a note, so as the lady knows who I am?'

'An excellent idea, Sid,' applauded Jack. He went to the door to summon Mrs Cracker to ask for paper and pen.

'There be some paper in that drawer there, and pen and ink in the cupboard. You're welcome to use it, ma'am,' said the landlady, ignoring the men and addressing Thalia, whom she knew held a respectable position of responsibility.

So Thalia sat down, Jack sharpened the quill and Thalia wrote a note to Emily, introducing Sidney Barton. Jack watched as Thalia wrote in an easy, flowing hand and had little doubt as to who had taught her her letters.

She and Miss Wright might now regard each other as friends, but the old relationship of governess and pupil was still evident for anyone with an eye to see. Her education had not been cheaply bought. Her father must either have made his money in trade or be a gentleman of some means. And now Miss Wright was teaching Thalia's daughter.

When the missive had been sanded dry, Jack folded and sealed the paper and handed it to Barton.

'We'll see you on Wednesday, Sid,' he said as they parted company.

'Aye, s—' Barton caught himself up '—Jack. I'd recognise 'is lordship if 'e turned up, seen 'im pass through the village a couple of times.'

'Including this afternoon, no doubt.'

Barton nodded. 'Soon after you went off for your walk across the fields.'

Thalia thought he almost added 'sir' but stopped himself in time. However much they tried to disguise it, the relationship between the two men was not simply that of friends. Sidney was used to taking orders from Jack. Oh, no, Jack Hamilton was not at all what he seemed.

She said nothing to Jack, however, and the walk to Stonar Hall passed in a pleasant discussion of the house, its grounds and the improvements Sebastian Tope had made since purchasing the estate.

'Were you with him at the time of the alterations?' asked Jack.

'Oh, yes! Mr Tope asked for my ideas and liked them

so much that in the end he gave me a free hand in most things.'

'So you were mainly responsible for the refurbishment of the place?'

She smiled. 'Yes. I did so enjoy the challenge!'

'I like what you have achieved.'

He sounded sincere and she forgot he was merely a footman who had no business passing judgment. She glowed at his praise.

'Thank you! The previous owner, the Earl of Eardley, had let the place run almost to ruin,' Thalia explained. 'In the end he was forced to let the place go to his creditors.'

Jack maintained an unusual silence after this, his expression brooding. 'Poor fellow,' he said at last. 'A pity he got into such debt.'

'So many of the nobility seem to,' sighed Thalia, thinking of her brother's fall from grace when he had come down from Oxford. Papa's wrath had been terrible to see, according to her mother's account of the affair. It had taught Arthur a lesson and now, despite his moving in Society, his debts remained manageable — or so Lady Marsh assured her.

She often wondered about Arthur. She supposed he would be marrying soon, but she did not expect to be invited to the wedding. It still saddened her to be cut off from her family.

'He must have regretted losing this lovely estate,' mused Jack, looking about him with a brooding eye.

'Yes. He must have had other estates, but he was still in such debt that a few months later, soon after Mr Tope moved in, he committed suicide. Mr Tope never met the Earl, of course—the place had already passed out of his hands and the transaction was done through lawyers.'

Jack grunted at this and changed the subject. By the time they parted, Thalia was looking forward to having his company for the walk to Asham on the following Wednesday. Having someone so agreeable to talk to made the miles seem shorter.

The journey, the visit, passed without unwelcome incident. Jack had armed himself with a stout, gnarled stick belonging to one of the groundsmen and, secretly, with a pistol hidden under his coat, but neither was needed.

They found Fanny in the back garden with Sidney. So absorbed had she been in a game of ball that she had not been waiting in the front with her usual impatience. However, the moment her mother and Jack appeared at the kitchen door the game was forgotten and she flew into Thalia's arms.

The child was having her fill of male company, thought Thalia, smiling at a sweating Barton, who wiped his brow before coming forward to pay his respects.

Emily had welcomed his presence and invited him to eat in the kitchen with them. Since they had visitors, though, they would all take tea in the front parlour. Barton helped to carry the food through while Jack amused Fanny.

I need not have bothered to come, thought Thalia wryly, an indulgent smile on her lips. Any jealousy she might otherwise have felt had been dissipated by Fanny's welcome and by the vivid happiness evident on the childish face.

It was strange how at home she herself felt in the men's company. Emily was looking surprisingly happy, too. Perhaps she enjoyed having a couple of attractive men about the place. Because, once you ignored Barton's disfigurement, you could see how attractive he must once have been and still was.

Much younger than Emily, of course. Emily was inclined to treat every one of them as children, despite addressing the men formally, as Mr Hamilton and Mr Barton, not as servants. Fanny did the same.

On the way home they spoke of the Church fête, due to take place on the Saturday in the grounds of the Hall. Sebastian Tope was to open it and so Jack would attend him. He had also been roped in to help run a hoop-la, while Thalia would assist with the cakes.

Thalia wished, not for the first time, that she could take Fanny to the annual event. The little girl would enjoy it so much, for the children ran races and had a fine time at the side-shows, but, of course, that was impossible.

She said as much to Jack.

'One day,' he said, 'it may be possible.'

'Not without revealing my shame for all to see.'

'Does it concern you so much, Thalia? No decent person, knowing the circumstances, would condemn you for what happened. And if you wed—'

'How could I?' demanded Thalia. 'No man of any consequence would marry me if he knew I had a bastard daughter!'

'Must it be a man of consequence?' asked Jack. He wanted to know her mind. Not that he wished to wed her himself—he simply wanted to keep his vow to bed her, though that possibility seemed ever more remote the more he discovered about Miss Thalia Marsh.

And yet, she had one indiscretion behind her—what could a second matter? He had to make her want him so desperately that another deviation from the path of righteousness would not seem to matter. Not such a tall order, he considered, since he had felt her instinctive, passionate response whenever he had kissed her. His pulses quickened at the thought of the battle of wills ahead.

The weather broke a little the next day, becoming unsettled and rather cooler. On Friday it rained in the morning and everyone became anxious for the next day.

'I only hopes as how we manage to keep the cakes dry,' said Mrs Gale gloomily as she prepared the mixture for yet another farmhouse cake.

The pantry shelves already groaned under a display of tarts, buns and sponges and she would be cooking for much of the day. The Hall, by tradition, provided most of the items for sale on the cake stall, though the more prosperous villagers contributed something.

Thalia had made a couple of children's bonnets for the needlework stall and and turned out some old clothes for the jumble. But most of the fun came from the side-shows organised by the vicar and the entertainments laid on by Mr Tope, who had arranged for the local Militia band to provide music, some travelling players to enact a masque, Morris and country dancing, children's races and a tug-of-war.

* * *

Saturday dawned fair and, as the morning progressed, became sunny and warm.

'Thank goodness,' said Thalia to Mr Tope as they prepared to depart for the large swathe of recently cut meadow where the groundsmen had already erected a marquee and set up wooden booths for the side-shows. Hamilton was fetching Mr Tope's hat and gloves and a large umbrella in case it should rain.

'I see you've brought your parasol. The ground will be damp—I hope you are wearing boots,' rejoined the elderly gentleman with a smile. 'You are looking extremely charming today, my dear.' He eyed her simple but fashionable gown approvingly. 'That green suits you. Have I seen the outfit before?'

'No,' admitted Thalia. 'I bought the muslin some months ago and decided to finish it in time for today. I trimmed the bonnet last night. I'm glad you approve, sir.'

'Damn sight more pleasant on the eye than the dismal colour you normally insist on wearing, m'dear.'

'Do you truly object? I think grey suits my position in your household. It underlines my authority.'

'It don't need any underlining, my dear. I'd prefer to look on a pretty gown any day. Wish you were m'daughter. Then I'd see you dressed as you were meant to be.'

'But I'm not, dear sir. We've spoken of this before. I am not your daughter and cannot presume to behave as though I were.'

'But you don't need to go about looking like a hedge sparrow. Please an old man. Wear some pretty gowns. If you haven't any, order some. Count 'em as uniform—you need some new things to wear about the house.

But I'm not paying for any more of those dismal grey things.'

'You are very kind. I'll think about it,' said Thalia and was glad to see Jack approaching, so putting a stop to an embarrassing conversation.

Her renewed instinct to make herself look as attractive as possible warred in her mind with her duty to Mr Tope and her fear of involvement with men of any description. What good could it do to attract Jack Hamilton, for example? If she succeeded beyond the dangerous degree already apparent, where could it lead but to disappointment, disgrace, extreme unhappiness and probably all three?

Yet she had finished the gown especially so that he should see her wearing it today. And the frank admiration in his strangely-coloured eyes as they met hers brought a bloom to her cheeks. The amber in his irises made his eyes seem to glow.

She walked beside Mr Tope's chair as Jack pushed it through the grounds towards the sounds coming from the meadow used for the fête. Everyone, it seemed, had taken an early dinner and arrived for the occasion in good time and full of high spirits.

As they emerged from a screening growth of shrubs and bushes, a scene of great activity met their eyes. People had come from hamlets and villages all around though, thankfully, not from so far afield as Asham. The more prosperous would buy from the stalls and so provide the church with funds, but otherwise everything was free.

Children were already running wild, their parents quite unable to control them under such exciting circumstances. The vicar stood on a small platform attempting to direct operations and keep order. He immediately descended to greet his benefactor.

Hamilton, after acknowledging Mr Wyndham with a respectful bow, pushed the chair up the ramp someone had thoughtfully provided. With Sebastian Tope settled on the platform beside the vicar, Thalia excused herself, going to find Mrs Gale and the cake stall.

From then on, everything went like clockwork. Mr Tope opened the fête, making a droll speech that had his audience laughing and clapping, and then the fun began.

Thalia scarcely had a moment to think, so keen were even the poorest of the women to buy Mrs Gale's cakes. From her station behind the laden trestle table, she watched Hamilton handing out hoops to both grown-ups and children who had paid a penny to attempt to capture one of the prizes.

When the races began he abandoned the hoop-la to walk towards her. Her pulses quickened but expectation abruptly ended in annoyance. Rose waylaid him to ask him to help organise the competitors and to fire a blank charge from one of Mr Tope's pistols to start each event.

'You'll do it, won't you?' she demanded, looking up at him with a flirtatious smile. 'See the little devils! Quarrelling and fighting to get in front!' She went on persuasively, 'You'd be able to keep them in order and manage the pistol better than anyone else.'

Jack looked round at the vicar and several of the men and their wives who were, rather unsuccessfully, trying to organise the children into a line. 'I've no wish to tread on anyone else's toes.'

'Oh, you won't! The Reverend sent me to ask you!'

At her suggestion, no doubt, thought Thalia sourly. Had they been closer Thalia would have been tempted to slap the girl. But the afternoon was a holiday for the staff and it would not be right to exert her authority under such circumstances. Hamilton was a free agent. He could do as he pleased.

He chose to go with Rose. Thalia had to admit it would have been difficult for him to refuse.

Custom at the cake stall had died away, for not only were the chief of the cakes sold, but everyone had gathered to watch the children have their fun. Thalia's eyes scarcely left Jack Hamilton as he brought order from chaos, primed the pistol and started the first race. The children recognised authority when they met it; few caused any further trouble.

Flat races, three-legged races, egg-and-spoon and sack races followed each other in rapid succession until the children, exhausted but happy, collapsed on the ground to drink lemonade provided by the organisers and await the presentation of the prizes later on.

Throughout it all, Rose had scarcely left Hamilton's side. But with the last race done he excused himself and once more set off for the cake stall.

'You still have some left, thanks be!' He winked at Thalia as he approached but addressed Cook. 'I'll have two of those tartlets and two rock cakes if you please, Mrs Gale.'

Having paid for his purchases he turned to Thalia.

'Could you be spared for a few moments, do you suppose, ma'am?'

His smile was blinding. Thalia blushed. Mrs Gale raised her brows as a knowing smile crept across her broad face.

'There's not much doing here now, Mrs Marsh. I can manage,' she told Thalia with such a bland expression Thalia felt even more uncomfortable. And then Rose appeared at Hamilton's side. 'Besides,' Cook went on smoothly, 'Rose can help me. You come and take Mrs Marsh's place, Rose my girl.'

Rose opened her mouth to protest, looked around at three unhelpful faces, and decided to accept the inevitable, though with bad grace.

At the place where lemonade was being dispensed Jack gave Thalia the food to hold while he acquired two full cups of the refreshing juice. Then, carrying them carefully, he led her to a quiet corner of the field, where he put them down, spread his brown coat—he was not wearing his uniform—and invited her to sit.

They were in full view of the entire gathering, yet isolated from it. Everyone would see their intimate tête-à-tête. She should not have followed him in so docile a manner. She should return to the crowd.

But that same rashness which had infected her the other day caught hold of her again. She accepted the offered seat and, when he joined her, sitting on a tail of the same garment, she was glad that she had. Her attitude to Hamilton had changed completely. Despite the doubts that still plagued her, she felt warm, secure, happy in his company.

The lively scene was like a play being enacted before

them. The masque—a pageant of historical figures—
had taken place earlier, but the performers were still
capering about in their costumes. The present scene
was more like watching an opera chorus, the figures
small, remote, in another world.

It was so long since she had been to a theatre, let
alone to an opera! She wondered whether Hamilton
had ever been to a proper theatre. He might have, she
supposed. Perhaps abroad in the army. He might even
be a gentleman's son. Off guard he gave that
impression.

She accepted a cake and her lemonade and for a few
moments they ate in silence. Then Jack stirred.

'I'm looking forward to our walk tomorrow. There's
no message from Sidney, so all is well at that end.'

'I feel much happier knowing he is with them. Miss
Wright seems to like him. So does Fanny.'

'Miss Wright is a wise lady and children don't take
the same notice of disfigurement as adults do. Fanny
sees only a kindly playmate.'

They spoke of Asham for a little, then went on to
discuss the events of the afternoon.

'Holding this fête here is an old tradition, I gather.'

'Yes, the village green is just not large enough.'

'It was kind of Mr Tope to carry it on.'

'He wanted to do everything he could to preserve the
old ways.'

'But stopped short of living in a depressingly
neglected house!'

'He wanted to improve everything. Even this event.
He introduced the marquee last year, in case of rain.

Before that everyone got soaked if the weather was bad.'

'He's been good for the estate, I think.'

Thalia looked at him. He seemed unusually thoughtful, almost sad. He felt her scrutiny and looked up. Their eyes met and he smiled.

'You know, I'd like to sit here with you for the remainder of the afternoon, but I cannot.' He heaved a regretful sigh. 'They've roped me in for the tug-of-war.'

'But you're not an outside man!'

'I know, but one of the fellows injured himself yesterday and they've no one else strong enough. And it really doesn't matter whereabouts I work, I'm still employed at Stonar Hall.'

'I suppose not. It's the usual challenge, the Hall's men versus the villagers but usually there's no one inside who is fit enough! Do you mind?'

'Only because I'd rather sit here with you. But I expect Mr Tope would need me before long anyway. He's bound to want to move around a bit.'

'Everyone else is having a holiday, it hardly seems fair that you shouldn't, too! He's a considerate gentleman. I don't think he will bother you unless he has to.'

'No, I'm sure he won't.' As he spoke the sound of a distorted voice reached their ears. 'There, you see, I must go. The Vicar is using his speaking trumpet to call for the teams.'

He sprang lithely to his feet and held out a hand to help Thalia to hers. She took it and he pulled her up, pulled her close. There was an instant's meeting of the eyes, a moment when time seemed to stand still as some intangible message passed between them. Then the spell was broken by a renewed bellow through the trumpet, which the Vicar had handed over to a villager with a huge voice.

'I must go,' said Jack, released her hand and bent to pick up his coat and the empty cups.

Thalia nodded. 'I'll walk back with you. Unless you are in a desperate hurry?'

'Not at all. Will you take my arm?'

More food for gossiping tongues, thought Thalia. They had avoided leaving together on Wednesday, had met beyond the village, although she had known that Jack had shadowed her from the gates. She was a little apprehensive of the consequences of being seen to favour Hamilton's company. She did not want to be forced to leave Stonar Hall to escape damaging gossip. Yet everything they had done that afternoon had been in full view of everyone.

No doubt their names would be linked and speculation would be rife, but if they provided no reason for the more scurrilous kind of gossip, what damage could a little conjecture do? She liked Hamilton and, it seemed, he liked her. She was, of course, alone in his company during the walk to Asham. But no one knew of that. Was she to pass her whole life fearing gossip?

'Thank you,' she said, placing her gloved hand on his brown sleeve.

He smiled down at her, his eyes holding an expression which told her he admired her courage and was glad she was prepared to acknowledge their more harmonious relations in public. It would, after all, raise his standing in the close-knit community of the servants' hall to be seen on friendly terms with the housekeeper.

What it would do to her standing she feared to contemplate.

But the die was cast. She had accepted Jack Hamilton for what she knew him to be in himself, not what he appeared to be or might turn out to be. She only hoped her trust would not be proved false.

Once they reached the centre of the field and he had replaced the cups, Jack took his leave and went to join the other members of the Hall tug-of-war team. Thalia rejoined Mrs Gale, who had left her post now that the trestle table was devoid of anything remotely edible, and found herself a seat on a bench. Rose had disappeared.

A child jumped up out of the way and Thalia sat beside the cook.

'The cakes were delicious,' she said.

'He's a good lad,' said Mrs Gale comfortably.

'Hamilton?' asked Thalia, as though Mrs Gale might mean someone else.

'Jack Hamilton,' confirmed Cook. 'Too good for the job here.'

'Do you think so? He does it well.'

'Should be a gentleman's gentleman or a butler. Couldn't you get 'im promoted?'

'Over Jenkins's head?' cried Thalia, pretending to be scandalised.

'Jenkins wouldn't mind,' declared Mrs Gale. 'He's too long in the tooth to care provided 'e's secure and comfortable. He likes 'amilton. You wouldn't have no trouble with him.'

'There are not enough staff to warrant Mr Tope

employing both a butler and a housekeeper,' protested Thalia.

'He could take on a married couple, though.'

Thalia took her eyes from the absorbing sight of Jack, in shirtsleeves, winding the end of the rope about his muscular torso, to stare at Mrs Gale.

'What exactly do you mean by that, Cook?'

'You make a nice-looking pair, my dear, that's all. Pity not to seize your chance. If you don't, he'll be off, mark my words.'

'Of course he'll be off! He's already given me notice but promised to stay until I can find someone to take his place,' said Thalia, remembering that she had done nothing about advertising for a replacement. She had had other things on her mind. And Jack did not seem all that keen to go now that their quarrel had been resolved.

'They've made 'im anchor man,' chuckled Mrs Gale. 'Trust them crafty devils to hive off the worst job! I see the bailiff has got hisself the best one, just yellin' at 'em when to pull. We'll all miss Hamilton when he goes. Keeps us in fits in the servants' 'all.'

'Does he?' Thalia could not imagine Jack telling funny stories. They must be clean, or Mrs Gale would ban them. 'How?'

'Tellin' us of blokes he met in the army. Some strange coves about, according to him. Officers and men.'

'I see.' So he was now talking freely about that phase of his life. 'Does he mention his family?'

'No. Nor 'is 'ome. Parents are probably dead and he 'asn't got one.'

'He came here from Sevenoaks.'

'But that's not to say he had more than a room there. On 'is uppers I reckon he was when he came 'ere. Godsend, this job must've been. Now he's got experience he'll be looking to better hisself. Ooh, look! They've started!'

They both jumped to their feet and moved nearer the action. It was to be the best of three pulls. With Mr Shepherd urging them on, the Hall men heaved, stamped their feet down on the grass, and pulled again, gaining a little ground.

Jack dug his heels into the soft, slippery turf and hung on for dear life while the village team gathered momentum. Every man in front of him strained to keep to their place, not to be forced forward, not to give ground; and then, as the villagers' strength faded, they stamped and pulled, stamped and pulled until the villagers collapsed. A cheer went up. First pull to the Hall!

The teams fell to the ground, exhausted. They were given five minutes' rest before the second pull. This time, despite determined resistance by the Hall, the villagers won. Everything would depend on the final tug.

Thalia found herself edging nearer and nearer; and when the third contest began she was almost alongside the bailiff, beating her clenched fists up and down in time with his calls to heave.

She wanted to shout encouragement, to urge Jack to dig his heels in deeper when the villagers seemed about to drag the Hall team forward, but decorum would not allow her to join in the raucous cheering all around her.

Her upbringing demanded that she preserve some dignity, even on an occasion such as this.

For what seemed like minutes the two teams strained in opposite directions without moving more than an inch or so in either direction. The rag marker was nearer the Hall's winning line than that of the village but the men did not seem able to make the final effort which would bring it over the line.

Then Jack visibly gathered himself. He filled his lungs with air and in a voice which would have carried across a parade ground yelled, 'Come on, lads! One, two, three, HEAVE! HEAVE!'

To a man, they responded. Muscles bulged, veins stood out on neck and forehead. They began to go backwards, the villagers slid forwards and, with one final effort, the rag passed over the Hall's line. The team fell over one another into an exhausted heap.

'Well done, well done,' cried Mr Tope from his position on the platform.

Thalia, unable to stop herself, went to help Jack to his feet.

'Where did you get that voice?' she demanded to cover her confusion at finding herself where she was.

'Came in handy, didn't it? A sergeant major taught me the trick. In case I ever got promoted.'

'And did you?'

'Not to sergeant major,' said Jack regretfully.

He brushed himself down and went to struggle into his waistcoat and coat. His forehead was beaded with sweat.

'Why don't you carry those for a while?' suggested

Thalia. 'I'm sure no one will mind. No one else is putting their coats back on.'

'But although I'm not in uniform I'm still in attendance on Mr Tope!'

'He won't be bothered. He's not the least bit stuffy.'

'Except about attendance at church,' rejoined Jack ruefully.

'That's a matter of conscience, not formality!'

'Agreed. So come and sit with me again.'

'On that bench,' suggested Thalia, indicating the seats she and Mrs Gale had left and which were, mercifully, still vacant. She did not wish to go off alone with Jack Hamilton again. 'If we hurry, we might secure them!'

They sat together to watch the children receiving prizes for winning their races, and clapped extra hard when Mr Shepherd went up to receive the medal on behalf of his team for winning the tug-of-war.

Afterwards they watched the Morris men dance with their bells, streamers and sticks, and then it was time for the country dancing.

Jack stood up and bowed before her. 'Come,' he said, 'I've recovered enough breath to dance a measure, I think. Will you do me the honour of standing up with me?'

Someone had taught him manners. Thalia rose with alacrity. It was so long since she had danced!

The occasion was informal, the steps familiar. In a ballroom, even a private gathering, it would be frowned upon for two people to dance together more than twice. But in a meadow on a summer's evening at a village fête, barriers came down and everyone danced with whoever they liked for as long as they liked. Jack seemed content to keep Thalia for his partner, simply smiling engagingly at all the young women from Hall and village obviously anxious to dance with him.

'You should stand up with Rose,' murmured Thalia at one point.

'Why? She does not lack for partners.'

'But she has a crush on you.'

'Foolish of her. I've done nothing to encourage it.'

'Except wink at her and make her blush,' pointed out Thalia tartly.

'Oh, but that means nothing. She should know that. In the army—'

'You winked and whistled at every passing skirt.'

He grinned, unrepentant. 'Something like that.'

'Well, you'd better watch yourself, Jack Hamilton, or you may find yourself committed to a young lady you have no desire to wed!'

'Is that a warning, ma'am?'

'Oh no. I have no one to produce a shotgun on my behalf.'

They were both smiling—the exchange was light-hearted, flirtatious badinage, but there was enough truth behind her words to give them both food for thought.

'You know I would never do anything to cause you hurt, don't you?' asked Jack.

He'd said something similar once before. She believed him. But he could not be held responsible for her foolishness in wishing for the impossible. For falling in love with him.

CHAPTER SEVEN

THE next day found them walking to Asham once more.
This time they set off together from the church. After
all, the entire village now knew they were friendly. Why
should she not take Hamilton to meet the other friend
she visited so regularly?

First they called in at the inn to confirm that Varley's
sword had been safely delivered to his commanding
officer.

The stable lad grinned cheekily and assured them
that he'd found the Colonel's lodgings and given the
sword into his lordship's own hands.

'His staff did not stop you?' demanded Jack
curiously.

'Couple of officers tried, but I was too smart for the
likes of them. Darted past while they was confabbing,
sir.'

Jack chuckled. 'Good lad. Here's another sixpence
for a job well done.'

The boy spun the coin, bit it to make sure it was
genuine, and went off whistling.

Jack also wanted a word with the landlord. While
Sidney had been staying at the inn Jack had fallen into
the habit of walking out to see him after helping Mr
Tope into bed. Now he went to see if Sid had left a
message.

* * *

The visit to Asham proved as happy as the previous one and even more satisfactory. Since she had company for the return walk, she was able to leave a little later than usual so that she could help to put a tired but contented Fanny to bed.

So it was dark by the time they approached the Hall, having kept to the road and entered by the main gates. As they rounded the house to reach the service door, Jack drew her into a patch of impenetrable shadow thrown by some bushes and gathered her into his arms.

Thalia did not protest. She met his kiss with keen anticipation and mounting excitement. She had never expected to feel this way, to enjoy the exquisite pleasure he evoked in her. She might never have another opportunity to delight in the attentions of a man to whom she could wholeheartedly respond. Most ladies of her class merely tolerated the advances of their husbands, that she understood. Only the ill-bred were supposed to feel passion, possibly, thought Thalia cynically, because the well-bred were unable to wed for love.

A few lucky ladies of her former acquaintance had found real fulfilment in the marriage bed and she had been determined to emulate them. Others, wed to men they hated, despised, feared or regarded solely with affection, defied convention and took their pleasure outside the bonds of wedlock. It might be all right for otherwise respectable matrons to do so—everyone knew Lady Jersey, for example, had a lover—but because she herself had been unwed, she would have been ostracised for stepping out of line.

But surely, because she considered herself cast out from Society, she need no longer think of herself as a lady! Jack Hamilton seemed to like her response to his advances; if that lowered her to his level, then so be it. The rules that had once bound her so strictly seemed stupid in the face of her present circumstances. Because of a momentary weakness under pressure, through no real fault of her own, those strictures had reduced her to the role of servant. For what was a housekeeper but a servant? So, if she wanted to, why should she not behave like one?

She wound her arms about his neck and returned his kisses with an ardency Jack found enchanting but frustrating. He knew her reaction was born largely of innocence and tried to keep his rising passion under control. But he could not prevent the deepening demand of his kiss, the response his body made of its own volition. God, how he wanted her! And how inconvenient to his plans was his growing regard for her!

His hands stroked her body, following the satisfying curves of shoulders, back and hips. She did not protest. Emboldened, he cupped a breast in his palm, felt her flesh respond through the thin layers of cotton covering it. She growled deep in her throat and sagged in his arms as his thumb stroked her hardened nipple.

He lifted his mouth from hers and took a harsh breath. It was more difficult than he'd imagined to keep his passion within bounds. Words which had been running around his brain since the moment he'd met her burst from him.

'I want you, Thalia.'

His mouth closed on hers again. The turf was soft and dry beneath the bushes. Keeping his lips clamped to hers, he moved to lower them both to the ground, ignoring the deeply-buried knowledge that Thalia Marsh was no ordinary creature and that he should not take her lightly.

Thalia desperately wanted to give herself to this man she suspected she loved. But, despite all her previous rationalisations, as he urged her down to the grass her upbringing rose to confront her, to forbid her from behaving as Rose might have done.

'No,' she whispered, finding strength to resist his downward momentum, 'no, Jack, please. I cannot.'

Her resistance, the agonised pleading in her voice brought Jack back to his senses. The devil! Was he no better than Varley?

With a supreme effort he controlled his breathing. His hold gentled. He held her loosely, kissed her lightly on forehead, cheeks, and finally her mouth.

'I'm sorry,' he murmured. 'I want you so badly I forgot myself. Can you forgive me?'

Thalia continued to cling to him as relief washed over her.

'Of course,' she answered him, and stroked his lean cheek to make sure he realised she understood and was grateful for his forebearance. 'It is I who should apologise. I encouraged you. I wanted you, too,' she admitted shyly, 'but I find I cannot lightly repeat what Varley forced upon me. The consequences were too shaming.'

'I would never allow—' began Jack, then stopped himself. He would never allow what? Her to bear another bastard? Her to suffer for yielding to his demands? But how should he prevent these things unless he were willing to wed her? And he could not enter into that kind of commitment with a woman who kept her true position in society so secret.

So he allowed his words to tail off and kissed her again instead. His passion had died to a pulsing undercurrent and he felt a great tenderness for this girl the world had treated so harshly.

'Come,' he said, tucking her arm beneath his. 'Allow me to see you safely to your room.'

He walked with her as far as the landing and watched as she moved on to a door and opened it. He made no attempt to follow her further and she did not beckon him on. He would have loved to see her rooms, to know how she lived, but both knew it was safer not to court temptation. He went up and joined a slumbering Jenkins in their attic.

Jack arrived at the King's Arms later than usual on Tuesday evening. There was no message from Asham but Mr Alfred Cracker touched his bulbous nose and drew Jack aside. The landlord's original suspicions of both Hamilton and Barton had been quite dispelled once he got to know them. Now he was prepared to be friendly, even helpful, to a good customer.

'Take care,' he warned Jack. 'We've 'ad strangers in 'ere tonight. Sea-cocks, I reckon, though not ones as comes this way regular.'

'Smugglers?'

'Aye, and nasty-looking coves they were. Maybe they've come over from Hawkhurst, part of that gang. Asking after the fancy footman who recently came to the 'all. Did you come regular, 'ad you been 'ere this evening and such. Told 'em no, but I don't reckon they've gone far.'

'What would they want with me?' wondered Jack. 'Does Mr Tope have dealings with them?'

'Not that lot.' He touched his nose again. 'Our local lads, maybe, though they have a hard time keeping out of the way of the big gangs. But Squire wouldn't deal with the likes of the Hawkhurst Gang. Steer clear, Jack, steer clear.'

'Thanks for the warning, Alf. I will if I can.' He thought and frowned. He had his pistol, but once that was fired it would be of no further use except as a club. 'How many of them are there?'

'Three, as I saw.'

'If you don't mind, I'll take one of your pitchforks with me when I go.'

'You're welcome,' said Cracker, showing all his blackened teeth in a gleeful grin.

'I'll try not to damage it,' promised Jack. 'If I do, I'll make it up to you.'

Jack remained for a few minutes while he drank his ale then departed via the yard. He found a wicked-looking double-pronged fork propped in an empty stable, tested it for strength and, satisfied, began his walk back to Stonar Hall. At least he had something with which to defend himself. But why would these ugly customers from another part of Kent be asking after him? What did they intend?

Jack had all the old soldier's instinct for danger and knew it was near. His senses heightened, he anticipated the coming confrontation with fierce joy. He had been living the soft life for far too long! But how he wished he had Sergeant Barton beside him, as he had so often been during their years in the army.

But, provided there were no more of them, the odds were not insuperable. And if he could reach the short cut across the fields he had discovered soon after arriving at the Hall, he would leave the open road, where he felt vulnerable.

The attack came before he reached the footpath, but far enough from the village not to rouse any inhabitants who might be tempted to come to his aid.

He heard the champing of a bit, the sound of hooves moving restlessly in the undergrowth and then a voice rang out.

'Now, men! This is the creature! But I don't want him killed!'

Jack recognised that voice. 'Come out, Varley!' he challenged. 'Be a man and meet me face to face.'

He could hear the snapping of twigs in the undergrowth as men crashed through. How many? Only the three, he thought, as he pulled out his pistol.

Varley's sneering voice came to him again. 'I'll prove I'm a man, fellow, when I take the Marsh woman from you! She'll come to me when she knows I have discovered her secret!'

Jack tensed. His fierce joy in a promised battle turned to cold fury. He had intended to fire to frighten the horse but now he aimed at Varley himself. He did not care if he killed him. Damn the consequences!

But as the flame spurted, the pistol recoiled and Varley screamed, clutching his shoulder, he knew he had only winged the Viscount; as common sense reasserted itself, he ruefully blessed the uncertain aim of his firearm. However, the horse had bolted and Varley was out of the game.

He had no more time to even think of Varley's fate because the three assailants were on him. He fended off the first rush with the deadly tines of the pitchfork, swung at a sideways attack with his clubbed pistol, thrust forwards again with the fork and felt the prongs catch cloth if not flesh, though a curse and bellow of pain told him he had damaged the man. He wrenched the weapon free and thrust with it again, catching a whey face and hearing the man scream in agony.

With their mentor gone, the creatures seemed disinclined to press home the attack against an armed and dangerous man so capable of inflicting serious damage. Jack backed away towards the inviting cover of the path and they did not follow. But then, just as he was thinking the danger over, a new element in the drama came on the scene.

A musket fired. A huge voice bellowed, 'Halt, in the King's name! Lay down your arms!'

The devil! thought Jack, seeing the dark shapes appear on the road behind his assailants. Revenue men! They'd be after the smugglers, brought to the scene by the sound of his pistol, and no doubt they'd think he was one of the gang! He'd be able to explain, to clear himself, but it would mean revealing his true identity. He was ready to do that only in an extremity, and it hadn't come to that yet.

He hoped to quietly disappear into the bushes, but the King's men were sharp eyed, used to spotting escapees in the dark.

'There! After him!' shouted their leader as Jack's shadow dissolved into the undergrowth.

So it would be a chase! He'd take it as far as he could, surrender if he must. But he knew the ground, had walked it most evenings. The track ended at a back entrance to the Hall's grounds, which in turn was quite near the kitchen and the service door.

One of the Revenue men was mounted, but thank God they had no dogs with them. As he fled along the narrow, rutted path, Jack could hear the sounds of his former assailants being rounded up and arrested. The pounding of hooves told him that the mounted officer was coming after him. He leapt the ditch and dived behind a thick screen of vegetation, cursing the recent rain as he sank down into the dank and muddy bottom of the drainage channel and pulled the cow parsley over him.

The horse passed his hiding place and pounded on. Jack crawled from the ditch and, leaving the path, pushed his way through a small gap in a tangle of branches and cautiously carried on in the field, behind the shelter of the hedge.

He heard the horse pull up ahead. Above the line of the hedge he saw its rider silhouetted against the lighter sky and melted back into the shadow of the bushes. From where the man sat, he could scrutinise an empty stretch of the path ahead. He had a pistol in his hand and Jack hoped he'd shout a warning before firing. He did not relish the thought of being spotted and brought down by a lucky shot. The man turned to shout over his shoulder to a couple of minions pounding after him on foot.

'He's gone. He must be here somewhere. Search the ditch!'

Doubled up, his brown coat invisible in the impenetrable shadow of the hedge, Jack continued on towards the horse and its rider, who was watching his men stab into the ditch with the bayonets attached to their muskets.

Almost holding his breath, Jack passed soundlessly within feet of the motionless rider. The horse shifted restlessly, sensing his presence, but the Revenue officer merely quieted it, as Jack had hoped.

If he kept to the shadow of the hedge which divided path from field, he could reach Stonar Hall without coming out into the open. If they came into the field he'd hide amongst the tall rye. He did not think they'd catch him now. Provided he kept hidden and they did not shoot first and ask questions afterwards, he was quite safe and enjoying the challenge of the chase. He thrust the pitchfork into the tangle of weeds at the foot of the hedge, from where he could recover it at leisure.

It was not until he was forced to leave the shelter of the hedge to cross an open patch of path to reach the postern gate of the Hall that he heard a distant cry and knew that he'd been seen. Damn! But they'd have descended upon the Hall looking for him in any case, guessing that he might be headed there. He should have taken a more circuitous route, deceived them into thinking he was making for the marshes. Too late to think of that now—he had not expected to be seen.

As he barred the postern behind him and loped across the kitchen gardens to reach the door to the house, which would not yet be bolted, he knew what he would do. All things worked together for good, he thought, as a broad and mischievous smile spread across his face.

Inside, he shot the bolt, hoping everyone else was already in, used the jack to remove his muddy boots and padded up the stairs in his stockinged feet, carrying the incriminating footwear. He did not hesitate but made straight for the door he had watched Thalia enter. At this time she would certainly be in her room.

He gave a cursory knock and stepped into what was clearly her parlour. She was not there. He crossed to a door that must communicate with the adjoining bedroom and opened it.

Thalia was propped up in bed, the bed-curtains tied back because of the heat, reading by the light of a branch of candles set on a table beside her. Even his present circumstances could not prevent his noticing how desirable she looked in a snowy nightgown with a white cap tied under her chin, her brown hair hanging loose beneath it to cloak her shoulders.

His heart leapt. He had the perfect excuse for joining her in the bed.

'Hush!' he ordered as she gave a startled cry. 'I need your help. The Revenue men are after me for reasons I'll explain later. But they'll be hammering on the door soon and I need an alibi.'

To Thalia's astonishment, as he spoke he was throwing off some decidedly muddy garments.

'But you can't stay here!' she protested.

'For God's sake, Thalia, do you want me to be arrested? You are the only one I can ask to lie for me.

If you don't, I can't be of help to either you or Fanny.
And you need help.'

'Why, what has happened?'

'Varley,' said Jack succinctly and saw the colour drain
from her cheeks.

He was sorry to distress her but it seemed she was
prepared to prove obdurate. Damn her girlish confusion, the prudery instilled in her probably from birth.

'Where can I hide these?' he demanded, indicating
his clothes and boots.

At that moment came a thunderous knocking on the
front door. His pursuers had not taken long to arrive.
Had the mounted officer climbed the wall? He could
easily have done so by standing on his horse's back and
letting himself down on the inside.

The sound seemed to galvanise Thalia into action. In
fact, she had been assessing the pros and cons of doing
as Jack requested and had decided that her reputation,
for so long carefully guarded despite being already
sullied, did not matter a jot in comparison with his
safety.

'Under the bed,' she suggested, leaping out and lifting
the drapes.

'Thanks.' Jack stuffed his outer clothes out of sight,
aware of the delicate scent of her as he bent down
beside her. He stood again, thrusting temptation aside.
'I'm afraid I'll have to join you in the bed to make it
look convincing should anyone come to call you. I've
been here for the last hour at least. Do you
understand?'

Thalia nodded, then walked calmly over to her wash-
stand and returned with a damp cloth.

'You have mud on your face,' she pointed out, 'and your hands are none too clean. Use this.'

With a grimace, Jack glanced in a nearby mirror and cleaned himself up. The muddy wet cloth joined his clothes under the bed. Thalia had already resumed her place on the mattress. Jack ran his fingers through his hair as he walked round and got in on the other side. Thalia, her heart pounding, waited to see what he would do.

He put his arm beneath her shoulders, drew her down and brought her head to rest against his chest.

Thalia, suffering acutely from anxiety and embarrassment, was intensely aware of his odour, the warmth of the strong body hidden beneath his shirt and linen undergarments. As he drew her to him she stiffened, resisting the urge to turn to him, to show how much she wanted him to make love to her.

Jack thought wryly that he was exactly where he had sworn to be, for all the good it was doing him! Her body was desperately desirable, but stiff as a board in his arms. Given time he felt certain he could melt her resistance, make her welcome him not only into her bed—

His erotic thoughts were abruptly cut off, and not before time, he thought wryly, subduing the urgent demands of his body as a frightened boy, left on duty by the front door as watchman, knocked and came stumbling into the room.

The lad stopped dead and gawped in amazement at the sight which met his eyes, for they had not touched the open bed-curtains.

With commendable calm, Thalia roused herself to

ask, 'What do you want, Binns, disturbing me at this time of night?'

'Oh, mum, it's the Revenue, wanting to search the 'ouse, mum. What am I to do with un?'

'Do not disturb Mr Tope, whatever else you do. Ask them to wait. I'll come down.'

The lad scuttled away, giving Jack an awed, disbelieving glance as he left. Jack dropped a quick kiss on Thalia's forehead and got out of the bed.

'I'm afraid our apparent dalliance will be the talk of the servants' hall,' he said wryly. 'I'm sorry. I hope it won't upset you too much. It is a pity that you were already in bed and that the boy actually burst in— though I must confess his seeing us together like that will make the alibi convincing! I must thank you most sincerely for laying yourself open to gossip on my account. And thank you for allowing me to stay.'

'How could I not agree to help you? I owe you too much.'

'You owe me nothing.' He tilted her chin and gently kissed her lips. 'I'd better go and make myself respectable.'

'Leave your things here. They won't search my bedroom but they will yours.' She was picking up her grey gown as she spoke, her voice as unsteady as her hands. 'I'll have to dress.'

'Wait for me.'

'Yes.'

He went. Thalia pulled on the gown. Fumbling with the hooks at the back and unable to reach some, she flung a shawl about her shoulders to hide the gap, then fastened the belt round her waist. She slipped house shoes on her bare feet and tidied her hair, tucking it under her usual austere daytime cap.

Yes, with the keys hanging from her waist she was back to being Mrs Marsh, respectable housekeeper. Outwardly. Inwardly she was far from calm and her thoughts were certainly neither austere nor respectable. Something dramatic had taken place in her emotions as she lay so tense in Jack Hamilton's arms.

The sweat of recent exertion had bathed his body in a manly scent which had sent her senses reeling. Why should she refuse to accept the pleasure he could give her just to comply with some stupid convention?

Convention? It would be a sin. She had sinned once before and suffered for it.

Jack walked back into the room and all her doubts disappeared in a tide of pure joy at sight of him. She smiled, and despite the austerity of her appearance, Jack felt the warmth of it and caught his breath. But Authority was waiting impatiently below. First they must deal with the Revenue men.

'Come.' He held out his hand. 'Let us beard the lion.'

Together, they descended to the hall where the officer was pacing. His men had caught up and stood in a group near the door.

Thalia introduced herself.

'Sorry to trouble you, ma'am, but the smuggler fellow we are after came here to the Hall, I'm certain of it. I must interview every man living here and search the place, too. Probably brought some contraband in with him.'

'Then you have a daunting task ahead of you, officer,'

said Thalia. 'I do not believe any of the staff here are involved with smuggling, but if you insist—'

'I do, ma'am, I do.'

'Very well. There are few menservants living in the house. Some outside and stable staff live in quarters there, while others live in cottages throughout the estate. Do you wish to rouse them all?'

'I'll begin with those in the house,' growled the officer. 'I think this is where he was making for. Who's this fellow, eh?' His bloodshot gaze rested suspiciously on Jack. 'He looks about the right build to me.'

'This,' said Thalia stiffly, 'is Hamilton, Mr Tope's personal footman. He cannot be the man you are after. He has been with me for the last hour.'

A snigger from the boy Binns made Thalia's cheeks burn but she kept her gaze steadily on the official, who glanced quickly from one to the other and gave a cackle of laughter.

'Enjoying yerselves, eh? Catch 'em at it, did you?' he asked the boy.

The lad went scarlet, threw Thalia a frantic look, and gulped.

'Do not worry, Binns,' Thalia reassured him. 'You will not suffer for what you saw. You would not have burst in upon me without excellent reason.' She turned to Jack. 'Perhaps you will be so good as to rouse Jenkins and the others. Bring them down here to my office.'

Jack bowed deferentially, amused by her small revenge. He did not in the least mind being made to appear in the guise of the housekeeper's fancy. 'Yes, ma'am.'

Jenkins had not stirred as Jack had crept in to don his uniform clothes, so would need waking. Jack mounted the stairs with all the dignity of a well-trained footman.

It took the officer and his men over an hour to question the servants and fruitlessly search their rooms. Thalia could see that the officer was still highly suspicious, but he could prove nothing. He would, Thalia hoped and expected, have a similar lack of luck in any of the cottages he decided to knock up. But you never knew. One of the groundsman might be involved in running contraband. It would be sheer bad luck if he were caught because of Jack's activities.

Jack wondered what the captured smugglers would say under questioning. Would they admit that they had been engaged in beating up a footman from the Hall, who had escaped them? He doubted it. They would protest complete innocence, insist it was a private quarrel and, if they had nothing incriminating on them, would escape justice. He doubted whether he would hear any more of the matter.

As the door finally closed behind the investigators, Thalia beckoned him to follow her.

'Come and tell me all about it,' she said quietly.

Yes, thought Jack. He would tell her what had happened and they must discuss the threat to Fanny. But not until they had made love.

Back in her bedroom, Jack told her briefly what had happened.

'Varley set a gang of smugglers on me. The Revenue

men had spotted them and mistook me for one of them so, having captured my attackers, they hunted me.'

'Oh, Jack, I'm so sorry! Supposing they'd chased you into the marshes!'

'Don't be. They didn't. I could have got away by telling them who I was and what the trouble was all about, but I preferred not to. I did not wish to involve you, or even Varley.'

'And who are you, Jack?'

He grinned, not about to be caught out as easily as that.

'Mr Tope's personal footman and that is why I made straight for the Hall, thinking I'd lost them. But unfortunately the officer spotted me by the postern gate. My only regret is that I caused trouble to everyone here. However,' he murmured as he pulled her into his arms and kissed her, 'I cannot pretend to regret my intrusion into your bedroom.'

Immediately, past tensions dissolved, all questions were forgotten. Swept along on a tide of relief, Thalia allowed her feelings free rein, accepting the flare of passion between them as inevitable. Everyone would think them lovers after tonight. Why not make it true? They would be hurting no one but themselves. Sins could be forgiven. And could it be so very sinful to give herself to the man she loved?

For now she was certain. Her fear for him, when she realised the danger Jack had been in, had finally convinced her that she was not mistaking a girlish *tendre*, born of gratitude for his protection, as something more. Her feelings for him ran deep.

She sensed that in Jack Hamilton she had discovered

an audacious, self-reliant individual possessed of the finer feelings she had despaired of finding in any man, let alone one she could love. It saddened her that he did not love her, could not trust her with his secrets, yet she knew—or thought she knew—that he would not treat her as despicably as Varley had.

She was doubtless piling up more misery for the future when his interest in her died and he left to better himself, but she'd found the courage once before to follow her own course and she would do so again.

So, when Jack plucked off her prim cap, ran his fingers through her hair to loosen it and then stroked it about her shoulders, she did not demur but returned the kiss that followed with enthusiasm. Nor did she object when he undid those hooks she had managed to fasten to push the gown from her shoulders, kissing the soft, creamy flesh thus exposed.

She'd not taken the time to don undergarments and so, as he removed her belt and the gown tumbled about her feet, she stood naked before him. Thalia, rosy now with excitement and embarrassment, instinctively crossed her arms to hide her breasts. Jack shook his head, his eyes blazing with admiration.

'Do not hide from me, Thalia. Let me look at you. You are so beautiful.'

'I am?' wondered Thalia, reluctantly allowing him to peel her arms away from her body.

For a moment he stood taking in her shapely form, the high breasts and narrow waist, the generous hips and slender legs.

'You should not hide such riches under those dreadful gowns,' he murmured.

Next moment he swept her off her feet and carried her the few steps to the bed, where he laid her down and removed her slippers.

Thalia watched shyly as he disrobed, her stomach clenched in knots of anticipation. Would he, like Varley, find her response unsatisfactory? He undid his hastily tied neckcloth, threw off the grey waistcoat and black coat of his uniform and followed them with his shoes and stockings. She caught her breath as he removed the grey breeches. Consumed by embarrassment, she averted her eyes. By the time she found the courage to look again, he was as naked as she.

The flames of the candles revealed highlights and shadows in the light growth of fair hair covering his broad chest and running down in a thin line to his slim waist and beyond. He was all male, and he wanted her. But although she felt shy, he did not frighten her as Varley had done. There was a certain look in his eyes, compounded of admiration, desire and tenderness, which melted her insides.

Thalia, beyond embarrassment now, gave a choking cry as she reached out to draw the strong, lithe body down to her.

dinexter, smoothing the roughness of his body-hair;
inadvertently she brushed one of his nipples and he
jerked, drawing a sharp breath.

'Sorry,' she murmured, snatching away her hand.

'Don't be—' he broke off, struggling to regain control,
will be over far too soon.'

to be calm, murmured

. . . .

CHAPTER EIGHT

THE bed shifted under his weight. 'Jack,' she whispered
huskily.

'Don't be afraid,' he murmured, 'I won't hurt you.'

'I know, I'm not. Whoever you are, you're more of a
gentleman than Varley will ever be.'

She saw his wry smile as he said, 'Thank you, ma'am.'

'Oh!' she cried in distress. 'Did I sound condescend-
ing? I didn't mean to.'

'Hush! It doesn't matter.' How could it, when it was
his own fault she thought him some lowly upstart? 'All
that does matter is that you are in my arms at last. You
cannot imagine how I have longed to have you there.'

'It's where I want to be,' admitted Thalia in a whisper.

Even if he was some misbegotten son of a whore she
would still love him. He might well be, for she guessed
he had some gentleman's blood in him somewhere. He
was neither coarse nor lewd and had dignity and
authority—all she had ever truly demanded in a man.

Besides, he was gentle, wooing her in a way Varley
had not. As his hands stroked her body and his lips
played with hers, her limbs trembled. Soon the long,
sweeping strokes changed into light, circling movements
of his fingers as he traced the shape of her breasts. Then
his thumb found a peak and she gasped and shuddered
with exquisite, piercing pleasure.

Her hands slid down his chest, rippling over his

muscles, smoothing the roughness of his body hair. Inadvertently she touched one of his nipples and he jerked, drawing a sharp breath.

'Sorry,' she muttered, snatching away her hand.

'Don't be,' he growled, 'but if you do not desist all will be over far too soon.'

There was so much she had to learn. 'Teach me what to do,' she murmured.

'My pleasure, ma'am.'

His unthinking choice of words might appear to reinforce his subordinate status but his actions certainly did not. He was her master, bringing her body to throbbing life with his expertise.

He lowered his head to her breast and took its peak into his mouth. When Varley had done that, he had hurt her; for an instant she tensed, but Jack's caressing of her breast was so different, so tender, that the spears of intense pain shooting through her were pleasurable rather than painful and made her want to pull him closer, to become part of him.

She shifted her hips and felt how much he wanted her. 'Jack,' she whispered. 'Take me, please.'

His hand travelled down to investigate the secret places between her thighs. She gasped again and, instinctively, sought to touch him.

'Don't,' he muttered. 'Wait. I want to give you pleasure first.'

And then, suddenly, all the strength drained from her limbs. She lay, completely enervated, utterly under the spell of his gentle exploration.

He moved and her legs parted to accommodate him. His weight as he lay on her, his hands cradling her head while he kissed her, infused her with fluid warmth. Unheralded, the strength returned to her muscles, her hips moved in patent invitation as she clung to his shoulders, urgent for his possession.

He stilled himself for a moment, looked down into her flushed face, her drowning eyes. His own need intensified at sight of her surrender, was almost uncontrollable, but he still had to ask. 'Thalia,' he murmured, his voice ragged, 'are you sure about this?'

He was giving her the chance to withdraw. His desire was so evident she wondered how he could. Her heart melted.

'Oh, yes, yes!'

'Then help me.'

He raised his hips and Thalia did as bidden. It was strange, but holding him, guiding him, seemed to make the act of possession as much hers as his. She was taking him just as much as he was taking her.

The long, slow strokes enticed, seduced and uplifted her. A strange quivering in her abdomen made her gasp before she became lost in a labyrinth of exquisite pleasure. She was in a new and golden world inhabited by no one but herself and her lover, who was taking her to Paradise. She wanted it never to end.

But of course it had to. She returned to herself to find him collapsed on top of her, his beloved, reassuring weight pressing her down into the mattress. The shattering experience had been no trick of her imagination. It had been real.

Jack, in tune with her responses, let himself go as she climaxed. He'd lost himself in a woman many times, but not like this. Why was this woman so different? he wondered distractedly before he stopped thinking and plunged into the depths of the most satisfying release he had ever known.

He expelled his pent-up breath and began to breath again. Slowly, he regained his strength and senses, to find that Thalia was pressing a multitude of warm, moist kisses on his shoulder and neck. He eased his weight from her and rolled from the bed.

'Jack?'

Thalia's bemused cry accused him but he thrust aside the guilt. If he did not immediately escape her seductive arms, he would do something foolish, like ask her to marry him.

At first he had sworn to take her to bed out of pique. Then he had discovered her hidden attractions and wanted her for herself. But he'd never expected to find in this outcast from Society a passion to meet his own, tempting him to throw caution to the winds and declare himself, to demand that she wed him.

But he could not. He did not yet know where his own future lay. He could not encumber himself with a wife, let alone one so bereft of family and friends, while he was so uncertain of his own position. If and when he did wed, he would probably be obliged to marry an heiress, a woman who could bring him a large, much needed fortune to restore his family's finances. The idea repulsed him—he wanted to wed for love—but if he must he would.

So he had to tear himself away from Thalia Marsh before he did something they would both later regret.

'Jenkins will wonder where I am,' he growled, swiftly pulling on his clothes. They had not drawn the bed curtains and she could watch his every move.

'The entire household knows by now,' declared Thalia. Tears of mortification gathered in her eyes. She had failed again. Lord or commoner, men found her disappointing in bed. Jack Hamilton could not leave her fast enough. He probably despised her now, for giving in so readily to his demands.

Jack noticed the sparkle of moisture spilling over to her cheeks and smothered a curse. But he must not weaken.

'No tears,' he ordered abruptly. 'I have to be up early in the morning. I must ride to Asham and see to your child's safety.' Dear God, he'd almost forgotten Fanny's danger in his preoccupation with her mother! At least it made a tolerable excuse for his hasty retreat. 'I need your authority to take a horse. I will say that you have sent me on an urgent commission.'

Thalia roused herself to sit up, keeping the covers tightly stretched across her breasts. She wiped away her unbidden tears, determined not to turn into a watering pot, not to let Hamilton know how foolishly weak she was. But oh, how his rejection hurt! She forced the pain of her breaking heart aside and made herself concentrate on what Jack said.

'Of course.' How cold her voice sounded. But at least it was steady. 'What exactly did Lord Varley say?'

'He informed me that he knew your secret. He probably guessed you left home because you were pregnant. It would not take him long to work out the rest.'

Thalia shivered. 'You think he knows where she is?'

'He will have asked around. If he has not already discovered her whereabouts, he soon will. Your secret has remained a secret because no one was interested enough to make determined enquiries. Varley will spread his net wide. He will have little difficulty in finding her.'

Jack was all brisk business now. Fully dressed, he stood at the foot of the bed, his hand gripping a post so hard that his knuckles became white, wishing he could touch Thalia to comfort her but unsure of his control and so not daring to. 'Both she and Miss Wright must be removed before he has a chance to plot some further mischief. He could use threats against her to force you, Thalia.'

And that idea was as repugnant to him as it obviously was to her.

Her face drained of colour, she gazed up at him, appalled, all thoughts other than for the safety of her daughter wiped from her mind. This unlikely footman was the only person she could turn to in her trouble. A man who had rejected her but who held all their fates in his hands.

'So what must we do?' Her voice had begun to shake, but the cause was evident now. She need not hide her distress.

'You do nothing. I winged him last night and I doubt he will be able to act immediately. I have time to ride out to Asham and arrange for Barton to take them to a safe place. He will know where to go and how to travel so that they cannot be traced.'

'Where will they go?'

'It is better if you do not know, Thalia. Varley will not be able to force the information from you.'

'But you will know?'

'I shall tell Sid where to take them.'

'That scarcely seems fair. How shall I know they are safe and happy? I shall not be able to see for myself!'

'Not for a while, though not for long, I hope. They must disappear until I have dealt with Varley.'

'You?' Doubt filled eyes rendered dark and mysterious in the dim, flickering light. He wanted to drown in their depths, to lose himself in her again. 'What can you do?'

He shrugged, both denying his need and admitting his lack of a plan. 'I'll think of something. Trust me, Thalia. Believe me, I have only your best interests at heart.'

She gazed steadily into his multi-coloured eyes and saw nothing to disturb her trust in his integrity. However disappointed he had been in her he was still prepared to help her.

His entire attitude spoke of a man used to making up his mind and allowing nothing to distract him from his purpose. The deferential footman had quite disappeared, replaced by someone who could well be a grimly determined officer, a leader of men. If he had indeed been an officer, then he had become a gentleman, whatever his origins. A comforting thought.

Not that it made any difference now. He had taken her and then as good as rejected her. Yet he was still concerned for Fanny's safety, and for her own if she read him right. Concerned for her, willing to help, but unwilling to admit that he had been as lost in their lovemaking as she.

Yet, now she had had time to recover from the shock of his sudden departure from her bed, and despite her limited experience, she knew that his passion had not been feigned, that he had been as overcome and delighted by the manner of their coming together as she had been.

A weight lifted from her mind. Perhaps it wasn't her. Perhaps his rejection had nothing to do with any failure on her part. So why was he breaking her heart?

Because she had proved herself to be no better than the whore her father had branded her?

If so, then all the joy she had experienced in his arms had been false. Her seemingly golden ascent into higher realms nothing but dross. The pain of it all brought a new pricking of tears to her eyes which she tried desperately to quell. Yet she could not regret her surrender. Once the pain receded, she would have the memory of bliss to sustain her through the rest of her barren life.

Jack moved round the bed and reached out for her hand as it clutched the sheet, trusting himself at last. She shrank away from his touch and he knew he had only himself to blame.

His voice thickened. 'Do not worry, Thalia, Fanny will be safe. Go to sleep, my dear.' He really could not stop himself from teasing her. The subterfuge was all so ridiculous, but necessary. A wicked, predatory grin lit his face. 'Dream of me.'

He bent and swiftly, lightly, his lips touched hers.

Thalia's whole body shook. Her trembling fingers gripped the sheet fiercely as she watched him leave her room. The arrogance of the man! Dream of him! She'd be lucky to sleep.

She didn't. She lay, dry-eyed, reliving the past hour,

its joys and disappointments, and worrying about Fanny.

How could she be so unutterably foolish as to entrust the care of her daughter to so cavalier a creature, a man who could so quickly change from lover to stranger to teasing seducer? She must see him, talk to him, before he left for Asham. The stables stirred at five. He would leave then, she supposed. He would not rouse the lads to tack up a horse in the middle of the night.

So, when she heard a stir in the house when the sky had barely begun to lighten, let alone display the first streaks of dawn, she rose and began to dress, wondering what had caused the disturbance, knowing that eventually someone would come to call her. She had just fastened her belt when Tilly, still in her nightgown but with an old cloak hastily pulled on over it, knocked and burst in. The child's crumpled nightcap had slipped to one side, giving her a rakish appearance.

'Oh, ma'am! Such a to-do!' Amilton sent me, ma'am. 'Tis the master, he's been took that bad.'

'Mr Tope?' asked Thalia, horrified. Apart from his injured spine and legs, Mr Tope had been in the best of health. What a night this was turning out to be! 'I'll go to him at once.'

Pringle must have rushed to rouse Jack and in doing so woken most of the other servants. Mr Tope must be bad for Jack to send Tilly for her.

Jack and Pringle flanked each side of the bed. Sebastian Tope was conscious. His face under his nightcap had become lopsided and he was struggling to speak. She rushed to his side as Jack stepped back to make room for her.

One of his hands moved in greeting. The other lay useless on the coverlet.

'Oh, sir,' she cried, grasping the hand that had moved. 'Whatever is the matter?'

'He can't talk,' said Jack, almost angrily. 'I think 'e's suffered a seizure. We should send for the doctor immediate, ma'am. I'll go if you like. There's nothing I can do 'ere that you or Pringle can't.'

In front of Tope and the other servants Jack still made some pretence of speaking roughly.

Thalia nodded assent. Jack bent over the bed and touched Tope gently on the shoulder.

'I'll be as quick as I can, sir,' he murmured, and Thalia wondered at the quiet reassurance in his voice, at the tone which implied a genuine fondness for his employer. But he had been Tope's efficient, faithful and gentle aid for some weeks now. He turned to her. 'May I beg a few words alone with you, ma'am, afore I go?'

Thalia squeezed Mr Tope's hand. 'I'll be straight back,' she promised, and allowed Jack to usher her from the room.

She sent Tilly, Rose and Jenkins, gathered in an anxious knot on the landing, down to the kitchen to make everyone a hot drink. There would be no more sleep for any of the staff now.

Alone with Jack, Thalia ignored the fit of trembling his closeness brought on, shut out memory of her mortifying failure to please him, and faced him squarely.

'Rouse the stables, take the best horse. The doctor lives in Sandwich. You know where to go?'

He spoke softly. 'Yes, Thalia, I do. And I will ride over to Asham before I return here.'

She flinched at his use of her name, just as she had when he'd touched her. Jack, feeling even more guilty at the way he had used his predicament to persuade her into allowing him into her bed when he could have managed quite well without implicating her, knew he deserved no less.

And then there was the way he had left her. His sudden withdrawal had hurt her in a manner he had never intended. Yet, at the time, it had seemed the only way to avoid complications he was not ready to face. He lowered his voice still further.

'Do not be at odds with me, my dear, I did not mean to hurt you by leaving so abruptly. Do not allow my insensitivity to spoil the pleasure we found together. And we must not set the tongues wagging faster than they already are. But the circumstances were unusual. We were both reacting in the aftermath of danger—and I thought you might regret. . .' He shrugged.

It was not quite an apology. Thalia looked up to meet his eyes at last and what she saw there reassured her.

'No,' she admitted. 'I do not regret what happened. But I thought I had not pleased you.'

His eyes widened in astonishment. 'Not pleased me? My dear—' his hands reached out to grip her shoulders '—I was so overcome I scarcely knew what I was doing.'

Thalia's smile was like the first pale glimpse of the sun after rain. 'Except that you had to leave me at once?'

Jack drew a breath. 'For the sake of my sanity,' he

admitted. His fingers tightened on the fine bones hidden beneath her gown. 'But. . .I long to visit you again.'

Danger lurked in continuing the relationship but, because he wanted her so much, Jack convinced himself that it would be cowardly to throw away present enjoyment for fear of some unlikely eventuality in the future. A pox on caution! If Thalia was willing he would take what she offered, as he would that of any mistress.

Thalia searched his face again and found no trace of the contempt she had feared. His eyes glowed with something far more reassuring. So she nodded. 'Come tonight if you are able. I must know what happens at Asham.'

He took her hand and lifted it to his lips. 'Until tonight, then, after Mr Tope has dismissed me. And do not worry about Fanny. I promise you she will be in safe hands.'

That had been almost a courtly gesture, considered Thalia, as Jack strode off on his errands. The rush of pleasure she experienced at the thought of the coming night shocked her. Her knees trembled and her heart hammered in her chest.

Dear Lord, the man had her behaving like a green girl, a hen-witted gudgeon! Where were her wits, the cool reactions she had so carefully cultivated over the last years? And where was her concern for her employer?

On a surge of guilt at her neglect, Thalia turned back to the bedroom and her duty to Sebastian Tope. Yet, even as she sat by his bedside holding the veined hand between both her own while they waited for the doctor to arrive, she could not concentrate on his needs. Her mind insisted on following Jack on his wild ride to Sandwich—where, God forbid, he might run into Lord Varley—and then on to Asham.

How would Emily react to a sudden demand to remove herself and her charge to a place of safety? Would she believe that Jack Hamilton had her authority to organise the move? She had not thought to write a note and Jack had not asked for one because, she realised, he knew Emily Wright liked and trusted him. And Sidney Barton would obey him without question.

Emily had said she might do worse than wed Jack Hamilton. The idea of becoming his wife no longer seemed as ridiculous as it had when Emily suggested the notion. He would be perfectly capable of bettering himself. Together they could look forward to a decent future, even if they both remained in Mr Tope's service. . .

But Jack did not have marriage in mind. He was simply indulging in an affair and, had she not been willing, he might well have turned to Rose. Perhaps he had already bedded the attractive parlour maid. She wouldn't be surprised. A stab of fierce jealousy made her tighten her grip on Mr Tope's hand. He made an inarticulate sound in his throat.

Thalia, full of contrition, leant over him. 'I'm sorry, sir! But do not fret. The doctor will be here soon.'

Tope managed a slight, lopsided smile and an almost imperceptible nod of his head. 'Don l. . .lee ee,' he muttered.

'You can talk!' cried Thalia joyfully. The words were indistinct, barely recognisable, but a great improvement on strangled grunts. 'Of course I'll not leave you! But you are recovering already. Can you move your other hand?'

A finger twitched in response. Thalia kissed the hand she held. 'You see, the feeling is coming back!'

Tope managed another smile, a sad imitation of his usual genial grin. But it was better than nothing.

The doctor came, examined his patient, bled him and said he would arrange for a couple of nurses to come to take care of the invalid's needs. The women should arrive during the afternoon, and he would call again on the morrow. 'Feed him liquids through a straw if he cannot manage slops,' he advised.

'Ha...ton,' murmured Sebastian Tope once the doctor had departed.

'Hamilton?' queried Thalia.

Tope tried to move his head in a nod.

'Can you blink?' Tope blinked, though one eye responded sluggishly. 'Then blink once for yes and twice for no. Can you do that?'

A single blink answered her.

'Hamilton had to go on another errand,' Thalia explained. 'He will be back before long. Did you want to be moved?'

Tope blinked.

'Pringle will manage.'

She knew Tope could not be shifted from the bed. Pringle had his ways of relieving his master's needs. Once the nurses arrived they would do everything necessary.

Pringle had retired to the dressing-room to prepare his master's shaving water. He would, Thalia knew, never allow his gentleman to become careless of his appearance, however ill he might be.

While Pringle administered to his master Thalia took the opportunity to return to her room and renew her toilet. She had risen at an early hour in a great hurry and had simply stuffed her hair under her cap. She wanted to look decent when Jack returned. And her new gowns, ordered on the insistence of Mr Tope, had arrived only yesterday.

Perhaps seeing her in a more cheerful colour would lift her employer's spirits, and wearing a new gown would certainly raise her own. She also wanted to see admiration in a certain pair of glowing eyes—eyes which changed colour according to their owner's mood as did a landscape with the shining of the sun and the passing of the clouds.

The pale mauve with the white polka dots would be best, she considered, as she surveyed her new gowns. It was more subdued than the blue or the green, though all the colours were muted and therefore fashionable. All three had been cut on much the same demure lines as her grey gowns but a higher waistline and the softer hang of the materials made all the difference to her appearance.

Surveying herself in the cheval mirror Mr Tope had insisted she move to her small suite, Thalia was pleased with the result. Jack would approve. But how would the other members of staff react to her new guise? Would she forfeit their respect, lose her authority, when they learned of her actions and saw her changed appearance?

Surely she had accumulated enough respect and

authority over the last years to draw on now? She was still the same person, if a little more relaxed in her manner. And she had gained a few years in both age and experience since she had first come to Stonar Hall as a nervous outcast, unused to earning her living. She had played the severe housekeeper for too long. Now, she must rely on her natural ability.

Meanwhile, her youth had almost passed her by. She was not quite past her last prayers yet, but no acceptable man would ever want her for his wife, not with a bastard child in tow, and she would never abandon Fanny. Even Jack Hamilton thought of her as a mistress, not as a wife.

So, she would accept this lesser joy, make the most of a transitory *affaire* and then settle down to being a spinster. It meant she would never have an establishment of her own, but at least she would be no stranger to the joys of the marriage bed.

She allowed a few more strands of hair to escape the confines of her still rather severe cap and tweaked them a little self-consciously into loose ringlets until she was satisfied with the result. Altogether, she looked less like the housekeeper than the daughter of the house, she thought wryly, the very thing she had been at such pains to avoid in the past. But Mr Tope would not mind, he had always encouraged her to behave naturally, and she had no intention of taking advantage of his kindness.

Just before dinner she went to the library to fetch a book to read to Mr Tope, who could listen even if he could not talk. The sound of a single horse approaching made her heart leap. She hurried to the window in time to see Jack cantering up the drive. He was no mean rider, he sat the horse well. But then, she'd guessed as much.

She stifled down the impulse to rush down to the servants' hall to meet him. First she must allow him time to eat, then she would summon him to Mr Tope's room. The master had been asking for him on and off all the morning. At least then she would be able to gain some idea of whether his journey had been successful, although she would have to wait until late in the evening before she heard the full details.

He needed an hour, she decided, to wash, change and eat, before she rang Mr Tope's bell.

She had no appetite for the food brought to her on a tray. She pecked at it while she waited. But ten minutes of that interminable hour still remained when there was a tap on the door and Jack entered.

He did not look as though he'd been up most of the night and then ridden to Sandwich and on to Asham, though as he advanced into the room she could detect a few tired lines. But she soon forgot everything else because his strange eyes were alight and held all the admiration and promise she could possibly have desired.

She could not know how her own eyes softened yet glowed at sight of him, or how the faint flush which rose to her cheeks entranced its beholder.

It was simply a look they exchanged, but it said so much.

Then, 'As you see, I have returned from successfully carrying out your commissions, Mrs Marsh. Did the doctor come? Is the master better?'

'He did, and there has been some small improvement in Mr Tope's condition. He has been asking for you all morning.'

Jack grimaced and strode over to the bed, where Tope lay apparently asleep. But Thalia knew that he was not.

'Sir?' said Jack softly.

Tope's eyes opened. One side of his mouth lifted in a smile while his good hand shifted impatiently. 'Ack,' he said.

'Yes, sir. Is there something I can do?'

Tope blinked.

'That means yes. Two blinks mean no,' explained Thalia. 'He's also writing with his left hand.' She handed the invalid paper and pencil.

Talk to me, wrote Tope. Men here last night. After you?

'They only thought they were,' said Jack quickly. Pringle must have informed Tope of the Revenue's visit. How much had he said? 'They had mistaken me for someone else. They found no one and nothing here to trouble them.'

'I'll leave you to explain,' said Thalia, making for the door. 'I have a number of things to see to.'

Jack bowed. 'Very well, ma'am.'

Tope could not see his face but Thalia could. His devilish expression left her in no doubt. He would give Tope a highly-coloured and fairly accurate account of his escape from the Revenue men, Which would have to include the fact that he knew about Fanny and that Binns had found them in bed together.

So be it. If he did not already know and Jack did not

tell him the last item, someone else would. If Mr Tope decided to sack her, she would simply have to find another position. But she did not think he would. Despite his insistence on church attendance he was no puritan. He would understand.

It seemed that he did. He said nothing to Thalia when she returned to his bedside later but the eye without the drooping lid smiled up at her and he held her hand for a long moment. Then he wrote: Hamilton a good fellow.

Thalia smiled back. 'I think so, too.'

She sent down to the kitchen for hot water to fill a tub and took a leisurely bath before donning a tucked lawn nightgown trimmed with lace, which she covered with a filmy blue peignoir. Tilly stroked the brush through her hair for her and tied on the most frilly nightcap Thalia owned. The child was bursting with curiosity but managed to contain it until the very last.

'Be 'amilton coming 'ere tonight, ma'am? Oh, ma'am, I thinks 'e's ever so lovely,' she sighed as she reached the door.

Thalia had never been so put to the blush. She was supposed to set a good example to the others! But how could she deny the expected visit? Jenkins would surely know that Jack was missing from his own bed.

In a household like Stonar Hall it was virtually impossible to keep a liaison like hers with Jack secret. She could not deny it with any hope of being believed, but she dared not admit her fall from grace, either. That would be to invite unbridled lechery amongst the other servants, something no conscientious housekeeper could condone.

She became uncomfortably aware that future insistence on morality in the others would be sheer hypocrisy. Oh, into what a moral morass her passion for Jack Hamilton had led her! What a deluge of unbridled lust she was probably letting loose in Stonar Hall! She had a duty to guard the younger girls' morality, but how could she, when she could not guard her own? She must, however, try.

She assumed a stern expression. 'Be off with you, girl. I'll not tolerate such impudence again.'

Tilly's face dropped. She dipped a nervous curtsy. 'No, ma'am. Give you a goodnight, ma'am.'

Thalia turned back to the mirror, her eagerness to be as beautiful as she knew how for Jack undiminished. Knowing their relationship to be sinful troubled her—she could not deny it—but nothing could dim the eager anticipation with which she awaited his coming.

She wanted to know how Emily and Fanny had greeted the news that they must go into hiding, of course she did, but Jack could have told her that during an interview in her office downstairs. Instead, she had invited him to her apartments and was waiting for him in her nightgown.

Colour flamed in her cheeks. She must be out of her wits! But, oh, so delightfully out of her wits! She had lived all her life by rules and regulations, by the dictates of good conduct.

On the only occasion she had been tempted and forced to deviate she had been betrayed and cast out. She had little to lose now except Emily's good opinion, for her daughter would not understand and so not condemn. Fanny had taken so readily to Jack. He would make her a splendid father. But he would never ask her to marry him. She'd been over all that before.

She spread her hair about the shoulders of her peignoir and sat in her parlour to wait for him to come.

When he did knock and enter, she was toying with her embroidery.

She thrust it aside and looked up. Jack stood just inside the door, a curious mixture of expressions flitting across his face. For a moment she thought she had seen regret, and her heart went cold. But then he was smiling, coming forward with all the assurance of a man certain of his welcome, the light in his eyes warming not only her heart but her entire being. She held out her hands and he dropped to his knees beside her chair as he took them.

'Never fear, Thalia. Miss Wright and Emily are safe now.'

'They are nearby?'

He shook his head. 'Not too near. They will reach their destination today. Sidney will return tomorrow and confirm that they arrived safely and without leaving an easy trail behind them.'

'How can you be certain no one knows where they went? He...' meaning Varley, as Jack well knew '...could ask the stagecoach driver—'

'No drivers were involved. I hired a coach and pair from Cracker at the inn, which Sid will drive back and return tomorrow. No one will know where he went and I think it highly unlikely that Varley will be able to trace Fanny when he realises she has gone. In any case, both she and Miss Wright will be well guarded.'

'Jack, how could you arrange all this?'

'Ask no questions, my dear. Suffice it to say that I did not waste my years in the army. I may be poverty-stricken—'

'So how did you pay for the coach?'

'Cracker gave me credit,' he informed her glibly. 'And I do have a few influential friends.'

Thalia glared at him in exasperation. 'Why can't you tell me about yourself?'

'Why can't you tell me who you are?'

She was tempted. What could it really matter if he knew that her father was a ruthless, self-seeking baronet with an unenviable reputation for double-dealing? A man she would rather not acknowledge as her parent for fear the stench should rub off on her? Why did it matter that, because Hamilton must be of a lower class than herself, she did not wish him to know that she was related, however distantly, to an earl? She wanted him to like or dislike her for herself. Not for who or what she had been born.

Jack, seeing her sitting there, a beautiful woman doing her embroidery, had longed to declare himself. But he had curbed his rash impulse and knew he had been right. He was in no position to even consider marriage at the moment.

She would grace any man's home, he thought, and make a charming hostess. But without the right breeding she would not do for his wife, however much he might wish otherwise. She must be ashamed of her connections, but this had not prevented her from treating him with haughty disapproval at first. Now she was prepared to welcome him into her bed.

Which, scoring as the conquest Sid had predicted, reminded him of just why he had initially determined to make her his mistress. That they now felt more kindly disposed towards each other was neither here nor there. Each was making use of the other. So be it.

So he stood, pulling her up with him.

'We should not be wasting time,' he murmured. 'Not when there is a bed waiting for us in the next room.'

Thalia couldn't help another blush. But she raised her lips willingly enough when he bent his head to kiss her.

CHAPTER NINE

JACK URGED her towards the communicating door and Thalia went blindly. She was too deeply committed in her mind to this man to balk at another interlude of intimacy. Just his touch had sent her senses into a whirl and, after the kiss, her mind simply refused to contemplate the simple expedient of saying no.

She still could not understand how it had happened, how she, the daughter of Sir Gilbert Marsh, Baronet, could fall in love with a footman, particularly an untrained and temporary one. But it seemed that the heart recognised no boundaries of birth or breeding or any other of the things the world thought so important. It simply recognised a kindred spirit.

He was an audacious, attractive creature and knew how to wield his charm, no doubt of that. She had not been proof against it for long and had been unable to deny the attraction he held for her. But then he had shown her an altogether more responsible side to his nature, had shown extraordinary courage in the face of Varley's threats, had been patient and understanding with Fanny, and she had been completely captivated.

These ideas were not clearly articulated in her head—she was too lost in the turbulence of her senses for coherent thought—but the knowledge was there, together with the recognition that the relationship could not last, that she must make the most of the time she could spend with him.

So, she threw off her inhibitions with her peignoir and helped Jack to remove his shirt and her nightgown then, in a rush of sudden embarrassment, ducked under the sheet. He chuckled as he discarded his smallclothes and joined her, throwing back the sheet with one sweep of his arm, thus making the bedside candles flare and flicker in its draught.

'Don't hide from me, I have every intention of exploring your body with my eyes as well as my hands. You should be proud, my dear, not shy.'

'I cannot help it,' protested Thalia. 'From my earliest days I was taught that modesty was a virtue, that gentlemen valued it in their...'

She trailed off, suddenly aware of where her sentence was leading. She was not his wife and no doubt gentlemen demanded different responses from their mistresses. And Jack did not even profess to be a gentleman.

'Few men are gentlemen in bed,' he growled. 'Unless, of course, their wives are so modest and unresponsive that they kill off all thought of anything other than a man's duty to beget an heir. Or,' he added hastily, 'so I have been given to understand. People confide in their personal servants, you know, and they in turn gossip with us lesser mortals.'

Thalia did not question what he was saying for she scarcely heard it. Her mind was fully occupied in following the path of the hands roving over her body in delicious sweeps and touches and finding sensitive spots to cherish that she had not imagined existed. He stopped talking to put his lips to better use, but even so he murmured now and again, small words of appreciation and encouragement.

The pleasure was so great that Thalia simply allowed it to wash over her. She shuddered and trembled, her hips rose in anticipation. Only when he moved over her did she clasp him tightly to her, murmur incoherent nothings into his shoulder, entwine her legs about him and dig urgent fingers into the muscles of his back.

Still he did not enter her except to explore her mouth with his tongue. Thalia answered his kiss with uninhibited passion. Her tongue tangled with his, rasped the rough top, slid past the silky underside, grazed against his strong teeth, tasted the cheese and ale he had consumed for supper.

He had not had the same opportunity to bathe as she had and the sweat of his long ride was still on his body but the musky odour, the strong male scent, roused her responses to new and ecstatic heights.

In the end she could not bear the waiting any longer. Her arms closed convulsively about him. 'Please, Jack,' she cried.

He gave a small laugh of triumph. 'Your wish is my command, ma'am.'

Spoken in an extremity of erotic delight, his comment was no expression of subservient status and Thalia did not even notice the words as he moved to join them together in the universal celebration of the mating instinct, oftentimes an expression of love, sometimes of duty, but frequently simply of lust.

It was no longer simply lust for Jack. There had been times in his youth when he had fancied himself in love with some female of the muslin company. He had even, once, been quite desperately in love with a chit acknowledged to be a beauty of the first water who had seemed to return his regard, but she had wed a marquess.

Then there had been those ladies of the demi-monde he had taken simply because he found them attractive enough to bed and had no liking for the life of a monk.

Thalia Marsh roused feelings in him he had never experienced before. He had never fancied himself in love with her and yet she meant more to him than a mere convenience.

He liked her, respected her and felt protective of her and her daughter. He could not simply use her.

Yet his desire was so great that he could not stop himself from taking her with unbridled urgency. Perhaps another time he would be able to consider her needs before his own, as he had yesterday, but not tonight, when the future had suddenly become even more uncertain, with Sebastian Tope lying between life and death. For everyone knew he might have another, fatal attack at any moment.

So Jack drove with all the strength of his passionate nature and to his delight Thalia responded with equal passion, her inhibitions lost in the maelstrom of his demands.

Afterwards he drew her into his arms, cradled her head on his shoulder and broke the news of his imminent departure.

Thalia shivered despite the warmth of his arms. She shifted to escape his hold. 'I thought you had decided to remain here.'

'I must go. I stayed for a while because I could not leave Mr Tope in the lurch and you were supposed to be finding someone to take my place. But my intention to leave did not go, and now, with two nurses to look after him, Tope no longer needs me.'

But I do! cried Thalia's heart. She did not utter the words. Instead she demanded, 'So when will you go? And—' suddenly urgent '—what about Fanny? I must know where she is!'

He drew her back down into his arms but she was stiff as a ramrod, rejecting him now as he had rejected her last night.

'Thalia, I must go, and it may take me a while to find—' He hesitated.

'Another, better position,' supplied Thalia resentfully. Dear Lord, was he really going off just like that, abandoning her and leaving Fanny in some unknown place where she could not find her? The tears would not be denied. They trickled damply down her cheeks to wet Jack's bare shoulder.

Curse it! He'd made her cry again. He stroked her hair and dropped a kiss on her wet cheek.

'I'm not abandoning you, Thalia. I'll come back, never fear. Er—' he thought quickly '—I shall not agree to start a new position straight away,' he improvised. 'Fanny has Miss Wright with her and will be happy enough until Varley's threat is eliminated. My dear, I shall keep my promises to you, every one. And I'll add another.'

He pulled her closer. 'Should you find yourself breeding, I will not desert you as Varley did. I will marry you, Thalia, that I swear. But until I know. . .until I'm more certain of the future, I cannot ask any woman to be my wife except if she is in need of the protection of my name.'

While he spoke Thalia had gradually relaxed. Perhaps it was not as bad as she'd thought, though she placed no real reliance on his promise to wed her. But he had made it. That much, at least, was in his favour. And it meant he did not entirely rule out the possibility of marrying her. A wraith of warmth began to circulate in her veins.

She shifted so that she was able to meet his eyes. 'I don't know what to make of you, Jack Hamilton. I just know I wish you were not so determined to leave Stonar Hall. We do need you here, you know.'

He stroked her hair again and pulled her face towards him. His kiss lingered on her lips, warm, vital, tender. She melted. But he clung firmly to his resolve. His future was at stake.

'I shall scarcely be missed.'

'By others, perhaps.' That implied something she'd rather not have confessed. But she could not take the words back.

Jack did not respond to her comment, preferring for his conscience's sake to ignore it. But there was a promise he must extract from her.

'Until you hear that Varley has left the district, promise me that you will not walk to the village alone. Take one of the grooms with you. You will not be able to get in touch with me directly, but Sidney will be back at the King's Arms tomorrow. I'll ask him to remain there until I return. He'll pass on any message you may wish to send.'

'He'll know where you are?'

'He'll know where a letter will reach me. And now, my dear, reluctant and comfortable as I am, I really must retire to my own bed. Jenkins will be expecting me.'

'He'll guess where you are.'

'Of course, but I shall deny it most strongly.'

She laughed suddenly. 'Am I speaking with the same man who only yesterday was anxious to be discovered in my bed?'

He had the grace to blush. 'The circumstances were rather different. Everyone knows we are lovers, but there is every reason to exercise discretion. We should study not to cause unnecessary embarrassment.'

No. It was enough that tomorrow she would once more have to face the knowing smiles, without adding to the speculation already rife. 'And you'll be gone— when?'

'I'll wait to see Sidney and make an early start on Saturday. So we'll have one more night, sweetheart.'

'Will you give in your notice to Mr Tope?'

'I'll tell him that I have urgent personal business and seek his permission to be absent for a time. It will be true, though he might disapprove if he thought I was looking for another place. Better to ask his permission than to simply disappear, he would think that highly irresponsible.'

He had called her sweetheart. Her heart thumped. Did that mean anything? 'Yes,' she agreed, 'he would. Mr Tope likes you, Jack. He'll be saddened to lose your company while he lies helpless.'

'When I return, I will stay to work out my notice.'

'He will think more kindly of you for that.'

He grinned down at her. 'I trust you will, too?'

She would not pander to his vanity. She simply gave him a cool look and said, 'Huh!'

That made him chuckle. His parting kiss threatened to turn into something more until he took a deep breath and regained his control. Then she found herself alone in the bed, again watching as he hurriedly donned his clothes.

He had said he'd come back to work out his notice. She hung on to that promise like a talisman as he blew her a final kiss and the door closed behind him.

Jack absented himself the following afternoon and Thalia guessed that he had gone into Stonar village to see Sidney Barton. From the window of Tope's bedroom she watched the men drilling with their muskets under the direction of Mr Shepherd, who had agreed to be Jack's second in command of the estate's small defence force. He'd learnt a lot in the intervening weeks and would be an able leader when Jack had gone.

When Jack had gone. The words rang like a knell in her mind. He shoulders drooped.

A sound from the bed brought her to Sebastian Tope's side.

'What is it, sir?'

He picked up his pad and wrote, Sad?

She smiled and patted his hand. 'What else would you expect, with you so struck down?'

He looked as sceptical as his poor face would allow and wrote, Hamilton is going away.

'I know. But he will be back.'

I wonder.'

'He promised.'

Tope wrote no more, simply grunted, implying maybe. But he looked at her with shrewd old eyes and Thalia shifted uncomfortably. Though her relationship with Jack Hamilton was no business of her employer, except insofar as he could dismiss them both for immorality, he'd shown no inclination to do that so far. She did not expect that he would, unless their liaison became too blatant and encouraged similar behaviour in others.

The doctor called and cupped his patient again. One or two of Tope's cronies called, too. This left Thalia free to go about her normal duties. She had not written up the household accounts for several days and the chore could not be neglected for much longer. So she settled down in her office with the bills and ledgers and was busy listing and adding figures when a tap on the door interrupted her. She called an invitation to enter.

Jack smiled a greeting, raising a conscious blush to tint her cheeks.

'You are back!'

'You look so busy,' murmured Jack, while his eyes roved over her appreciatively. 'Perhaps I should not intrude. Did I say how much I admire your new gowns?'

'No,' said Thalia tartly, while the colour in her cheeks deepened as he gave her the benefit of his most teasing grin. 'But please remember that, despite my change of attire, I remain the housekeeper here. Discipline must be maintained. You did not ask my permission to leave the Hall this afternoon. I did not realise you were absent until I watched the men at drill without seeing you there.'

'I mentioned it to Mr Tope,' said Jack, raising his brows in surprise at her tone. 'And it will do Shepherd good to take the drill on his own. As for not telling you, my dear—' he closed the door, stepped forward and dropped a kiss on her nose '—you knew I had to visit Stonar. I may be a footman here, but I never met such a shabby excuse for a reprimand in my life!'

She didn't know why she'd done it, except that his self-assurance nettled her. However much she loved him—perhaps because she loved him so much that she was afraid of becoming his slave—she felt bound to exercise some remnant of her authority over him.

He was only half-serious in his protest, she could tell. Yet he had taken her acquiescence in his absence for granted. She felt vindicated in raising the issue. But— tomorrow he would be gone. The matter was not worth quarrelling over.

He had moved behind her chair and she stilled his hand as it wandered towards her breast. 'Not now, Jack. I have a position to uphold. You should have sought my permission before you went.'

'Should I? I apologise, madam.'

Now he did sound offended and went to step back, but she held on to his hand. 'It doesn't matter. They arrived safely?'

'Ah! You've remembered why I had to leave the house! Capital!'

'Don't be sarcastic, Jack. I'm sorry.' Though why she should apologise she couldn't imagine. 'It's just that I

am worried and upset and—I do not see why you have
to go,' she confessed in a rush.

'I cannot explain more than I already have,' said
Jack, cursing again the need for deception. 'I've asked
you to trust me before, Thalia, and I ask you again.
Both our futures depend upon the success of my
search.'

His certainly did, and hers might well be bound up
with his in a way he had not initially envisaged. But he
could no more wed her for the wrong reasons than he
could use her and abandon her. He had already committed himself to her more fully than he had intended
and it was as far as he was prepared to go.

All the same, it would not be easy to turn his back on
Thalia Marsh when the time came. Her safety and
happiness had somehow become of prime importance
to him.

'Because your place here is not good enough for
you?' Her strained voice interrupted his thoughts.
'Coming here as a footman was only a temporary
expedient for you, I suppose, and you think your talents
warrant a more responsible position.'

'Something like that.' His hands rested on her
shoulders. He could not seem to prevent himself from
touching her whenever she was within reach. It would
be unwise to say it, but perhaps it would ease her hurt
if he did. 'I cannot take a wife, Thalia, unless I can find
a more lucrative occupation.' Huh! That was putting it
mildly! 'And I could never ask such as you to wed a
mere footman.'

Her pulse quickened in hope. 'Why not?'

'It would be presumptuous of me.'

'Nonsense! You would marry me were I to find myself with child.'

'I have said so, yes. But that is not to say it would be what either of us truly desired.'

Stupid creature! Did he not realise that she would marry him whoever he was? Perhaps she should hope that their union did prove fruitful. But that would mean she would tie herself to a reluctant bridegroom, a husband who had wed her from a sense of duty. Her pride forbade that.

She gazed blindly at the column of figures she was supposed to be adding. 'I would not consider a proposal presumptuous.'

The devil! How was he to evade parson's mousetrap now without appearing a cheat? His foolish concern and bad conscience had forced him into a corner from which it would be difficult to escape.

'But,' she went on quickly, feeling the sudden resistance in the fingers resting on her shoulders, 'that is not to say I should accept. Or that I should refuse. Since you have not posed the question, I am not required to give you an answer.'

He gave a short laugh, released her shoulders and went round to perch on the corner of her desk to face her, sweeping a couple of papers aside so that he would not crumple them.

His thigh, in the tight-fitting grey breeches, was too near. The temptation to touch it was cruel. But she resisted it.

With a finger under her chin, he lifted her eyes to his. A shiver ran through her. A pleasurable shiver, one of anticipation. Would he kiss her?

He ran the ball of his thumb across her slightly parted lips. 'You confound me,' he said. 'Would you truly consider marrying a footman?'

'Were I asked, yes. But not any footman. Only one who was remarkably irregular and singularly superior.'

Now he shouted with irrepressible laughter, though his heart had leapt at her words, for was that not what he had secretly wanted to hear? That she wanted him for *what* he was, not *who*? 'Irregular and superior! I like that! I cannot conceive that you are describing me!'

'I did not say so,' said Thalia demurely. But her eyes betrayed her.

She meant it. She would wed him for the man he was, not for any position he might hold. So, against the odds, his wish had been granted. It changed nothing, except that he felt strangely exhilarated and devilishly guilty.

The strain of discord between them unwound. But another kind of tension ran from him, along his arm and into her chin. From there it invaded every fibre of her being. She saw his strange eyes change to gold and slate as the desire rose in him.

But he controlled it. He leant forward to place a featherlight kiss on her lips before he stood up.

'Fanny and Miss Wright are safely installed where Varley will never find them. I'll tell you about it later. I may come to you again tonight?'

Thalia simply nodded. To deny him now would be unthinkable.

Jack had been gone almost a week. Mr Tope had recovered some use of his hand; his face appeared a little less twisted and he could formulate a few words.

Thalia visited him as often as her duties would allow, but he was so well cared-for by the nurses the doctor had engaged that she needed only to keep his spirits up by appearing cheerful as she read to him.

Appearing cheerful was not easy. She had little realised how much she would miss seeing Jack about the place, let alone how much she would crave his presence in her bed. The ache of frustration sometimes became unbearable. She needs must rise and pace the floor of the bedroom for a while before she could return to sleep. Blue smudges developed beneath her eyes.

Time and again she wondered what Varley would do next, how Jack Hamilton could possibly be expected to deal with an officer in the British army. Jack Hamilton. Her thoughts constantly returned to him, her lover, her hope of safety and protection from Varley.

He also represented her only hope of a future as a respectable and happily married woman, if he could only be brought to declare himself. Did he fear that she would make him feel inferior? Was that why, despite his obvious infatuation with her, he still refused to consider marriage?

Infatuation. Was that all it was? If so, he was wise to eschew matrimony. Were her own feelings just as insecurely based? Was all the warmth and love, the tenderness and caring, so intimately wrapped up in the sensuous delight of their love-making, merely transitory? No more than an expression of her longing for a husband, a home and children? Did she really love Jack, or was she deluding herself because she so much wanted to be in love with someone?

She truly did not know. But she did know that it had

almost killed her to let him go after their last time together. He had been gentle, tender, had roused her to such heights that she had not been entirely certain whether he had experienced the same pleasure as she. She had not felt the same desperation in him as she had the previous night. He had seemed, almost, to be saying a sad and tender farewell, which did not reassure her at all as to the future. If his passion had died. . .

That he would return she no longer doubted. He had promised Mr Tope. And there was the question of Varley to be settled and Fanny and Miss Wright to be rescued from their exile. But when he came back, would he still wish to come to her bed?

The uncertainty pecked at her nerves, worried at her self-possession. She had received no letter from him, had only seen Sidney Barton once, when she'd walked to the village with one of the stable hands in attendance. He had had no news, either.

But she had been able to gain at first hand an account of the flight from Asham and the settling of Fanny and Miss Wright into their new quarters in a wing, presumably the servants' wing, of a large house, though Sid was frustratingly vague as to their whereabouts and the nature of the place in which he had left them.

'They be safe and comfortable, ma'am,' he assured her, 'and that's all that matters. The—Jack'll bring 'em back when 'tis safe.'

With that she had to be satisfied. But she grew ever more tense as the days passed with no word from Jack. So, when Jenkins found her in her office and informed her that the desperate-looking cove called Barton, who was a friend of Hamilton, was asking to see her and should he show him in or send him about his business, her heart leapt.

It could only be a message from Jack!

'Send him in!'

Barton came in and a frowning Jenkins closed the door behind him. Sid stood for a moment, uncertain whether to come further into the room. He looked anxious, and Thalia's nerves began to twitch.

'Do come in, Sidney,' she said. 'Do you bring a message from Jack?'

He shook his head. 'No, ma'am. 'Tis a letter from London, addressed to you, but it's not from 'im.' He delved into an inner pocket and produced the missive. 'Came by the carrier and I offered to bring it out to you, ma'am, seeing as 'ow all Mr Cracker's lads was busy.'

He held out the letter, sealed with a wafer and franked in a bold hand. Thalia recognised the hand that had written the direction and the familiar signature of Lord Wharton, her mother's friend's husband. Disappointment swamped her. She was always glad to hear from her mother, but she had so wanted the letter to be from Jack!

'Thank you, Sidney.' She took the letter from him and tugged at the bell rope. 'I'll ask Jenkins to show you to the kitchen. Mrs Gale will give you some refreshment.'

'Thank you, ma'am.'

She couldn't help herself. 'You've not heard from Jack?'

'No, ma'am. Not a word.'

She nodded as Jenkins knocked and entered. 'Show

Barton to the kitchen, Jenkins, and ask Mrs Gale to give him refreshment.'

Once alone, Thalia broke the seal and spread the single sheet of paper. The letter was not long and as she read the blood drained from her face.

Her father, dead? She could not take the information in. He had been so hale and hearty, so occupied in attempting to buy himself a seat in the House of Lords. But apparently there had been an accident. His carriage had overturned and he had been killed by a kick from a panicked horse's hoof before he could be drawn clear.

Arthur was now the head of the family. Sir Arthur Marsh, a young man scarcely more than one and twenty years old. But, her mother wrote, he had agreed that Thalia should return to Bruton Street. Her mother needed her. She longed to see her daughter and arrangements could be made for her to meet Fanny later.

Thalia discovered that she had little real wish to return to Bruton Street. But her mother had never completely abandoned her, had done her best to help her so, if Lady Marsh needed her support during her time of grief, Thalia could not deny it.

She must go for a visit, during which she could discover exactly how she would be received by Society. Not that her family had often moved in first circles, but Lady Wharton's influence did occasionally result in an invitation to some splendid event, where she had been received with courtesy. She had been given vouchers for Almack's during her come-out Season. That was where she had met Lord Varley.

But what a time for her father to choose to die!

There was enough chaos in her life already. She must reply to her mother's letter, send Jack a message, and write another for him to forward to Emily and Fanny. She rang the bell again.

When Jenkins appeared she told him to ask Barton to wait before he departed. He could carry the letters back to the village with him and dispatch them from there. She had no means of getting them franked; the recipients would have to bear the cost of their delivery.

With the letters written, she sent for Barton.

She held out the letter addressed to her mother. Sidney could not read, so would not be able to decipher the direction. 'This must go, and so must these. You know where to send the two which must reach Jack?' she asked him.

'Yes, ma'am. Leastways, Jack left me some papers with an address on. I'll put 'em all together and send 'em off this very day, ma'am.' He hesitated. 'Were it bad news, ma'am?'

'I'm afraid so, Sid. My father has been killed in a carriage accident. My mother asks me to go to her. I must seek Mr Tope's permission, which I know he will grant, and prepare for the journey. I shall travel on Monday. I believe Mr Tope will allow me the use of his carriage as far as Canterbury. From there I shall take the stage, unless I can catch the mail.'

'To London?'

Thalia nodded. London was a large place. To admit that much would give nothing away.

'If you will permit it, ma'am, I shall escort you. H—er—Jack would wish it, ma'am.'

His face had reddened. He looked embarrassed.

What had he been about to say? It was not the first time he had stumbled over Jack's name. They were hiding something between them. And although they were on friendly, even intimate terms, it was not a friendship between equals. Sidney Barton was definitely of an inferior order. If Jack had risen to be an officer, perhaps Sid had been his servant from the ranks.

But she had no time to pursue such thoughts now. He'd probably been used to using his surname in the army. That was it. He'd been going to call him Hamilton. She put the matter from her mind.

Having thought for a moment, she nodded. 'Very well, and thank you, Sid, I shall be glad of your escort. No doubt Jack will be glad to have you join him and, if I am not here, there would be little purpose in your remaining at the King's Arms. I will leave here at six and call at the inn to pick you up.'

Sid beamed, and Thalia no longer noticed the grotesque appearance of his face when he did. 'Thank you, ma'am!'

With Sidney gone, Thalia began to plan in more detail. She had a few sovereigns put by, enough to take her to London and to pay Sid's fare if necessary, but she suspected that Jack, who had been paid what was owing to him before he left, had provided Sid with the means to pay his way at the King's Arms and to travel to join him if necessary.

Sebastian Tope was far from happy at all the favourite members of his household leaving Stonar Hall together, but was too generous a creature to forbid her to leave his side.

'Go if you feel you must, my dear,' he mumbled. His

speech was improving every day. 'But promise me you will return?'

'I promise, sir.' Thalia bent to kiss the furrowed brow. 'I know no other home but Stonar Hall now.'

'May it always remain so,' he said, clasping her fingers.

Passing through the drawing-room on her way back to her duties, Thalia glanced up at the familiar portrait of the sixth Earl of Eardley. His heir had died shortly before he had committed suicide, so she'd heard, but what had happened to the family since no one knew. Presumably some male member had inherited the title and what remained of the lost estates and fortune. The portrait had been painted in the Earl's younger days, when wigs were worn by every gentleman and lady on formal occasions, before powdering one's own hair had become the thing. Even that had fallen out of fashion since the introduction of a tax on the powder. Nowadays only very old gentlemen, lawyers and footmen wore wigs.

She was reminded again of Jack Hamilton, whom she'd seen only twice dressed in full fig. She stared hard at the portrait, suddenly tense. Then she laughed at her own folly. It was the wig that did it, of course. Any man of today would look remarkably like the man in the portrait, if wearing a similar periwig. Even Jenkins, were he younger.

She was beginning to see Jack Hamilton everywhere. He'd become an obsession. At least returning to London would take her mind off him for a while.

It suddenly occurred to her that Jack might be

looking for a position in London, since Sid was prepared to escort her there.

Supposing he was offered a job in one of the houses her mother visited? Of someone who knew her? The possibility had never entered her head before, but now dread touched her spine with cold fingers.

If he did and insisted on taking the position, she could not marry him, even were he to ask her.

CHAPTER TEN

ON HIS way to London Jack called in at his home near Sevenoaks to collect a servant and apparel fit to be seen in Town. He wished Sidney Barton had been able to accompany him, for Sid was used to his ways, but Thalia needed his protection at Stonar. William, an eager lad of some twenty summers, would have to serve in Sid's stead. The boy was still untutored as a valet but Jack did not account himself a difficult man to please.

Trotting up the weed-strewn drive of Five Elms Manor, he eyed the mellow exterior of the modest mansion which had been the much-loved home of his youth. Signs of decay afflicted parts of the stonework, particularly about the mullioned windows. This estate was all that remained of the Eardley possessions that he had so unexpectedly inherited, and badly needed repairs which he could not afford.

His sombre mood lifted and a grin spread over his face as he saw Fanny rush out and down the steps from the massive front door.

'Mr Hamilton!' she cried, dancing in her excitement. 'Oh, Mr Hamilton, you've come to see me! Isn't this a splendid place? Where is Mama?'

Jack dismounted from the hack he had hired from the King's Arms and gave the reins to a stable hand to lead away. Lady Eardley and Miss Wright, who had both come out to stand on the step to greet him, exchanged an amused smile.

'Fanny, my love,' reproved Emily gently, 'you must learn to call the gentleman Lord Eardley.'

Fanny's mischievous face dropped in shame. 'I'm sorry,' she muttered. 'I forgot.'

Jack swung her up into his arms. 'It doesn't matter, sweetheart. I shall be very happy to remain Mr Hamilton to you. I'm glad you like it here. But I'm afraid your mama is not coming.'

'Why not?' demanded Fanny, pouting.

'Because, Fanny.'

'Fanny, don't ask so many questions,' admonished Emily at the same moment.

He carried her up the steps and still held her while he kissed his mother.

'How is it with you, ma'am?'

The Countess of Eardley's warm smile of greeting lacked assurance, as though she was not certain what his coming portended, but her eyes rested fondly on the strong, roughly clad, tumble-haired figure of her son. The events of the past few years had left their mark on Lady Eardley and the lines of anxiety seldom left her face.

'I'm well enough, Eardley. It is an age since you were last here. Where in the world did you find those clothes?'

He looked down at himself and smiled indulgently. 'I'll change immediately, Mother.'

He put Fanny down and greeted Emily before going on, 'As for my being here, I'm afraid I'm away again almost at once. I have to go to Town.'

'Hmm,' said Lady Eardley, leading the way indoors while a footman picked up Jack's bag, which had been unstrapped from behind his saddle, and followed them in. Emily, the embodiment of discretion, took a reluctant Fanny away to leave mother and son together.

Once in the privacy of her small sitting room, Lady Eardley took a seat and pursued her train of thought. 'It seems to me you would do better to avoid London and all its rackety ways. It was the ruination of your poor brother.'

Jack, slightly stiff and saddle-sore after his journey, paced the small room, seeming to fill it with his presence.

'Marcus had no call to spend so freely, to drink to excess or to gamble away the family fortune, Mother,' he proclaimed forcefully. 'I know you loved him as a mother should, but he was a frippery fellow. His debts left poor Father in an impossible situation, though Papa might have have pulled through but for being tricked out of his property.'

Lady Eardley sighed. 'Poor Eardley! I had no idea of his difficulties, you know. He never confided in me.'

'He wished to protect you from unpleasantness.'

'I wish he had not. Things would not have come as such a shock. And I was left all alone. You were not here to take up the reins.'

Her voice quivered and she dabbed her eyes with a dainty lace-edged handkerchief. Jack sympathised with what had been her predicament, but smiled slightly at her display of feminine helplessness. She had shown remarkable courage and determination in the face of disaster.

'You held the fort splendidly, ma'am.' He strode over to gaze out of the window. 'I regret that I was not here to assist Father or to support you in your sorrow, but as the second son I was packed off to the army before I had properly finished my schooling. I was given no choice in the matter. A second son could look for no more than a small allowance and must earn his own living, I was informed, and the army would make a man of me.' An edge of bitterness entered his voice. 'If I lived.'

'It did that, my dear,' murmured Lady Eardley, 'and I thank God that you did live.'

'Marcus was the eldest.' Jack made a gesture towards the parkland, the line of trees in the distance and the nearer planting of roses and flowers about the arbour where his mother loved to sit. 'He would inherit all the estates I had loved since childhood and he would need the bulk of the money to maintain them. I understood and accepted that. But he threw it all away. He killed himself with his drinking and whoring and reckless, rackety ways and squandered his inheritance before he died.'

'Your father was devastated when he discovered the full extent of Marcus's debts,' murmured Lady Eardley. 'He was quite in despair.'

'He tried hard to pick up the pieces. After he shot himself, it was months before I discovered that I had become the next Earl. I could not immediately resign my commission even then. The military situation was too difficult and I was abroad. But I sold out as soon as the Peace was signed.'

'And set about putting the estate to rights with the

proceeds of the sale of your commission. I know, my dear boy, do not think I do not appreciate your efforts.'

Jack turned away from the window and resumed his pacing. 'Which, so far, have been nowhere near enough. The money has gone and we are mortgaged up to the hilt. The only recourse left was to try to discover the cause of the disastrous losses my father suffered after Marcus's death and to seek restitution. I think I have succeeded in the first, Mama. I have seen a document which confirms my suspicion that Father was cheated out of much of his property, but not by Sebastian Tope, as I had thought.'

'Then by whom?'

'A crooked lawyer in London.'

'Can you do anything about it now, Jack? It all happened so long ago.'

'Not that long. The man concerned must still be alive. That is my reason for going to London. I must confront him, and if possible, recover the family possessions he stole from Papa. I shall leave tomorrow.'

'You will be careful?' demanded his mother anxiously.

'I shall not be in any danger, ma'am.'

His mother, he noted, seemed happier than he had known her at any time since his return. Jack wondered whether her improved spirits were due to the presence of others in the house.

'I trust it does not inconvenience you too greatly to have Miss Wright and Fanny to stay?'

'Indeed not, my dear. Do stop pacing, Eardley, it quite makes me dizzy.' Obediently, Jack came to rest before the fireplace. 'I am delighted to have them,' went on the Countess once he was still. 'They have brightened my life considerably. Emily Wright is a most agreeable companion and Fanny a delightful child. Are you in love with her mother?'

Jack continued to stand before the hearth, in which a small fire burnt, its heat welcome since the early autumn day had turned chilly. He blinked at the blunt question but was quick to deny the charge. 'Good Lord, no, Mother!'

'But you are interested in her, are you not? Who is she, Eardley? Would she not make you an agreeable wife?'

Jack put an elbow on the mantelshelf as he turned to face his parent. 'I know your dearest wish is to see me leg-shackled, Mother,' he drawled, 'but I shall choose my own wife in my own good time! Thalia Marsh is Sebastian Tope's housekeeper, as you must know. She was not wed when Fanny was conceived and was thrown out by her father because of it. Hardly a suitable wife for me, do you think?' he added drily. But as he waited for his mother's reply, a strange tension invaded his body. Her opinion on this mattered.

'I know her story, my son. Emily has told me everything. If she approves of Miss Marsh, then I am sure I must, too.'

'But Society, ma'am—would they readily accept the mother of a bastard into their hallowed circles, even if she were the Countess of Eardley? I think not.'

'She would only need to be bold at first. If she is as beautiful, gracious and sweet-tempered as I am given to understand, they would soon forget her past once her rank as your wife secured her a place in Society.'

This was something Jack had been tempted to rely upon himself, for it was not beyond the realms of possibility that he would be forced into parson's mousetrap by his own rash promise. He drew a breath. His mother could be devastatingly clear-sighted when she chose and the relief her words had brought with them almost overwhelmed him. Did she know more about Thalia than he did?

'Miss Wright has told you all about her, you say, so you should know who she is, and can tell me! For I swear I know nothing of her breeding or background.'

'Do you not? No, I suppose you would not, for Emily tells me Miss Marsh is ashamed of her father and of her relationship to him. She will admit it to no one.'

'The devil! Is he a criminal?'

'Mind your language, Eardley!'

'My apologies, Mother. But what else could have made her so desperate to hide her relationship to this man?'

'You will have to ask her that, for I am sure I do not know. But the child has this bee in her bonnet and has sworn Emily to secrecy, so I know little more than you of her origins. Although Emily did let slip that there was some distant connection with the Earl of Whitbourne on her mother's side.'

A rush of such relief swept over Jack that he almost fell into the fire. The foolish creature! Why had she not said? That connection alone would make her an acceptable match for an earl... Of course, he should have guessed something of the sort, for otherwise Viscount Varley would never have declared an interest in her. But she had thought Jack Hamilton a low-born footman. Her connection to an earl must have seemed irrelevant, even disadvantageous.

And he was still in no position to wed, even if he wanted to, and he was still uncertain whether he did. But the fact that the possibility was there gave him a subtle sense of satisfaction.

He heaved himself from the mantel. 'I see. I did not know.' He wanted to end this conversation, to be alone for a while to think. He spread his arms to indicate the dishevelled state of his attire. 'I apologise for coming in here in all my dirt, ma'am. I will go and change.'

'I wished to speak with you, my dear! But you do not have too much time. Dinner will be served in an hour.'

'If I ring, will you order hot water for me, Mother? I declare, it will make an excellent change to be bathed, shaven and wearing my own clothes again, and not to be expected to wait at table! But you would have been proud of my appearance clad in full and splendid livery!'

'My dear boy,' said Lady Eardley as her son pulled the bell rope, 'I still consider your masquerade a shabby trick to play on Mr Tope!' She gurgled with laughter. 'But I should so love to have seen you serving dinner!'

'In a periwig!' added Jack lightly as he bent to kiss her powdered cheek. It was good to see her laughing again. He left the room whistling.

Thalia reached London late on Thursday, having accomplished the journey in a day. Small torches, huge flambeaux and several oil lamps were already flickering about the street as she alighted from the stage.

Sidney Barton, who had been riding outside, jumped down from the roof quickly in order to help her.

'Thank you so much for your escort.' She smiled as he made an awkward bow. 'I shall be safe now. You will wish to join Jack as soon as possible. Do you have far to go?'

'I shall walk, ma'am.'

'I see. So he is somewhere in Town?'

'I don't exactly know, ma'am. I'm going to the place where he said I could contact 'im.'

Sid lost some of his aspirates when he became agitated. He did not intend telling her where he was going and was nervous of making the necessary evasions. She, in turn, had no intention of letting him know her destination.

'Then we must part. I hope we meet again when I return to Stonar Hall. You will accompany Jack again?'

'Aye, I expect so, and so do I, ma'am. But I can't leave you before I know you're safe. Let me escort you 'ome, Miss Marsh.'

His tone held pleading, but Thalia ignored it. 'I have the money to hire a hackney, Sid. I will not put you to further trouble.'

''Twouldn't be no trouble, ma'am.'

'Yes, it would, and you are being over-protective, Sid. Lord Varley cannot trouble me here! No, you can find me a cab, and then be off to find your own bed for the night!'

Sid accepted defeat but still raised a protest. 'Very well, ma'am. But there's others like 'im about in town.'

'The cab driver will keep me safe.'

'I 'opes so, ma'am. Jack'd never forgive me if anything 'appened to you.'

He handed her into the cab and stepped back. Thalia made sure he was out of earshot before she directed the driver to Bruton Street. She looked behind once, turning to peer from the tiny, obscured window above her head. She could see no sign of Sid and sank back thankfully into the smelly interior of the cab.

At the town house in Bruton Street, she found all the servants changed from those who had attended the family before her ignominious departure. Perhaps it was as well. She would not have to face old retainers who knew her history. But she had to tell the footman who answered the door who she was.

'Ah, yes, Miss Marsh. Her ladyship is expecting you.'

'Then I'll go straight to her,' declared Thalia. 'Where is she?'

'In her boudoir.'

'Is Sir Arthur at home?

'No, ma'am. I believe he went to his club.'

'I see. Thank you.'

Thalia swept past the servant and up the stairs. She was not going to allow him the chance to insist on announcing her in what was her own home, however long she had been banished from it. And she did hope that Arthur had kept his head and was not out gambling away the fortune left him by his exceedingly rich father.

She found Lady Marsh reclining on a sofa, a lace handkerchief in one hand and her hartshorn in the other. Her eyes and nose were reddened, as though she had been weeping. A filmy house-gown enveloped her ample figure.

Her mother had always been a timid creature who had picked at sweetmeats to console herself for the necessity of living with a man she detested and feared. Thalia had been surprised but thankful that she had found the courage to keep up a correspondence with her daughter and to send her money, in the form of bank drafts drawn on Lady Wharton's account.

She must, surely, be feeling relieved by the death of her domineering husband. So why the show of grief?

'Well, Mama,' she greeted her brightly. 'Here I am at last! How are you?'

She crossed the pretty room, decorated in silks and satins in shades of pink, to bend and kiss the cheek her mother presented.

'Thalia! My dear child!' Her mother's hand, still clutching the handkerchief, came up to touch Thalia's face. 'How you have changed!'

'Is it any wonder, Mama? I am six years older and have a daughter of five. And I have been responsible for the running of quite a large household for much of that time. But what of you? Are you well? Why are you weeping?'

The tears welled again and had to be dabbed dry. 'It is wretched being a widow, Thalia. You cannot know how it affects one's life! Arthur is the head of the family now, I must defer to him in everything! And if he marries, I shall be turned out of my home!'

'You have your jointure, Mama. I believe the settlement was quite generous.'

'But it will not be the same. Widows are not much regarded in Society, you know.'

'Do not refine so, Mama! Think of all the widows you know of who move in the first circles of Society.'

This did little to comfort Lady Marsh. 'I did not realise I would miss your father so much!' she wailed.

'Neither did I. I though you would be relieved to be delivered from his ill temper.'

'Well, of course, I did not enjoy... But he was not all bad, Thalia. He made me a generous allowance. Otherwise I could not have sent you the sums I did.'

'For which I heartily thank you, Mama. I was able to make it easier for Miss Wright to support both herself and Fanny. My salary would not have gone far.'

'Servants receive very little above their food and board. I did not like to think of you reduced to becoming a servant, my love. You would surely have been better served to wed Lord Stimson. He died, you know.'

'No, I did not know—you must have forgotten to inform me. When did he die?' demanded Thalia.

'Oh, last year some time, I believe. You would have become a rich widow, Thalia. But a young one, which would be so much more agreeable than being *old*!'

'But I would have been forced to endure his attentions for five years at least. I could not have survived it, Mama. I would rather have spent the time in Mr Tope's service. He is a true gentleman.'

'He is a *Cit*.'

'So was Papa. He made his money in the City.'

'But he was a gentleman, a baronet, my love!'

'Mr Tope behaves with more charity and dignity than my father or many other men born as gentlemen! I have become very fond of him, Mama, so do not decry him to me. Especially as he has been struck down and lies at home ill. I must return to him soon. I cannot simply desert him now my fortunes have changed.'

'But I thought you had returned for good! Arthur is willing to have you here and he has promised a substantial dowry should you wed.'

Thalia supposed she should be grateful to her brother but her mother made his intentions sound like charity and her resentment rose. So her voice was slightly acid as she asked, 'How is Arthur? I had thought he might have been here to keep you company.'

'He is young, my love, and trying his new wings. But at heart he is a sensible boy, and though he has inherited something of his father's temper he is by no means brutal. I believe you will get on well with him. He is not normally late home.'

'Good. When is the funeral?'

'Oh, that took place yesterday. I did not write to you immediately, my love, for there seemed so much to do and I was persuaded that you would not wish to be here for the obsequies. Receiving everyone's condolences brought my loss home to me. That is why I am so in the hips today. Of course, afterwards the Will was read.'

Thalia said nothing for a moment. Then, 'Everything to Arthur, no doubt.'

'Except for my jointure and the income from a few securities for life. The servants received small sums.' After an embarrassed pause, 'He left you nothing, my love.'

Thalia smiled. 'I did not expect he would. So Arthur is a very rich young man. He will have to beware of fortune hunters.'

'Do not speak of it! I dread his marrying! He is bound to choose quite the wrong sort of girl!'

The handkerchief came into play again. Thalia decided she had had enough of her mother's self-pity.

'I assume they will have carried my luggage to my old room?' At Lady Marsh's nod Thalia rose. 'Then I shall go and change. Have you taken supper?'

'Yes, dear. I am unable to eat much.'

Eyeing the almost-empty bowl of sugared almonds beside the sofa, Thalia smiled to herself. 'Then I will ask for a tray to be brought to my room. I will see you in the morning, Mama. May God give you a good night.'

'And you, my love. I will send Martha to help you. We must see about finding you a maid of your own. Arthur will be generous, I know. He has already spoken of making you an allowance. Tomorrow we must see to your wardrobe and I do so want to hear all about Fanny. I do long to see her, you know.'

Thalia bent to kiss her mother again. 'Yes, I know, Mama.'

Sidney Barton knocked on a door in St James's Street. William answered and greeted the newcomer with a cheeky grin.

'Yer place 'as been took, Mr Barton, I'm 'is lordship's personal servant now.'

Sidney merely pulled a face, which did not frighten William for he was used to Sid's disfigurement. But he stepped back and motioned the older man to come in.

'I hope you've been looking after him properly while I've bin away?'

'Done me best, Mr Barton. But I can't get the shine

on 'is 'essians like you do,' confessed William sadly. 'No more'n I can tie 'is neckcloff to 'is satisfaction.'

'Been doin' it hisself, has he? He'll probably be glad to see me then. Is he upstairs?'

'Yes. Taking supper wiv Captain Jeffries.'

'Go and let him know I've arrived, then.'

Minutes later Jack was greeting his man with eager warmth.

'You know Captain Jeffries. He will not object if you sit down and have a bite to eat while we talk.'

Jack grinned at the short, stocky young captain clad in the splendid uniform of a Guards regiment, who was his host. Frederick Jeffries, the son of a Lieutenant-General employed at the Horse Guards, rose languidly to his feet.

'I've finished my supper. I'll be off to my club, leave you to talk. See you in the mornin', Jack.'

'Thanks, Freddie. Don't play too high.'

'Pockets to let. Shan't have the chance, my dear fellow. But I shall hope to find the General there. May have news for you when I return.'

'If you have, don't wait until morning to inform me of it!'

Jeffries grinned. 'The West Indies, I think you said?'

'As far away as possible!'

The Captain picked up his hat and sword. 'I'll tell William to bring in some ale for Barton, Jack,' he promised as he left the room.

Sid looked enquiringly at Jack. 'What was that about, sir?'

'General Jeffries is arranging a new posting for

Captain Varley. It pays to have influence in high places, Sid.'

'So it does sir. Good riddance to bad rubbish, I say.'

Jack dismissed Varley with a shrug. 'I received Miss Marsh's note but it told me little except that her father had died. What is your news now? She must have travelled to Town for you to be here. Where did she go?'

'Bruton Street, sir. She dismissed me at the coaching inn but I followed her hackney, it was easy enough. The house is in mourning, drawn blinds and a wreath on the door instead of a knocker. Thought it must be her father's and it is. But the funeral is over, sir, took place yesterday.'

'Come on, man! Did you discover who was buried?'

'Sir Gilbert Marsh, financier of dubious repute and known as a bully, though he didn't whip. The servants are all glad he's gone. Not a nice man, sir.'

'Who did you speak to?' demanded Jack with interest. With a father like that, no wonder Thalia preferred not to acknowledge her relationship!

'Footman from next door, sir.'

He suspended his report as William knocked on the door before entering with a flagon of ale.

'Pour some, take a drink—you must need it,' said Jack after the lad had gone. He sat in one of the padded chairs which furnished the comfortable bachelor's rooms and motioned Sid to sit by the table, which he did.

Sid took a long pull at his glass. Jack leant forward.

'What did this footman have to say?' he demanded.

Sid put the glass down and wiped the froth from his lips.

'The son has taken over and he ain't too bad, apparently. Only a young sprig, but he's more'n one and twenty so he came straight into his father's fortune. Seems unlikely he'll squander it.'

'But you can never tell what the sudden acquisition of wealth may do to a man,' said Jack thoughtfully. 'Will he carry on his father's business?'

'Couldn't say. But he kept clear while his papa was alive. There's enough to keep the family in luxury 'till kingdom come if he acts sensible.'

Jack leant back in his chair and crossed his long legs, assuming a negligent pose. 'And Miss Marsh? She is well?'

'Lively as a cricket, sir. Glad to be going to see her ma, glad her pa's dead if you asks me. But she'll not abandon Mr Tope. She's only come up for a visit. Or so she says.'

'She's better away from Stonar at the moment. Once Varley has been posted she can return without fear. And Miss Wright and Fanny can go back to the cottage.'

'All will be as it was before, eh, sir?' asked Sid innocently, not deceived by Jack's apparent indifference to his news of Miss Marsh.

'Maybe. For her. But I shall not return as Hamilton the footman!'

There ensued a short silence while Sid consumed the remains of the gentlemen's supper and quaffed more of the ale. Jack wondered what Thalia's reaction would be when she discovered his true identity. He was not exactly certain what to make of the revelation of her paternity. It put her firmly in the ranks of a suitable, if not brilliant, match as far as he was concerned.

'Have you done anything about recovering Stonar Hall, sir?' Sid broke into his thoughts to ask, wiping his lips and fingers with one of the crumpled napkins left on the table.

Jack watched the performance with hidden amusement. Being allowed to eat at the master's table was an unusual privilege and Sid was determined to show his best manners.

'I've tracked the fellow down,' Jack answered him. 'That was easy, his offices are still at the same address. And he is living in our old town house in Grosvenor Street.'

'So he kept that, did he?'

'Yes. You know, it was most considerate of him to leave us Five Elms.'

Sid acknowledged the irony in Jack's voice with a grimace. 'What can you do, sir?'

'Confront him. Tell him of the morally indefensible document I have discovered under the terms of which he was able to steal the properties from my father, and which I shall make public unless he does as I demand. He will not know I don't have it in my possession, and I do know exactly where it is, in Mr Tope's desk. It is safe enough there.'

Sid nodded. 'Lucky you found it, sir.'

'Yes, it was with the documents relating to Tope's purchase of the place. Thank God he keeps them there instead of with his lawyers. My father could not have read the document properly or he would never have signed it. I collect that he was so desperate for the money he would have agreed to anything to keep the creditors off his back. He had been bailing Marcus out for years and when he died could not allow the name of Eardley to fall into disgrace by refusing to honour his son's debts.'

'Suicide don't do much for a name.'

'No. And he left me with a shocking mess to clear up and without a feather to fly with. However—' Jack straightened up in his chair and grinned. With luck, his struggle against penury was almost over '—I have had my lawyers draw up documents which I can use to regain possession of all the properties. I cannot simply reclaim Stonar Hall, for Sebastian Tope purchased it quite legally. So I must obtain the money from this scoundrel so that I can buy it back.'

'Do you reckon Mr Tope will sell?'

Jack shrugged. 'If not, I shall have to bide my time. But I would not turn him out. He could live there as though the property were his.'

'When are you going to do it, sir?'

'Tomorrow. You had better accompany me. We shall need witnesses to the signatures. Lawyer Salloway must have a clerk who can act as the second.'

Sid gave his dreadful grin. 'He won't know what's hit him when we gets there, sir!'

'I hope you are right, Sid, I hope you are right. By the way, I've decided to accept an invitation from Lady Jersey to attend her rout next week. I must send her a note. Remind me tomorrow.'

'Yes, sir. Trying to come by a bit of Town bronze, are we sir?'

'Don't presume on my good nature, Sid!' Jack's smile

as he spoke the reprimand was broad. 'She was most pressing, keen to be the first hostess to take my scalp now I've appeared in Society. And I have decided she can do me a favour in return.'

'And what would that be, my lord?'

'Wait and see, Sid. Wait and see.'

Thalia heard her brother return. She was not in bed, although she was in her nightgown and Martha had left her for the night. It was not that late and she wanted to see her brother. So she donned her peignoir, went to her door and emerged on the landing in time to see the new baronet, Sir Arthur Marsh, pull himself up the last few stairs by the banister. He was, she decided, slightly foxed, but not enough to matter.

'Good evening, Arthur,' she called. 'Come in and say hello.'

'Shaylia?' His speech was slurred but he walked straight towards her. 'Sho you've arrived. How are you, you big bad shishter?'

Next moment she was enveloped in a bear hug. Immediately, any resentment Thalia had felt against her brother dissipated. His breath smelt of wine, not spirits, his clothes of sandalwood. As she emerged from his embrace Thalia straightened his neckcloth. He was only a little dishevelled and his linen was clean; he had obviously supped and wined well and was in a cheerful mood.

'Arthur!' she exclaimed. 'It is good to see you after all these years! But my, how you've grown!'

Arthur chuckled. 'I wash a shtunted wee thing until I turned sheventeen, and then I shot up! You've not grown much, and you look ra-ravishing, my dear shish-ter! We must see if we cannot find you a husband.'

'Mama said you were making me an allowance and would give me a dowry. I am grateful to you, Arthur.' She did not think it politic to say that she intended to return to Sebastian Tope and remain with him while he needed her, or that she had no desire to look for a husband. Not at the moment. Not until the situation with Jack Hamilton had been resolved. If Arthur would give her a dowry regardless of whom she chose to wed, it would improve their circumstances—if the proud Hamilton would accept it.

'Mama says we must visit the modiste tomorrow. I need new gowns if I am to move in Society at any level. She assures me that you will meet the cost.'

'Willingly! I,' announced Arthur with a grin, 'made many friends at Oxford. I can number lords, earls and viscounts among them and claim acquaintance with a duke or two. We shall move in first circles, dear shister.'

'That was Papa's aim.'

'Which he never achieved because he didn't sh-shet about it the right way. Thought money could buy anything and the way he made it and his bullying ways caused him to be much disliked, you know. But people will soon forget him. Come and sit down, Thalia.'

'You did not like him, either.'

Arthur pulled a face. He had collapsed on her chaise-longue, though it seemed that his inebriation was passing off; he was speaking more clearly now. He patted the seat beside him. That brought back uncomfortable memories of Patrick Varley and, although Arthur was her brother, she chose to sit in a chair facing him.

'Has it been bad?' he asked. 'I couldn't do anything to help, you know. Papa would have cut me off, too, which would have done neither of us any good.'

'Mama did her best, Arthur. And, no, it has not been too bad. I have enjoyed working as housekeeper at Stonar Hall. Mr Sebastian Tope is a thoughtful and kindly employer. I told him everything and he did not condemn me.'

'Neither do I. Could happen to anyone. Varley, wasn't it?' Thalia nodded. 'Never could cotton on to the fellow,' Arthur went on. 'Too smooth by half. But the women liked him.'

'I fell for his looks and charm. I didn't truly love him, but he was the most exciting of my suitors during my Season. He said he intended to marry me.'

'Never believe a man when he says that. Easiest way to get what you want from a respectable filly, you know,' said the newly worldly-wise Arthur.

'But I have my daughter Fanny now. Having her makes it all worthwhile.'

'You daughter, yes.' Arthur stroked his chin and his stubble rasped against his fingers. The last time she'd seen him he'd been a beardless boy. 'Most fellows wouldn't want to be saddled with your love child, my dear.'

'Then,' said Thalia, disappointed in Arthur's reaction to Fanny, 'I shall have to wait until I find one who does not object. Or remain unwed.'

Arthur yawned. 'Pity if you did. Still, there's time to talk about this another time. I'm deuced tired. Must be off to bed.'

He climbed unsteadily to his feet and made his way

to the door. 'Goodnight, Thalia. Glad to have you back.'

Thalia went across and kissed his rough cheek. 'Sleep well, Arthur. I'm glad to be back.'

But inside she knew a great disappointment. Arthur did not fully understand her problem. He would prefer for her to let Fanny go. He did not realise that she could never do that.

CHAPTER ELEVEN

JACK, with Sid close behind him, mounted the stairs to the the lawyer's rooms, a warren of dark, stuffy offices which indicated that Salloway, Medlar & Co. was a large and prosperous firm whose head did not believe in expending money on improving the premises. Jack had already ascertained that Mr Medlar had been dead these last ten years and that Salloway was in sole charge.

They entered an office in which two clerks, perched on high stools, worked at sloping desks surrounded by mountainous, untidy stacks of paper.

'I wish to see Mr Salloway,' announced Jack in his most imperious tones.

A scrawny man dressed in rusty black, after first glancing apprehensively at Sid, focused on Jack's undoubtedly elegant appearance and noted the unconscious arrogance which stamped him as Quality. He bowed, swallowed nervously, and asked whether the gentleman had an appointment.

'No.' Jack removed his kid gloves and slapped them into the palm of his hand, allowing the man to detect impatience. 'But he will see me. Kindly inform him that the Earl of Eardley wishes to speak with him on a private and confidential matter.'

The man glanced at his younger companion who, after a swift glance at the newcomers, had returned diligently to his work. Finding no help there, the man bowed again, rather more obsequiously, acknowledging both Jack's rank and tone of authority.

'Perhaps the chief clerk—?'

'No. I will see no one but Salloway.'

'Very well, my lord.'

The man knocked timidly on one of several inner doors and entered, closing it behind him. Jack, to reinforce his illusion of impatience, began to pace the floor. The other clerk did not look up but his pen stopped scratching. He stared at the page before him while stroking his chin with the feather.

Jack did not have long to wait. Muted voices behind the closed door ceased as it opened and the clerk emerged. He stood to one side and indicated with a wave of his hand that Jack should enter.

'Mr Salloway will see you, my lord.'

'Capital.' He handed his hat and gloves to Sid. 'Barton, wait here until you are called.'

Gravely, Sid ducked his head. 'My lord.' Jack could always rely on his man to behave with perfect formality and rectitude in public.

Jack strode through to face the creature who had caused his father to commit suicide. In his eyes, his father's murderer.

To his surprise the fellow appeared personable, of around five and forty years, tall, thin-faced with a beaky nose, dressed in austere black and wearing a wig, the marks of his profession. Jack did not exactly know what he had expected but supposed he had anticipated the villain's cupidity and deviousness to show in his demeanour.

The lawyer rose to greet Jack with a small bow and an insincere smile.

'My lord! I am honoured by your call. Will you be seated?'

He indicated the stuffed leather chair facing him across his desk. Jack, determined to appear at ease, lowered himself into it with languid grace, crossed his legs and flicked a hair from the arm of his green superfine coat.

'In what way can I be of service to you?' enquired Salloway, seating himself.

Jack did not beat about the bush. He gave the lawyer a seraphic smile. 'By returning the Eardley properties you stole from my father.'

Salloway went very still. He had not expected such a direct accusation. He recovered quickly. 'I fear I have no idea what you mean, my lord. My transactions with the late earl were perfectly legal.'

'Oh, yes,' agreed Jack. 'In perfect accord with the letter of the law, of that I am fully persuaded. But I am also persuaded that should the full details of the transactions become known, your name would become anathema, you would lose all your honest clients and most probably not be allowed to continue to practise your profession. In short, Salloway, you would be ruined.'

'You would never be able to prove trickery, my lord. The late earl was given the documents to peruse before he signed.'

'The law is so often blind, Salloway, more blind than my father was at the time you cheated him. It can only apply the rules, it cannot distinguish between right and wrong. But all the same, my lawyers believe that, if challenged, the legality of the document would be overturned. Its contents are so obviously morally wrong. A truth that ordinary people would immediately appreciate. It is quite possible that other victims of your perfidy would come forward to bear witness were I to publish the document I hold.'

That had pricked the lawyer's bubble of confidence. Jack saw the worry enter the man's small, rather bloodshot eyes, though it was quickly banished. 'May I ask what document?'

'Of course.' Jack maintained his pretence of indolent courtesy with an effort. He wanted to jump up and punch the fellow on the nose.

'I can produce the deed of mortgage which forced my father into such an impossible position that you were able to foreclose on both the Kentish estate and our town house. You knew my father would be unable to repay the sum within the time stated in the mortgage. A month, Salloway, only a month, the due date written in small and badly-formed characters which he would find difficult to read.

'What did you tell him, I wonder? Or did you tell him the truth, but make verbal promises of leniency and accommodation which you had no intention of honouring?'

Salloway opened his mouth to speak but no sound came.

Jack gave a wolfish smile as his patience ran out. 'And the money you loaned him amounted to only a fraction of the combined value of the properties.' Jack stood and leaned over the desk, staring fiercely into the other man's eyes. 'You took advantage of a half-blind, elderly man out of his wits with worry, Salloway, and you are going to pay for it.'

Salloway blanched, but he had recovered his voice. He managed a sneer. 'The Earl was a fool, Eardley. He should have called in another lawyer to vet the agreement.'

'*You* are a lawyer—he trusted *you*. It never occurred to him that you would cheat him. It was because you knew he wished to repay my frippery brother's scandalous debts without sullying the name of Eardley that you were able to perpetrate your deception. He *trusted* you,' Jack repeated, slamming his fist down on the desk and making everything on it, and the lawyer, jump.

'You knew he would take what you said as truth, would not peruse the document, which he would probably not understand, with any care. You stand accused, Salloway, and I want restitution.'

Salloway leaned back in his chair. He had recovered sufficiently to give every appearance of ease. 'You may want it, my dear fellow, but you will not obtain it.'

'No?' Jack recovered the sang-froid he had never lost. He perched on the corner of Salloway's desk and swung an elegant leg. 'You have no objection to having your name blackened throughout London?'

'I shall sue you for libel, slander, defamation of character.'

'And I shall produce the proof,' said Jack with an absolute certainty he was, at that moment, far from feeling.

The paper was safe enough in Sebastian Tope's desk, but he wished he had gone all the way and extracted it, put it somewhere where no one could possibly find it. But Salloway did not know that the evidence was not actually in his possession.

'Where did you discover the document?' demanded Salloway, thus admitting it existed.

Jack's hopes rose. 'It forms part of the legal documents Sebastian Tope holds as proof of his title to the property of Stonar.'

'Ah. I made a mistake in allowing a copy to leave my possession. But—'

'You did not expect the new and impoverished Earl of Eardley to question the transaction and search for evidence. Exactly,' Jack finished for him. He reached into an inside pocket in his jacket and produced documents of his own.

'You will sign these, Salloway, if you wish to retain your good name and continue in practice as a lawyer. But be warned: should I hear of any other unfortunate creature being cheated out of his property, I shall immediately acquaint him of my knowledge and advise him to take similar action. And my lawyers are fully cognisant of this matter. Should anything unfortunate happen to me, they would continue the action on behalf of the family.'

Despite Salloway's surface recovery of composure Jack noted the man's fingers clenching and unclenching around an ebony ruler, and that he had not regained his normal colour. When the lawyer did not respond to his demand, he smiled. It was not a friendly smile.

'This,' he said, thrusting a legal document under his nose, 'is a promise to repay a loan I have made to you. You will remit the money to my bank by this day week, or your Hertfordshire estate becomes mine. By repute it is,' said Jack carelessly, 'a prosperous estate left you by your father. I should delight in claiming it as mine in lieu of Stonar Hall.

'However, if you pay me the sum indicated in the document, which will enable me to purchase back from Sebastian Tope that which he bought in good faith but which should by rights be mine, I shall be satisfied. One week, Salloway, or your property becomes legally mine.'

'Preposterous!' exclaimed Salloway. 'You accuse me of double-dealing but this is positively evil! Your father owed me a considerable sum—'

'Consider it as defraying the rent you owe for use of the properties!' Jack cut in.

'And you have made me no loan!' went on Salloway as though Jack had not spoken. 'Of course I shall not sign!'

'You will, or your reputation will be ruined, sir, and my lawyers believe you would lose a fight in the courts.' God knew where he would find the wherewithal to go to court, but he would. 'Which is the most valuable to you, your good name, the future of this thriving practice, or a small part of your wealth?'

He watched the struggle taking place in Salloway's mind and held his breath. The man only had to prize his ill-gotten gains above his reputation and Jack knew he had lost. But Salloway's good name was essential to his future livelihood and without it, however wealthy, he would be a nobody, condemned to live in friendless obscurity. He'd likely as not take refuge in the bottle and drink himself to death.

'Very well.' Salloway's agreement came at last. 'I will sign. You shall have your money within the week.'

He dropped the heavy, round ebony ruler with which Jack had feared he might attempt to clobber him, picked up his quill and dipped it in the ink.

'Wait!' Jack put a restraining hand on the document. 'There is more.' He brought out his soft leather purse, untied the drawstring and spilled five golden guineas on the desk. 'This is the price I will pay you for the house in Grosvenor Street. Here is the contract for its transfer to me. You will sign that, too. But we need witnesses to the signatures, sir. If you will call your clerk, I will summon my man.'

Salloway reached out to strike a brass bell standing on the corner of his desk. He had lost the will to fight. Jack, when he wanted to be, and he wanted it very much at that moment, could be most persuasive. His personality had completely intimidated a lawyer more used to imposing his will on others.

The clerk entered in response to the bell and was told to come in and bring his lordship's servant with him. With the utmost solemnity the two men witnessed the signing and sealing of the documents. In duplicate. Jack was taking no chances.

'You may have the money transferred to my bank account—' he gave the details '—and I shall check to see that it is there. As for the town house, I will give you two weeks to vacate it. Dismiss all the servants. They may apply to be taken on again once I am installed and have appointed a housekeeper.' He tucked his copies of the documents into his pocket. 'Good day to you, Salloway.'

'Curse you, Eardley,' growled Salloway. 'May you rot in hell!'

Jack made a mocking bow. 'A fate which would be too good for you, Salloway. I trust we need never meet again.'

Out in the street once more Jack gave a great whoop and clouted Sid on the back. 'I did it, Sid! Next week I can return to Stonar Hall and offer Tope a good price for it, and still have some cash left over to equip myself with a decent outfit—we must visit Tattersall's soon and look over their cattle—and begin to restore Five Elms!'

'Aye, sir,' responded the more phlegmatic Sid. 'But do watch that coach, sir, and mind where you are walking.'

Still chuckling, Jack stepped over a pile of horse dung and took evasive action as the coach and pair approached at a smart clip, scattering hand-carts and pedestrians before it.

'Do you really think he will pay, sir? And what happens if he don't leave Grosvenor Street?'

'Then I shall take him to court, Sid. It would yield the same result, but take much longer and probably be costly. My solicitor urged me to go straight to court, so certain was he of victory. But I do not altogether trust the courts. I would rather do it my way.'

'And now all you can do is wait.'

'And enjoy a little of Town life. I believe I deserve a holiday after the arduous toil of these last weeks! I need to visit Weston if I am to be up to snuff, and Hoby can make me a pair of boots.'

'You could do with some new headgear, sir,' offered

Sid with a wry glance at Jack's rather battered town beaver.

'Then I shall visit Lock and Lincoln, too. I haven't had much practice at cutting a dash in Town, but one cannot do it without running up a few tradesmen's bills, I collect.'

'No, sir. But you won't be one to venture too far into dun territory. Not like your brother, sir.'

'Marcus,' said Jack with scant respect for his dead sibling, 'was not only an expensive fellow but reckless and a fool to boot. Mixed with the wrong set and was led into the briars. Look how he died! I account it the height of foolishness! Racing his curricle while in his cups for a wager against a known nonpareil!'

'Well, sir, he didn't suffer. Broke his neck and died immediate.'

'And left poor Papa with a mountain of debt to settle. Ah well, that is all past history now. Let us discuss more cheerful subjects! There is to be a mill out at Maidenhead Thicket tomorrow. I have never seen Cribb fight, I think I shall accompany Freddie. He is driving out in his curricle. Want to attend us, travel on the step? Freddie's man won't wish to go, too much of a daisy,' said Jack scornfully.

'Wouldn't miss it, sir,' grinned Sid.

In confident mood, planning the week ahead, they trod their way back to St James's Street.

Thalia found her time much taken up with fittings and shopping in Bond Street. Her mother, no longer languishing under the restrictive parsimony of her husband, insisted on spending lavishly.

'But, Mama, I shall not need all these gowns, bonnets, shoes, fans, scarves, gloves, petticoats, reticules or parasols!' cried Thalia in an attempt to curb her parent's extravagance. Most of the gowns were quite unsuited to immediate wear, for although she in truth did not mourn her father, he was too newly buried for her to ignore the necessity of showing some respect for the dead.

'White with black and lavender ribbons,' decreed her mother. 'That will be perfect for Lady Jersey's rout! Oh, my dear child! What an honour to be invited to an event of the first significance! Only think, it is because of my friendship with dear Dorothea Wharton! She could not put my name forward in first circles while Sir Gilbert was alive, for no one would receive him.

'But now...oh, my dear, I am so flattered! She believes I may be able to accompany her on most of her social engagements! I shall need an entirely new wardrobe! And while you are in London, the invitations will be extended to you!'

Thalia could not truly enter into the excitement as her mother did. She had little liking for the formal occasions so dear to her mother's heart. And she missed Jack Hamilton.

It dismayed her to discover quite how much. She had already known that she loved him, but had not realised quite how bereft she would feel when she did not see him each day. And at night she found it difficult to sleep. In the end, after several almost sleepless nights, aware that her looks were suffering, she accepted a posset from her mother's maid. By the day of Lady

Jersey's rout, the blue shadows had almost disappeared from beneath her eyes.

She dressed with care, for she did not wish to discredit her mother, whose first appearance among the *ton* for many years was of such importance to her. She wanted Lady Marsh to be happy so that she could leave her and return to Stonar with a clear conscience. She wanted to be back there when Jack returned, when they could resume the relationship. . .

Her mind went no further along that track. She had refused to engage a maid to tend her and Martha, having completed her mistress's toilet, came to put the finishing touches to hers. She submitted while her hair, already shortened at the front, was tweaked into fashionable curls over her ears and the long hair at the back was gathered into a chignon and covered with a lacy headdress consisting mostly of black and mauve ribbons.

'There you are, Miss Thalia. You look a treat,' Martha assured her as she stood back to allow Thalia to view herself properly in the mirror.

'Thank you, Martha. That will do very well.'

The white silk dress was in the first stare of fashion, with a high waist into which a narrow skirt had been gathered. The skirt flowed into a train the length of which reflected her rank. She looked, she considered, rather like a classical statue of a goddess. Almost ethereal.

But the moment she saw her mother, who had rapidly regained her looks and vigour since Thalia's arrival in Bruton Street, Thalia knew that, despite her undeniably plump figure, that epithet belonged to no one but Lady Marsh.

She floated down the stairs to the carriage in a cloud of grey chiffon, from underneath which peeped an under dress of oyster satin. She wore black gloves—as did Thalia herself—and a small black cap on her slightly-faded but still abundant chestnut hair.

Any impressionable gentleman of a certain age would be in raptures over her, thought Thalia wryly. The self-pitying woman who had greeted her on her arrival had quite disappeared. It had taken only the assurance that she would in future be accepted in first circles to revive Lady Marsh's spirits.

'After all, my dear,' she said as the coach rattled them to their destination, 'I am a distant cousin to the present Earl of Whitbourne. Our grandfathers were brothers. I have every right to move in first circles and I did, until after your come-out. But once that Season ended—well, your papa was never popular and made himself positively disagreeable. So I was dropped.'

Her voice and shoulders drooped for a moment but she soon perked up again. 'But I shall renew the acquaintance with my cousin. And you belong, too, my love,' she went on brightly. 'And of course, no one except dear Dorothea knows of your true reason for leaving home.'

'But they will, once Fanny joins me.'

'Must she?' faltered Lady Marsh. 'I do not blame you in the least for what happened, but it was such a disgrace! Your father could not bear the thought of it! It was that which made him so very disagreeable.'

'Ha!' exclaimed Arthur, elegant in evening clothes,

who was escorting them. 'I do not remember any time when Papa was agreeable!'

Thalia drew a deep breath. Her mother and Arthur must be made to understand. 'I would not deny my child then and I will not do so now. If people accept me, they must accept Fanny, too.'

'Oh!' wailed Lady Marsh, 'you were always so head-strong, Thalia! Fanny would be perfectly all right with Miss Wright. You could visit her whenever you wished—'

'No, Mama. For a start, any man I may marry must accept Fanny, too.'

'But no man of consequence will!'

'Then I must marry a man of no consequence or remain single.'

'You could say you had been married!' put in Arthur.

'Of course! How clever of you, Arthur! That is what we must say!'

'No,' said Thalia shortly.

Lady Marsh groaned. 'There's no bending her, Arthur! And that Patrick Tolley! The charming, agree-able Viscount Varley! Able to cozen all the mamas into believing him serious about their daughters—I confess, I was quite taken in by him!—but in the end he did not marry anyone, as far as I have heard.'

'Probably not, Mama.'

Thalia had not told her mother or brother of her recent meeting with Varley or of his threat to Fanny. Jack Hamilton had promised to solve that problem for her and she trusted him to do so. There could be no occasion to worry her mother, who had expressed no urgent interest in meeting her granddaughter. Thalia hoped to put that moment off until Fanny was back in Asham and she knew where to find her.

Like all Lady Jersey's entertainments, the rout had developed into a sad crush. Thalia, used to the dignified dinners hosted by Mr Tope in his spacious dining-room, almost suffocated. Myriad candles added to the heat, and the smell of candle grease mixed with those of perfumes, powders and sweat to render the atmosphere almost unbreathable.

Lord and Lady Wharton had already arrived and immediately began to introduce Thalia and her mother to a selection of their friends. Arthur gravitated towards a group of other young men and soon disappeared in the direction of the card tables.

A slight commotion at the door heralded the arrival of a latecomer. Thalia glanced across and saw an elegantly dressed gentleman bending over the hand of his hostess. Her trill of laughter reached Thalia's ears; as the late arrival straightened up, she saw shining fair hair topping a familiar face.

The room swam about her. She swayed.

'Are you not feeling well, Thalia, my love?'

Her mother's anxious voice came to Thalia's ears as through a thick blanket.

'The heat,' she managed to utter, bringing her fan into play.

'My love, you have gone white as a sheet! Here, sit on this empty chair!'

Gratefully, Thalia took the proffered seat.

'I'll fetch you a drink,' offered Lord Wharton gruffly.

'No! I am quite recovered now,' said Thalia quickly, pulling herself together by a supreme effort of will. No one must suspect that her indisposition had been caused by sight of the man Lady Jersey was leading towards her. She could do nothing but wait for the quite dreadful moment when she would be introduced to Jack Hamilton as a stranger.

Although this was not the Jack Hamilton she knew. This man moved amongst the *ton* as though he belonged there. He did not appear to be well known—for he had been away in the army, that much was the truth, she supposed—but several people greeted him as he moved inexorably towards her.

Lady Jersey came to a halt by their group.

'Lady Marsh, Miss Marsh,' she said, 'may I present Jack Hamilton, the Earl of Eardley? He is most desirous of knowing you. Lord Eardley, Lady Marsh.'

Her mother, looking pleased and flattered, made a deep curtsy. 'My lord!'

'And Miss Marsh.'

Thalia automatically executed the required courtesies as Jack bowed. He was then introduced to the Whartons. While these civilities were being exchanged, Thalia sat as though turned to ice.

She should have suspected. Had she not thought how like the portrait of the previous earl the footman looked?

But how dared he? Making game of them all with his impersonation! She would never forgive him, never!

'Miss Marsh. Will you do me the honour of taking a turn with me?'

Jack's voice, holding a hint of laughter which added to Thalia's annoyance, sounded through the surrounding hum of conversation and the subdued strains of an orchestra in the next room, to tease nerves already stretched to breaking point. But she could not cut him in this company—it would show a lack of conduct she had no wish to display. So she nodded and placed a hand on his offered arm.

Immediately, the feel of him under the black superfine of his splendid yet austere evening coat sent a frisson of awareness to squeeze her heart. However diabolical his behaviour, she still foolishly longed to be in his arms. And that made her angry. How could she love a man so depraved as to perpetrate such a wicked deception on Sebastian Tope?

'I'm sorry, Thalia,' came Jack's low voice as he bent his head towards her. 'I wished to surprise you but it seems I have offended you instead.' They had walked towards a door at the end of the room which gave on to a terrace. Jack steered her towards it. 'We cannot speak freely here. Let us go outside.'

Thalia halted. 'And have all the tabbies gossiping about us, my lord? Remember, we have met but this instant.'

He eyed her quizzically. 'There are others on the terrace. It is well lit. But we can better converse there without being overheard.'

'Very well.'

Thalia gave in reluctantly but, if the *ton* imagined she had made an instant conquest of the Earl of Eardley, her stock might rise. She was, after all, at her last prayers as far as marriage was concerned and his interest must be flattering as well as giving rise to gossip. Unless, of course, the *ton* attributed less honourable motives to Jack's obvious wish to further their acquaintance with all possible speed.

Either way, he had made it perfectly plain that she had fixed his interest. That, it could not be denied, was gratifying.

For, in his own milieu, Jack was impressive. His upright bearing, his face—undeniably handsome despite an irregularity of feature—his striking colouring—his fair head shone amongst the more usual browns and blacks—his exquisite tailoring, all rendered him superior to any other gentleman present. In Thalia's eyes they paled to insignificance. The mamas must be falling over themselves to bring their daughters to his notice.

But he was a cheat.

'You deceived us all,' she accused in a low voice once they had reached the comparative seclusion of the terrace. 'I suppose it afforded you immense amusement.'

'Some,' agreed Jack equably, 'but I did not set out on my impersonation with amusement in mind. And I failed to play my part with much conviction, did I not? You suspected from the first that I was not who I pretended to be.'

Thalia removed her hand from his arm. She could no longer endure his touch, it was too disturbing. 'So did Mr Tope.' That, she could see, surprised him. 'But never, for one moment, did I imagine that the Earl of Eardley would stoop to deceive a man like Sebastian Tope! You entered his employment in order to spy on him!'

'That, my dear one, I cannot deny.' Jack stopped and

leant on the balustrade. They were in a public spot lit by a flambeau. Others were passing by within a few yards, yet they were isolated in a short widening of the terrace which formed a niche. 'But at that time I had reason to suspect that Mr Tope had cheated my father out of the property. I knew someone had, and it seemed likely that the present owner was responsible. It did not take me long to discover my mistake.'

'When you searched his drawers in the library?' guessed Thalia, remembering their encounter and how he had covered up his devious actions. And kissed her.

And said he was leaving. 'You did not leave,' she accused. 'If your search was successful, you had no further need to prolong your masquerade.'

'No. I should have done so straight away, for my business lay in London, but by that time I had other motives for remaining, at least for a while.'

He moved to place his hand over hers as it rested on the coping. Her lips quivered but her eyes remained guarded. 'I wished to solve the mystery of Mrs Thalia Marsh. You were flying false colours, too, my dear. And then I found you and Fanny needed my protection. I could not leave you to Varley's mercies.'

'You could have told me who you really were!'

'So could you have told me,' he countered.

'But my deception was born of shame. Yours, I collect, was practised for altogether less worthy motives.'

'Less worthy? To right a wrong done my family? When you merely did not wish to own your own father?'

That was not exactly what she had meant, although it might have sounded like it. He could have owned his true identity before he left for London, but had not. He had simply wished to seduce her. And had succeeded. While she had avoided what she had thought would be the erection of a barrier of breeding between them.

It was there now, but in reverse. As her father had once said, no earl would wish to wed a mere baronet's daughter for herself. Lord Stimson had wanted her unborn child.

'Thalia.' His voice was low, intense. 'My enquiries have borne fruit. I am no longer quite penniless. I have regained some of my family's lost property and have the means to purchase Stonar Hall should that become possible.' He drew himself up and made her a bow. 'Because of this, I am now in a position to address you. Miss Marsh—Thalia, my dearest girl, will you do me the honour of marrying me?'

Her emotions ran riot at sound of his words but she met his gaze with cool dispassion. He had so carefully avoided asking her to wed him while he had thought her a nobody. Now, it seemed, she was considered fit to marry an earl.

She could not ignore his deception, which seemed so much worse than her own. She had merely concealed a part of the truth. He had entered Stonar Hall under false pretences on a spying mission.

'My lord,' she said stiffly, 'had the Jack Hamilton I knew as a footman asked me that question, I would gladly have accepted. But, sensible as I am of the generosity of the offer, I regret that I cannot consent to marry the Earl of Eardley.'

CHAPTER TWELVE

By the shock on his face she might have hit him, as she once had. But his reaction was not the same. No punishing kiss followed. Tight-faced, he gave a formal bow and strode away.

Thalia leant against the balustrade and took a series of deep breaths, but they could not fill the hollow feeling inside her as she watched his departure. But—how dared he play such tricks? How dared he think that because he was the Earl of Eardley, she would fall into his arms as she had fallen into Jack Hamilton the footman's?

Memory of those nights he had spent in her bed rose up to taunt her. How could she have been so naïve? How could she not have guessed that he was a high-ranking gentleman bent on seducing a mere servant?

Yet his true status had been cleverly concealed. He had pulled the wool over her eyes most successfully, presenting himself as a charming, resourceful man, a man she had come to trust. And—dear Lord! She had no idea where Fanny and Emily were! He had them hidden away somewhere and she was helpless to find them!

Yet surely Emily would write to her. Perhaps there was a letter waiting at Stonar Hall even now.

She had been in London for little more than a week but her return to Stonar could not be delayed. Mr Tope needed her. And she must be there to receive any message from Emily. If she did not learn of their whereabouts soon, she would have to discover it for herself. Not that she did not trust Jack to do the right thing, even though piqued. Discovery of his true identity only served to reinforce her opinion that he was, in essentials, a gentleman of honour.

Her chaotic thoughts came to a halt. Why, then, had she reacted so violently to the disclosure? Why had she immediately accused him of deceit and perfidy, rejected his hurriedly given explanation as of no account?

The initial shock was over. She could think more clearly now. The Jack she had come to know would not have entered on the escapade without good reason, but his irreverent, audacious spirit had allowed him to enjoy it. A young gentleman of his quality, especially an officer in the army, would be up to any lark. Playing the servant had afforded him great amusement, while at the same time serving a useful purpose.

She could understand. Her judgement had been too hasty.

But she had rejected him out of hand. His pride must have been hurt. He would not ask her again. The sense of emptiness inside her grew.

But there was no denying that he had used her ill. He had seduced her. Not like Varley—oh, no, he had used their mutual attraction to enlist her willing participation, and then left her with vague promises of marriage should the necessity to protect her name arise.

But tonight—tonight he had not attempted to seduce her, had not prevaricated. He had asked her to marry him. But—he was an impoverished earl and he had discovered that she came of a rich family and could probably command a substantial dowry.

Had that had anything to do with his proposal?

That mortifying thought brought bright spots of colour to burn on her cheeks. He had most certainly deserved her instinctive set-down!

She had been in shock, she had scarcely known what she was saying. But she had been right!

Though—he had said he had regained at least part of his family's property and had the means to purchase Stonar Hall. If his own fortunes had changed, then perhaps he had no need of hers. But even if she could come to terms with his deception and disregard his possible desire to command her fortune, it was of no use regretting her impulsive refusal—although she might have become mistress of Stonar, which she had come to love.

But she did regret it, for above all else she would have shared his life. The very thing she had so longed to do only a few hours earlier! How could she still love him? But she did.

In one, impassioned moment, she had thrown it all away. Wearily, she heaved herself from the cold stone of the balustrade and forced her limbs to take her towards the salon. She must go back to join the company; they would be wondering where she was. Had they noticed Jack's sudden return alone?

As she approached the door Lord Wharton appeared, silhouetted in its frame.

'My dear Miss Marsh! We thought you must be still out there! His lordship passed swiftly through the salon and took immediate leave of our hostess. Is anything amiss? Did he attack you? Don't know the fellow, he ain't much in Town, but I shall deal with him for you—'

'No, please! I am perfectly well. His lordship was most gentlemanly in his conduct. It was I who offended him. Please return me to my mother. I shall leave immediately. Would you be so kind as to call the carriage? It can come back for Mother and Arthur.'

'My dear child!' exclaimed Lady Marsh moments later. 'Of course I shall accompany you!'

'No, Mama. I am perfectly well, just rather fatigued. I know you have been looking forward to this evening and I would not deprive you of your pleasure simply because I am not feeling quite up to snuff.'

Her mother's gaze was keen as she eyed her. 'Lord Eardley appeared to form a sudden and most particular partiality for you, Thalia. It was almost as though you had known each other before.'

Thalia said nothing.

Lady Marsh, her curiosity unassuaged, went on, 'I trust you did nothing to offend him? I discover that he is a most eligible gentleman, apart from the sudden loss of much of the family fortune and the consequent scandal of his father's suicide, but you cannot afford to be too nice in your choice, my child. Some mothers might decry his lack of fortune and the scandal attached to his name, but I do not.'

With a grand sweep of her arm, Lady Marsh waved these peccadillos aside as of no consequence. 'You would be well enough served to gain the title of Countess.'

'Yes, Mama,' murmured Thalia, who had no desire

to enter into an argument with her parent at that moment. 'If you will excuse me? I see Lord Wharton approaching. He has doubtless secured our carriage.'

The relief of emerging from those stuffy rooms swept over Thalia like a flood. A slight breeze touched her cheeks as she descended the steps; although the air was tainted with chimney smoke and whiffs of ordure, it acted like a vinaigrette on her jaded senses.

Thoughts still churned round in her mind, see-sawing her emotions. His lordship was trying to reverse his family's fortunes. If he had been moved to offer for her because he now knew that she would command a substantial dowry, the idea still did not sit well with her. She had been wise to reject him! How could she ever hope to find happiness with one who had treated them all shabbily?

She would not refine over her loss but, as soon as she could, would begin to remake her life.

With this determination firmly fixed in her mind, Thalia went straight up to her room upon her return, drank the posset left by her bedside, and quickly dropped into a deep, drugged sleep. But that did not prevent her from dreaming of Jack Hamilton.

Jack dismissed his carriage and walked back to St James's Street. He needed fresh air and exercise to quell the tension in his limbs, to settle the emotions boiling inside him.

Absently, he threw a penny to the child sweeping a crossing. A carriage clattered past, light spilled and noisy laughter echoed from many a window or door. But he was oblivious.

All he could see in his mind's eye was the utter scorn on her face as she'd delivered her stinging rejection of his offer of marriage.

He had sadly miscalculated her reaction to discovering his true identity. His need to gain entry, incognito, to Stonar Hall and to unearth the truth of its passing from his family's hands had appeared so overwhelmingly justifiable to him that he had not considered in what light such a deception might be viewed by those he had gulled.

And to appear before her in all the splendour of his new evening clothes and the dignity of his title without warning had been an egotistical indulgence which had badly misfired. She would think him vain, unfeeling. Possibly—the thought shocked him—a fortune-hunter? For word had already circulated amongst the *ton* that the new and extremely wealthy baronet had promised his sister a substantial dowry upon her marriage. What a ramshackle creature she must think him!

And his proposal had been unplanned, the impetuous result of seeing her again, of the realisation of how much he had missed her, of how much she had come to mean to him, of the certainty that she would grace the rank of countess like no other woman he knew. And she had scorned his addresses.

Politely, with perfect civility. She did not lack conduct.

There seemed to be only one certainty left in his suddenly chaotic world. Thalia Marsh was the only woman he wished to wed. Her rejection had hurt his pride but it had devastated his emotions. If he lost her through his rash foolishness—

But he would not. He had lost a battle, but not the war.

Despite all her mother's pleas, Thalia travelled back to Kent two days later, promising to visit Bruton Street again in the near future and to bring Fanny with her when she did. She still had not acquainted Lady Marsh with the complicated circumstances caused by Lord Varley's reappearance in her life. She had to trust that, by the time she was able to visit her mother again, the situation would be resolved.

That largely depended on Jack. The day following their meeting at Lady Jersey's a note had been delivered to her. She had never seen Jack's writing before, but the boldness of the hand and the elaborately decorated 'E' impressed on the wax seal told her immediately who it was from.

Her fingers trembled as, in the privacy of Lady Marsh's coach, which her mother had insisted she use for the journey, she unfolded it to peruse his words again.

'Madam,' she read, 'I do not write to trouble you further with my unwelcome suit, but to inform you that your daughter will be safe under my care until the question of Varley's presence in Sandwich has been resolved. He is shortly to be posted to the West Indies, where he will be unable to trouble you. Be assured that you will be reunited with your daughter at the earliest possible moment. Until that time, please believe me that both Miss Wright and Fanny are well and happy. My only object in this matter is to serve you. Eardley.'

Her initial reaction had been one of relief that she

had been right—he was not so small-minded as to abandon her and Fanny to the mercy of Lord Varley. But now, as she read the words again, the import of his revelation of Varley's future struck her more forcibly. Jack must have arranged the posting through his army contacts. Men of rank and influence, since he had achieved such a result so quickly.

She had to feel sorry for Varley, despite what he was, for service in the West Indies was almost as fatal as a death sentence. The fever killed more men than the enemy.

She dismissed the carriage at the Post Inn in Canterbury, where the coachman and footman would spend the night before returning to town, and engaged a post-chaise to take her on to Stonar. She had no wish to cause a stir by arriving in an expensive carriage which, drawn by four splendid, showy match greys, had been her father's declaration to the world that he was a rich man.

The greys had been left at the first stage but the coach itself was of a quality to cause comment and had the Baronet's coat of arms emblazoned on the doors. She wanted to slip back into her role as housekeeper without bringing attention to herself. She had enough problems to deal with without adding the curiosity of her fellow servants. They knew her father had died, but still did not know who he had been. It was better so.

She arrived late to find the house still and dark. The only light she could see in the front came from Sebastian Tope's suite. The post chaise circled to the rear of the house and drew up by the servant's entrance, where light did spill from the kitchen windows. Ben

Treddle came running across from the stables to greet her while other hands untied her luggage from the back of the coach.

'It's well you're back, Mrs Marsh,' he told her. 'Master's been took even more poorly. Doctor don't hold out much hope for him.'

He looked anxious; everyone she could see appeared worried, subdued. If their employer died it would mean changes. No one knew who the new master would be. Mr Tope had never even hinted at the identity of his successor. He had no direct heir and no relations he ever saw, so speculation had been rife. The most likely thing was that the place would be sold, though some male relative might appear from nowhere to claim the inheritance.

'I must go in immediately!' cried Thalia. 'Oh, poor Mr Tope! And I thought he was recovering so well!'

She hurried indoors, greeted Mrs Gale and others gathered in the kitchen and then, without bothering to go to her room, went to the sick man's side. On her way she could not help glancing at the portrait of Jack's mother, in the dining-room, and that of his father in the drawing-room. How could she have been so blind? The likeness was there for anyone to see, and Jack in his footman's wig looked a great deal like his father!

Crossing the landing to Mr Tope's room, it occurred to her that, if he died, Jack might find it easier to purchase the property from the heir, whoever that might be. The problem did not concern her as it did the other members of the staff. Whatever happened, she would return to Bruton Street once Mr Tope's need of her had gone.

Surprisingly, that prospect did not greatly enliven her spirits. She had come to the conclusion that she would probably never marry. Few men would be able to stir in her the response Jack did and, despite everything, she loved and admired him more than she thought it possible she ever would any other man.

To enter into a loveless union for the sake of an establishment of her own and more children in the nursery seemed not only undesirable, but unlikely, since no other eligible gentleman was likely to agree to accepting Fanny into his household.

So, she would have to find something else to fill her life. The prospect of endless days spent in idleness or socialising did not appeal to Thalia, who had found her duties as housekeeper both interesting and fulfilling. She could not face living long in Bruton Street, although once her mother had met her granddaughter she would not refuse to have her live with them, Thalia felt certain. And she would be able to sway Arthur, whose approval would be decisive in the matter.

But she would prefer to have an establishment of her own to run. She doubted whether Arthur's generosity would stretch to setting her up in great style, but a small house would suffice, preferably in the country, where Fanny would thrive, and where Emily might be persuaded to live with them as governess and companion.

She almost wept to see Mr Tope, lying in his bed completely helpless. The nurses fussed about him and Pringle hovered nearby, aching to serve his master but unable to do anything to relieve his condition.

Yet the ill man did recognise her. His eyes it up and he managed a twisted smile, though he was unable to speak. And now both hands lay useless on the bed. She gathered them into her own.

'I had thought to find you recovered,' she whispered. 'My dear sir, are you quite comfortable?'

Mr Tope blinked.

Thalia squeezed the fingers she held. 'I am back now, my father is buried and the family well situated. I shall not leave you again.'

The nurse intervened. 'You must not tire him, madam. You should leave him now.'

Tope blinked, twice.

It was his only method of communication. But his meaning was clear.

'He wishes me to stay a little longer,' Thalia told the nurse firmly. 'My presence will do him no harm. Why do you not take the opportunity to rest? Your duties here must be excessively onerous.'

'Well—five minutes, then ma'am,' agreed the nurse, a formidable woman of heavy build and considerable strength. 'Nurse Mays is off duty. I will be in the next room if you need me. Not that it'll be much pleasure to sit with Mr Pringle.' She snorted, rather derisively. 'Thinks he owns his master, he does. Don't like us intruding on his preserves, but he'd never manage on his own, not a skinny fellow like him.'

'He has served Mr Tope most faithfully for many years, Nurse. He has grown fond of his master. You must allow for that.'

With the door closed behind the nurse, Thalia launched into a censored account of her time in London, not mentioning her meeting with Jack or telling Tope of his true identity. Let Jack deal with that.

She had no wish to pre-empt him and cause her employer pain by so doing.

It was clear that Sebastian Tope was glad to have her back and Thalia knew that her decision to return had been right. In a way she loved Sebastian Tope. She would sorrow for him when he died, whereas her father's death had left her unmoved.

Mrs Gale knocked on her door later that evening.

'Come in, Cook,' invited Thalia.

She would rather have tumbled straight into bed, for she felt fit to drop after her journey and the harrowing experience of talking to Mr Tope, though whether she'd have been able to sleep was a different matter. She was still wrung out emotionally over her feelings for Jack. At least the visit put off the moment when she'd have to take to the bed, with all its memories.

So, having settled Mrs Gale on the sofa, she demanded, 'Tell me everything that's occurred while I've been away.'

Mrs Gale gave her a dramatic account of the upset which had followed Mr Tope's second stroke, lamented the fact that a third one was going to kill him, and wondered what any of them were to do then.

'I shall lose me place, so will you, Mrs Marsh. We'll be out on the street, sure as eggs is eggs!'

'Not necessarily, Mrs Gale. You are an excellent cook, you'll probably be asked to stay on, and in any case you have no need to fear the future. You may have my enthusiastic reference, if needed—you'll never be short of a place.'

'Maybe,' admitted Mrs Gale, 'but there's others as

won't be so fortunate. If there's a mistress, she may not want a housekeeper! Had you considered that?'

'I had. And I must tell you, Mrs Gale, that my father's death means that I have command of a small competence. I shall leave here as soon as Mr Tope no longer needs me.'

'Well, now! I always suspected as how you was a cut above the rest of us. What made you come to work here in the first place?'

'I quarrelled with my father and had to leave home. But now I can go back. Except that I do not really wish to. So I shall set up a small establishment of my own.' She tried to change the subject, not wishing to go into further detail. 'Has nothing else of any interest happened while I've been away?'

'Well, it looks like we'll be losing Rose. She's met a soldier, a sergeant she says, and according to her he's going to wed her. Course, he'll probably move off and leave her stranded, but there's no talking to her. Hamilton was the fellow she wanted, and since she couldn't catch 'im, she's found herself another.'

'You haven't heard from Hamilton?'

There was just a chance that he'd been in touch.

'Not a word. But you don't know! And here was I almost forgetting to tell you!'

'What, Mrs Gale?' prompted Thalia, her nerves tensing. From Cook's tone this was news of some import.

'There's been murder done!'

'Murder?' repeated Thalia faintly. But it couldn't concern Jack or Sid or Fanny or Emily, and who else's death could trouble her? She relaxed again.

'You know that Captain fellow who came here to dinner? The one Rose said you'd met afore?'

'Captain Varley?' asked Thalia, remembering the occasion without pleasure. His appearance on the scene had signalled the beginning of all her troubles. But how could this concern him?

'That's 'im! Found dead he was, beaten up first and then shot dead.'

Thalia's mind began to reel. Varley, dead? 'But who killed him?' she gasped. Thank goodness it could not have been Jack or Sid, who were both in London.

'Ruffians belonging to the dishonourable company of sea cocks, at least, that's what the Revenue men reckon.'

'Killed by smugglers?' wondered Thalia faintly.

'Aye. Must've crossed 'em somehow, betrayed 'em or cheated 'em, the Revenue men reckon. Anyways, he's dead and his body's been sent back to his family in Ireland.'

'Well, fancy that!' said Thalia inadequately.

She tried to keep her voice even, to appear tolerably unconcerned by this astonishing news. No one must suspect how nearly it affected her. She doubted whether Jack knew. News had not reached him two days ago. There was nothing, now, to prevent Fanny and Emily from returning home!

Except that she did not know where they were and Jack was ignorant of the circumstances.

Once Mrs Gale had left, Thalia sat down and attempted to write him a letter. But the words would not come and in the end she burned the paper in the flame of her candle. She would have to wait for Lord Eardley to keep his word and contact her.

She shivered. It was nearing the end of September. Winter would be upon them soon and she must order more fires to be lit about the place. But it wasn't the lack of a fire making her shiver tonight. The cold was inside her.

For she had turned Jack away and however devious he had turned out to be, she did not know how she was going to live without him.

Saturday was the first day of October. Thalia took the feathers of her quill gently between her teeth as she struggled with September's accounts. They were out of balance by two pounds and seventeen shillings. It took her a while to discover that she had written a three in the wrong column, making the sum shillings instead of pounds. With that put right, she sat back and puffed out a sigh of relief.

It had been a long day and she was glad to set her books aside, call in to bid Mr Tope a goodnight, and retire to her room, warmed now by a bright fire, for the weather had turned chilly. Tilly would be up soon with her supper.

She had been back at Stonar for a week and still there had been no word from his lordship. Had he learned yet of Varley's death? News of that kind took time to travel but there should have been an announcement in the *Gazette* or in one of the London papers. He may not have seen it. And the Horse Guards, even if they knew, might not think it necessary to inform Jack.

The waiting and the uncertainty were unravelling her

nerves. She sighed as she returned Fanny's portrait to her drawer, wondering when she would see her child again, and sat down to gaze abstractedly into the leaping flames.

She turned as Tilly knocked and came in with her tray, her face shining with delight.

Placing the tray on the table beside Thalia, she exclaimed, 'Oh, ma'am, 'amilton is back!'

Thalia's stomach turned over. She clasped her hands together to stop their trembling. 'Hamilton?' He'd come back as Hamilton?

'Aye, ma'am. Says he'll be leaving, though, 'cause he's found hisself a better place in London.'

'I see.' Thalia swallowed. 'We shall miss him.'

Tilly looked at her askance. 'Thought as how you might be going with 'im, Mrs Marsh.'

'I shall remain with Mr Tope,' stated Thalia flatly. 'When did he arrive?'

''Bout an hour ago. Walked in from the village. Probably fetched hisself a lift from Canterbury on the haulier's cart. Anyways, he's 'ere for a couple of weeks while he works out his notice, he says.'

'He hasn't handed it in yet,' observed Thalia primly, though her heart was crying out. An hour ago she'd still been down in her office. He could have come to her there. But why should he? She had rejected him so angrily.

Yet he had returned as Hamilton. She had expected him to arrive in style when he did, and request that Lord Eardley be admitted to Mr Sebastian Tope's presence, for he would not know that Mr Tope had suffered another stroke.

And, on being informed of that circumstance, he should then have sought an interview with her.

She was glad he had not. But what would he do? They must talk.

With a nod and a strained smile, she dismissed the child. 'Thank you, Tilly.'

She ate little of her supper; the dryness of her throat prevented her from swallowing and the lump in her stomach had taken her appetite. The tea, she thought gratefully as she sipped it, might save her life.

She expected someone to come for her tray and so when, half an hour later, someone tapped on her door she had no hesitation in calling out for them to come in.

She glanced up. Immediately, her muscles turned to jelly.

'Good evening, ma'am,' said Jack gravely. 'I have come to collect your tray.'

His expression matched his tone but his eyes held uncharacteristic uncertainty as they met hers. Something in her face must have encouraged him for the assurance came back and the corners of his mobile mouth twitched.

'I see that you are surprised at my return in this guise, my dear Thalia. I had not intended to continue my masquerade, the more so since it displeased you, but you once said you would wed a footman, while in London you rejected a lord. So—' he stepped quickly across to drop on one knee beside her, where she sat transfixed in her chair '—you see before you a man anxious only to address you once more with a view to securing your hand in marriage.'

Thalia's mouth opened but no sound emerged. She had been regretting her outburst, yet now he knelt before her she could not find her voice to tell him so.

After waiting hopefully for a moment and receiving no response, Jack went on. 'I acted rashly that night, gave you no time to recover from the shock of discovering me. Can you forgive me? Can you excuse my deception? I acted from necessity, my dear, not wickedness or mere frivolity. Now my object has been achieved, I should like to take my proper place in Society.'

He reached out to take her hands between his. Thalia shivered at the contact. The effect of his touch upon her had not changed. If anything, it had intensified. She had not been able to stop loving him. Warmth and strength began to flow back into her limbs.

'But seeing you at Lady Jersey's,' Jack went on, 'I knew immediately that my happiness would never be complete without you at my side as my Countess. That I desired you I already knew. That I loved you I discovered that night.'

Her hands fluttered in his. He held them more tightly. 'And so I made my premature declaration. May I hope that you may learn to return my regard? Tell me now if my hope is vain, and I will trouble you no further with my feelings.'

'I do return your regard, Jack,' whispered Thalia.

He gave a cry of pleasure and began to draw her nearer.

'But there are things that must be settled before I can consent to become your wife,' she added firmly.

CHAPTER THIRTEEN

JACK lifted her imprisoned hands and pressed them to his lips.

'My dear love,' he murmured. 'You have almost made me the happiest of men. What are the things that must be settled before my happiness is complete?'

'Varley,' murmured Thalia.

'Ah!'

Jack rose, drawing Thalia up as he did so, and led her to the settee. Once there he threw off his coat, settled himself beside her and took her into the circle of his arms. Thalia stroked the white cotton of his shirt sleeve, thinking how relaxed and terribly attractive he looked.

'What of Varley?' he asked.

She stilled her fingers. 'He is dead. Did you know?'

'Yes. The news reached me before I left London. I was informed because my friends knew I was interested, having asked for him to be posted abroad.'

'He will never see the West Indies,' commented Thalia grimly. 'I cannot say I was saddened by the news. My only regret is that such a man was Fanny's father.'

'She takes after you, my love; there is no vicious streak in her, you may be sure.'

'I do hope so, though I cannot help but worry. You know the Revenue men think he was murdered by smugglers?'

'Yes. He caused trouble for those criminals he set on me. They spent days in custody being questioned before being released. In addition, he may have refused to pay the leader of the gang the agreed sum, since I escaped his vengeance.'

'Knowing him, I believe you may be right.'

'Their leader will command the allegiance of hundreds of men and be quite ruthless. I imagine it to have been a revenge killing.'

Thalia nodded and her cap tickled Jack's nose. He removed it, tossed it aside and sunk his face in her hair.

'That's better.'

The arm behind her shifted so that his hand could cup her breast. The exquisite pain of it speared through Thalia and she could not control the little gasp of pleasure which escaped her.

Jack nuzzled her neck. 'Isn't it?' he demanded.

'Yes. Oh, Jack, I have missed you! How could I have been so stiff-necked the other night?' She snuggled closer. 'But how did you dare to come here under your own name? Did you not fear someone would recognise it?'

'Not really. I had not been here since I was a child. Few would remember the ten-year-old brother of the heir, Marcus, Lord Craymont. I was merely Lord Jack! Eardley, Craymont—people would remember those names, but not the family name of Hamilton, which was seldom used. And Hamilton is not an uncommon name. It could simply have been coincidence that the new footman bore it!'

'I suppose so, but it was a risk!' Thalia quickly passed on to a matter close to her heart. 'But now Varley is dead, Fanny is safe. Can she not return home so that I may see her?'

'You may see her tomorrow, my love. Sidney took them back to Asham while I came on here.'

She twisted in his arms to lift her radiant face to his. 'Oh, Jack, how wonderful! Are they both well? Where have they been?'

'They are both blooming. They have been with my mother,' Jack told her wryly, gazing down at her eager face, wishing the expression of love and joy were for him, longing to kiss her. But not yet. He still had bridges to rebuild. 'Mother lives on our only remaining estate, a small entailed manor near Sevenoaks.'

Unable to truly believe it, 'They have been staying with the Countess of Eardley?' gasped Thalia.

'The Dowager Countess, yes.'

'What an imposition!'

He chuckled. 'Not at all. Mother has come to love Fanny and she and Miss Wright dealt famously together. She needed companionship, and they gave it to her. She was sad to part with them when I brought them away today. But she knows that Fanny's mother is the dearest object of my heart.'

'Oh!' Thalia blushed in confusion. 'I'm glad they caused no trouble. How Fanny must have loved it there! But, Jack. . .' Thalia braced herself. This was the crucial question. Her stomach churned as she asked, 'What of Fanny if we wed? Where will she fit into our lives?'

Jack tightened his arm about her. 'I love her as my own daughter, Thalia, and I believe she is fond enough of me. Would you object if I took out adoption papers? If she became legally my child?'

'Object?' Her voice wavered. Jack would have the legal right to determine Fanny's future. Yet how often had she thought him the perfect father figure for her child? He would soon eradicate any faults in her character bequeathed by Varley. But could she let full responsibility for Fanny go?

Yes, because the child would then be in precisely the same position as any offspring they might have together. Children belonged to both parents but, first and foremost, to the father. Varley could have claimed Fanny and taken her away since she had always acknowledged his paternity.

Besides, were anything to happen to her, Fanny would be safe with Jack.

'No.' Her decision was firm. It echoed in her voice.

'So, my love, what is your answer? Will you wed a bogus footman who is in truth a comparatively impoverished earl who may not be able to negotiate the repossession of Stonar Hall until its owner either recovers or dies? I am sorry to find that Mr Tope is much worse. I could not possibly trouble him now.'

'Indeed not.' She grimaced. 'I must confess that I still disapprove of the deception you practised on us.'

Jack chuckled. 'But admit it, my love, having an affair with a footman afforded you an additional thrill, did it not? Perhaps,' he added wryly, 'the thought of marrying a mere earl seems tame by comparison?'

'How can you believe that, when the man is the same? No, my dearest one, I soon found that, whatever your faults, I could not bear to lose you. I love you, Jack. I will marry you with all my heart.'

He drew in a sharp breath and let it out in a sigh of

relief. 'Then I am the happiest of men, my heart's delight.'

At last he kissed her. His lips sought hers in a tender, loving caress of dedication. Thalia responded, her fingers tangling in clean, fair, wavy hair as she opened her soul to her lover.

After a long interval he sighed and withdrew his arms.

'I must take your tray down. Otherwise I shall earn a reprimand from Mrs Gale.'

'Will she not guess that we had much to discuss? She knew at the fête that we had engaged each other's affections. Our affair came as no surprise to her. But do you not intend to tell everyone who you are?'

'Not yet. I confess to enjoying the deception too much, and it does no harm. You have not told them your true status, have you, my love? So neither shall I. But we shall announce our engagement, if you agree?'

'They have been expecting it, I think.' Thalia laughed. 'You are a rogue, Jack Hamilton, but I must admit that I shall enjoy gulling them all! You are making me as bad as yourself! When shall we tell them?'

'Tomorrow. And I have a special licence ready. We can be wed as soon as it pleases you.'

'You have? You were so certain that I would change my mind?'

'Once I had realised my fault in taking you so much by surprise and springing my proposal on you—unintended, I assure you, but I was so overwhelmed by the sight of you that my feelings overcame my judgement—I was determined to woo and win you.'

'And never doubted a successful outcome of your

suit!' teased Thalia. 'It did not take you long,' she admitted ruefully. 'I quickly realised that my first reaction had been wrong. But do we announce our engagement as between housekeeper and footman? Or as between the Earl of Eardley and Miss Marsh?'

'Tomorrow, as members of Mr Tope's staff. We can always surprise them later.' He regarded her quizzically. 'Do you wish for a Society wedding, my love?'

Thalia shook her head. 'No, I should prefer a quiet wedding in Stonar. But our mothers may feel cheated if we wed secretly, without consulting them or inviting them to the nuptials. And although he has no real say in the matter it would be polite to ask my brother Arthur for my hand. He is now the Baronet and head of our family. He has promised me a dowry should I wed.'

She watched his face closely. Would the prospect of a dowry influence him? He had confessed himself in need of funds.

He sighed and shrugged, 'My preference would be to wed first and sort out the settlement later. But I agree that good conduct demands that I should approach your brother and inform our parents of our intention. Whether they agree or not will make no difference to me. I shall marry you, my love, come what may.'

This required another kiss to seal the bargain. Then Jack picked up her supper tray and, after a final peck on her cheek, carried the dirty dishes back to the kitchen.

Thalia picked up the coat he had left behind and sat for a while with it pressed against her breast. When she began to prepare for bed she did so in the certain knowledge that he would be back. Otherwise, why had he left the coat behind?

That night he remained with her until dawn, for it no longer mattered that others knew of rather than suspected their liaison. Their engagement would be official in a matter of hours.

They went together to inform Sebastian Tope. Unable to express his approval in any other way, he gave a wry smile, accompanied by an almost imperceptible nod.

They were alone in the room with the invalid. 'I have a confession to make, sir,' said Jack in a low tone. 'I have perpetrated a grave deception on you for all the time I have been here. I must tell you that I am in fact the Earl of Eardley.' There was little reaction from Mr Tope. But he attempted another smile and nod. 'I believe you guessed I was not who I professed to be, sir?'

Tope blinked.

Jack nodded. 'Thalia said as much. I came here to try to discover how this property came to be lost to my family. I have done so, and know that the fault was not yours. You are the legitimate owner and I fully accept that.'

Tope blinked.

Jack took hold of Thalia's hand. 'We shall neither of us desert you while you have need of us, sir. But I must return to London on Monday to make certain arrangements. I shall not be gone for long and Thalia will remain here. We have yet to finally decide where to hold the ceremony, but wonder whether it would be possible to be married from here?'

Tope's face seemed to light up. He managed a definite nod and struggled to achieve speech.

Jack frowned as he tried to interpret the sounds Tope made but Thalia understood what he was trying to say. 'You wish us to treat the place as our own?' she suggested gently.

And Sebastian Tope blinked, nodded and then shut his eyes as he let go, his message understood.

Later that morning, as the staff gathered to walk into Stonar to attend church, Thalia and Jack entered the servants' hall together.

After a few moments of general greeting and conversation, Thalia, in her capacity as housekeeper, called for attention.

'Hamilton has an announcement to make,' she told the assembled servants and, in the most mortifying manner possible, blushed.

Jack placed a black-clad arm about her shoulders. He smiled round the company as he told them, 'Mrs Marsh has done me the great honour of consenting to become my wife.'

A buzz filled the room; whoops, whistles and more genteel exclamations from Cook and Rose filled the air. Ben Treddle, walking into the village himself since Mr Tope had no use for the carriage, came over to shake Jack's hand and offer Thalia his best wishes.

Tilly cried, 'Oh, ma'am! How romantical!'

Then Jack cut off the avalanche of congratulations with a reminder that they would all be late for church.

Naturally, news of the engagement spread through the village; after the service they received the congrat-

ulations and best wishes of so many people that Thalia
was surprised. She had not realised how well-liked she
was, nor how quickly Jack had become a welcome
member of the local community.

She wondered what the reaction would be when they
discovered that he was the Earl of Eardley. Many of
them should have been and might become his tenants.
They had not approved of his father or brother. She
thought they might turn out to be more tolerant of the
new Earl.

'Felicitations, felicitations, my dear Mrs Marsh!'
offered the Reverend Wyndham, shaking her hand,
while his wife smiled and nodded her bonneted head in
agreement with her husband. 'May I hope to have the
pleasure of officiating at your nuptials?'

'Probably, sir,' said Thalia, still blushing rosily
because of all the attention her engagement had
brought. 'But my mother lives in London. She may wish
me to be married from there.'

They had decided not to make up their minds until
Jack had been to London, where he would announce
their intention of being wed in Stonar. If this decision
caused too much dismay in certain households, they
would reconsider. But they wanted to be married
quickly. There seemed little point in delaying the
ceremony and although Thalia had so far not fallen
pregnant, the possibility of its happening was upper-
most in her mind, if not in Jack's.

Afterwards, they walked together to Asham once
more, there to be greeted exuberantly by Fanny and
calmly by Emily Wright. Sid, still with them, treated the

new arrivals to the terrible grin that had no power to frighten those who knew him.

'Well,' said Emily once the greetings were over. 'I can tell by your faces that you have news for me?'

'Indeed we have, dear Emily!' Thalia hugged her old governess as she had in adolescence when something exciting had occurred. 'We are to be married!'

Emily smiled. 'I urged you to wed your footman, Thalia. I'm glad you have decided to take my advice.' She turned to Jack and gave a small curtsy. 'I congratulate you, my lord. I need scarcely say that I thoroughly approve your choice.'

Sidney Barton looked as pleased as his poor face would allow. 'Congratulations, my lord! And may I wish you every happiness, ma'am?'

Before they could respond to Sid's felicitations Fanny intervened.

'Mama! Mama!' Fanny tugged at Thalia's skirt. 'What will happen when you marry Mr Hamilton? Shall I live with you? All the other children live with their mamas.'

Thalia stooped down to Fanny's level, reached out and touched her daughter's soft cheek. 'Yes, my love. You shall live with us. And once we are wed, you may like to address his lordship as Papa. Would that please you?'

Fanny turned a radiant face to Jack. 'Truly? Will I truly be your little girl?'

Jack swept the child up into his arms. 'Yes, Fanny. It will be as though I had always been your father. If you have no objection?'

Fanny flung her arms about his neck. 'Oh, no, dearest

Mr Hamilton! 'Cause,' she added in muffled tones as she buried her face in Jack's cravat, 'I do so love you.'

'And I love you, my poppet. But will you not be sorry to leave Aunt Wright?'

'Oh!' Fanny had not thought of that possibility. Torn by the prospect of having to part from Emily, her surrogate mother, she squirmed from Jack's embrace and ran to fling loving arms about her. 'But I do not wish to leave you, Aunt. I love you, too!'

Jack had not missed the sadness on Emily's face while Fanny had been exploring the terms of her new life. His question had a purpose behind it.

'Then we shall have to do something about it, shall we not?' He smiled at Emily. 'Miss Wright, Fanny will need a governess for many years yet. My mother would welcome an agreeable companion. Will you do me a great service and consent to live with us at Five Elms? Thalia and I may spend part of our time either here or in London and you would be a familiar anchor for Fanny while we are away.

'Dear Emily—I may call you Emily?—you are so much a part of Thalia and Fanny's life that I consider you to be family. You would be more than welcome to join our household. Am I not correct, Thalia?'

'Indeed!' Thalia's face was radiant. How thoughtful of Jack to include Emily in their happiness! 'I know you have been content in this cottage, but you will be among friends and must be happy at Five Elms! You will know better than I if this is so, for I have not yet met Lady Eardley or seen my future home!'

The tears were streaming down Emily's cheeks. 'My dears,' she mumbled. 'How can I thank you for thinking of an old woman's pleasure? Of course I will come with you! And you will delight in both Lady Eardley and Five Elms, Thalia!'

'Capital!' exclaimed Jack. 'Then that is settled. All we have to do now is fix the date of the wedding, to which you are both invited. As are you, Sid! I could not wed without my faithful Sergeant Barton at my side!'

Sid grinned. 'I'd given up hope of ever meeting the lady who could leg-shackle you, sir!'

Jack had the grace to look embarrassed. Then he laughed. 'It took being under the thumb of a prim housekeeper to lure me into parson's mousetrap. I became addicted to that perverse pleasure!'

'While the housekeeper,' retorted Thalia mischievously, 'found it quite impossible to keep the new footman under control! I found him giving orders instead of taking them,' she added plaintively to Emily.

Jack chuckled. 'I wonder you put up with me.'

'I had little choice,' Thalia reminded him severely. 'Mr Tope had need of your strength.'

Jack clenched his fists and flexed his muscles. 'Aye, poor man, he did.' Then, soberly, 'It is a sad shame for him to be so helpless now.'

Sebastian Tope's predicament did not lower their spirits for long and the rest of the visit was spent talking of future plans. Thalia and Jack returned to Stonar Hall happy in each other and quietly content.

'I cannot wait to make an honest woman of you,' murmured Jack as he slipped into her bed that night. 'I hate having to leave you again so soon, my love, but it is necessary for me to return to London.'

'I trust Mama and Arthur and Lady Eardley will be willing to travel to Stonar Hall and be Mr Tope's guests for the wedding. It is such a pity that he will not be able to attend the ceremony. I have come to look upon him almost as a father these last years. Certainly as an uncle.'

'I know, my love.' Jack gathered her to him and began to stroke her satin-soft skin. 'You will miss him when he goes.'

'Do not say it! I cannot bear the thought of his dying.'

'He would be better dead,' said Jack sombrely. 'Do you truly think he enjoys lying helpless in bed? He was a valiant and cheerful man, but even so the disability he suffered irked him. Imagine what he must feel now, for despite his helplessness his brain remains active.'

'I know. It is selfish of me to want to keep him with me, I know. But I shall miss him sadly if he does not recover.'

Jack said no more but murmured sounds of comfort in her ear as he led her again into the realms of passionate delight they so joyously shared.

Thalia woke, sated and content, in dawn's first light. When she realised that she was alone in the bed, her contentment vanished.

Jack had already gone! She had slept so soundly that he had not wakened her when rising. She had not bidden him a proper farewell!

Yet perhaps it was just as well. She snuggled back under the covers, for the autumnal dawn was chill. Instead of a sad leave-taking to remember, she had the warmth and togetherness of the night lingering in her memory. How truly wonderful was his love-making! How amazing her own response. And to think that such ecstasy could be theirs for the remainder of their lives!

Tilly knocked, bringing her morning chocolate. She swept back the bed and window drapes and set about lighting the fire.

'Mr Hamilton 'as gone off again,' she informed Thalia chattily. 'Left best part of an hour ago, he did.'

'Yes, I know.' Thalia sat up to sip at her cocoa. 'He will not be away for long.'

Sid had stabled the coach and horses, in which Fanny and Emily had returned from Five Elms, in Asham. He was to meet Jack outside Stonar Hall and the two men would drive to Five Elms and then on to London. His business would take a couple of days at the most, Jack had said. He should be back by Thursday, as Lord Eardley, with the wedding date fixed. Whether the marriage settlement could be agreed so quickly would largely depend upon Arthur and the lawyers. But nothing, Jack had vowed, could stop him making use of the special licence in his pocket to wed her at the first possible moment.

So Thalia anticipated Thursday with quiet happiness.

But on Wednesday afternoon Sebastian Tope suffered another stroke and died.

CHAPTER FOURTEEN

STONAR HALL lay shrouded in darkness and sunk in reverential dejection. Windows had their curtains drawn across and the front door knocker had been wreathed in black crepe.

Most of the staff, who had valued Sebastian Tope as a kindly employer, genuinely regretted the old man's demise. Pringle was prostate with grief. Uncertainty added to the general feeling of gloom. No one knew what would become of them.

The doctor, responding to an urgent summons, had come at once, to find that his patient had already breathed his last. He contacted the lawyers. Their representatives arrived on Thursday morning to take charge.

Thalia, swamped by responsibility, wanted Jack. He was still in London and no message would reach him in time if he kept to his proposed plan. She must simply cope until he came.

Her attention was required everywhere. The lawyers made the funeral arrangements, but she had to provide food and shelter for them and prepare for any guests who might arrive to attend the obsequies, which had been fixed for the following Tuesday.

'Are you expecting any relatives to attend?' she asked Mr Quiller, the senior lawyer, who, with a couple of clerks, was to take up residence until all the business was settled. 'No one visited him while he was alive.'

'He had none that our firm is aware of, Mrs Marsh. He made no bequests to any relation. By the way, we have his Will in our possession, but do you know where we might find his copy? He may have changed it without our knowledge; although it seems unlikely, we must check. It will be with his papers, no doubt, and I shall need to examine all his documents.'

'Of course. He kept them in the drawers of his desk, in the library.'

The dried-up little man glanced at her covertly from the corners of eyes half-hidden behind a pair of pince-nez. 'He never discussed the contents of his Will with you?'

'Never, Mr Quiller. I was but his housekeeper.'

'Just so. Just so. Ahem. Perhaps you will show me where our client kept his papers?'

'I have the key here.' Thalia removed it from her bunch. 'I thought it safer to take it from the box by his bed where he kept it.'

'Thank you, ma'am.' Quiller accepted the key from her. 'The library, you say? You realise I shall need to inspect all the estate accounts?'

'The household accounts are in the housekeeper's office downstairs. I will have them sent up to you, if you wish to work in the library, and ask the bailiff, Mr Shepherd, to deliver the estate accounts.'

As the arduous day wore on and Jack did not return as expected, Thalia's spirits sank to zero. Was Arthur arguing, holding Jack up? Or had he been delayed by one of the thousand-and-one other things which could have gone wrong?

A dreadful thought flew into her mind. Had he suffered an accident on the road? Was he lying somewhere injured, or even dead? Now she had found a man she could truly love, she simply could not bear the thought of losing him. All her new-found freedom and happiness would die with him. She would never be a whole person again.

The fears grew in her until she had to take herself firmly in hand, telling herself that they would all be groundless, there would be some quite innocent explanation for his tardy return.

But convincing herself of this was easier said than done and he still had not arrived when she retired late that night. Despite an anxiety she was certain would preclude sleep, so exhausted was she that she dropped off almost immediately. It must have been hours later when a small sound woke her.

Through a crack in the bed curtains she saw the moving glow of a candle.

'Who is it?' she demanded, struggling to bring herself wide awake.

'It's only me.' The bed-curtain was swept aside and, by the light of the flaring candle he held, she saw Jack's dear, welcome features smiling down at her. He was safe!

She sat up, suddenly wide awake, glowing with the warmth of relaxed tension, swept by a flush of awareness. She opened her arms to receive him. 'Jack! Oh, Jack, how glad I am to see you!'

He kissed her in a most satisfactory manner and kept

his lips on hers as he reached for her comforter and draped it about her shoulders.

'You must not catch cold, my sweet.'

Thalia clung to him. 'You know Mr Tope is dead?'

Jack perched on the edge of the bed and she released her hold on him while he removed his coat, waistcoat and neckcloth. He wore country clothes, but those of a gentleman, not the rough garments he had assumed as Hamilton the footman.

'The boy who let me in told me. My poor love, I wish I had been here.'

'So do I—it has been a vastly disagreeable day! But the lawyer has arranged everything. The funeral is to be on Tuesday of next week.'

'And I,' said Jack wryly, 'had arranged our wedding for the Friday.'

'So soon! Oh, Jack that is incredible!'

'Yes. Your brother was most obliging and had his lawyers draw up a marriage settlement immediately. I remained in London until late this morning, until my lawyer had approved the document. We wanted no wrangling and there was none. Everything is signed, sealed and settled.'

Thalia had had no hand in it. Although she knew that the bride seldom had any say in an agreement which was normally made between the two fathers, she had to thrust down a feeling of resentment at being so ignored. However, she was as anxious as anyone else to hurry things along so did not protest. But she had to ask, 'Was Arthur generous?'

'He agreed to a sum of twenty thousand pounds, my love.'

Such a splendid dowry! Larger than she had dared hope. 'Dear Arthur!' she exclaimed. 'I am so thankful to him.'

'Your brother and I got along famously. Your join-ture will include possession for life of the town house, of which, incidentally, I now have the keys. I have installed a butler who will take on a temporary staff until we can deal with the matter ourselves. I ensured that all the family furniture and heirlooms were left in place, so the establishment will be ready for us when-ever we choose to go there.'

'That dishonest lawyer did everything you demanded, didn't he? How you must have cowed him!'

Jack grunted as he stood up. 'I did my best. He had much to lose had I exposed his crooked dealings. I suspect he got off lightly.'

As she watched Jack undress, her senses swum with such a surge of desire that she found it difficult to carry on their conversation, however important it might be to their future. She swallowed and said, 'I long to see the house.'

A frown gathered between Jack's fair brows. 'If we do go ahead with the wedding, I doubt the ceremony could take place here. We would have to travel to London, in which case your wish would be granted. But, as you can imagine, it may not be convenient to leave here so soon after the funeral.'

He hesitated. 'I do not like to say it, but it appears better that we postpone the ceremony for a short time. If you agree, I will send messengers to both our families. They were to arrive here on the Wednesday. That would be far too close to the funeral for comfort.'

'Oh, Jack!' wailed Thalia. 'Do we really have to postpone our wedding?'

Jack had finished disrobing and now he removed the comforter from her shoulders and flung it aside as he slid into the bed and took her into his arms. He kissed her briefly but hard. 'We could simply go down to the church and ask Mr Wyndham to marry us. Emily and Fanny would be there, of course, and Emily and Sidney—he is at the King's Arms—could be our witnesses. We could visit our families at a later date. Would you prefer that?'

'Yes,' said Thalia slowly. What possible reason could there be for her to delay her union with the man she loved? 'Yes, I think I would.'

'Then I will see the vicar tomorrow. We could be wed quietly this Saturday. Before the funeral.'

Thalia turned his face to hers, the stubble on his chin rasping her fingers. She looked into eyes shadowed by the flickering light of the single candle. 'Yes,' she said, and pulled his head forward so that her lips could reach his.

There seemed to be a strangeness about Jack, a detachment she had not noticed before. His lovemaking was as sensuous, as passionate as ever, leading her along the paths of sheer delight she had come to know so well.

Yet some element she could not name was missing. He was withholding part of himself. So it came as no surprise to her that, despite the erotic abrasion of his beard on her soft flesh as he ran his mouth over her breasts and down her body, her own response was not as complete as usual. After the many times they had come so wholly and satisfyingly together she could not but notice the lack, though Jack did not appear to.

She supposed she must be imagining things, that the strain of the last days had told on her more than she'd realised.

As she snuggled down and fell asleep in his strong arms her unease lessened.

When she awoke to the feel of butterfly kisses on her eyelids the unease evaporated altogether.

'They'll be wondering about the strange coach and team of horses in the stables,' he murmured. 'A stable boy sleeping in the loft helped me to unharness the beasts and put them in some empty stalls, but I offered him no explanation. I must attend to the matter as soon as I can.'

At that moment a tap on the door heralded the arrival of Tilly with cocoa and coals. Jack reached out an arm and pulled the bed-curtains close. It was not that they were ashamed of their relationship, but did not wish to flaunt it before the innocent Tilly. Once she had left the room, Jack chuckled.

'We shall not have to hide behind curtains after Saturday. You have not had second thoughts, my sweet?'

'No. But once they know who you are—'

'And who you are, Thalia. Will you introduce Fanny, or would you rather keep your secret? If Fanny attends the church, the village will see her and wonder. Word will spread—'

Thalia sighed. 'After all these years of keeping my secret, it would be sheer heaven to be able to acknowledge my daughter at last! But I am still a little concerned that Society will not receive me if they know I am Fanny's mother—I did not mention her existence when I was in London, although I intended to take her there as soon as possible and told Mama that I would never deny her. But I would not wish for you to be burdened with a wife ostracised by Society—'

'I thought we had settled the matter, Thalia. You will be my Countess, Fanny our adopted daughter. We do not need to paint the full picture for them, details will be unnecessary. Officially, to the villagers and retainers here, she will be your ward, living with Miss Wright for convenience. If Society ostracises you or casts a shadow over Fanny's future, then I shall bring certain persons to account for their own secret liaisons, which are many, according to friends who know.'

Thalia shifted uneasily. 'I should not like you to do that.'

'Nor I. But it will not be necessary. Your secret will be buried under a fabrication of half-truths and speculation which will soon die. For my sake the leading hostesses will accept you. Lady Jersey invited you and your mother to her drum at my request, you know— and I predict that you will soon be all the rage in London. The hostesses will be falling over themselves to entertain the Earl and Countess of Eardley.'

'You arranged the invitation? We had no idea!' Thalia gave a quiet chuckle. 'I shall not inform Mama! She would be vastly mortified!'

'I trust you are not?'

'It was naughty of you, Jack, but I have already forgiven you for the events of that evening. So,' she went on thoughtfully, 'I must trust that, if you, my lord, can ignore my ruined state, others will not dare to enquire too deeply or to criticise. Oh, Jack, Fanny will be legitimately ours—I shall not have to deny her before the world and will not suffer for my folly! How will I ever be able to thank you enough?'

'My dear girl, you have done nothing you need feel ashamed of! It was your courage in facing adversity and overcoming it that first won my admiration. As for thanking me—you have done that by agreeing to marry me.'

The sensation caused by Hamilton's announcement that he was, in truth, the Earl of Eardley and therefore the lord who would have been their master had his father not lost the property, shot through the household like the blast of an explosion.

'Oh, ma'am!' squeaked Tilly in complete awe. 'He's a lord and you'll be a lady!'

'We hope to be wed quietly, on Saturday, in Stonar church,' Jack told them. 'I hope to arrange the matter now. You are all invited to the ceremony, though—' he glanced at Thalia for approval before going on '—some must remain behind to keep vigil—arrange it among yourselves. There will be refreshments available at the King's Head afterwards, since it would be unseemly to return here to celebrate with Mr Tope still lying in his coffin.'

Jack left then to ride into the village. He had arrangements to make and letters to send by express mail.

Thalia tried to give some answers to the anxious questions thrown at her by Mrs Gale and others.

'We do not know who will inherit the estate,' she told them, 'but his lordship hopes to purchase the property back from whoever is the owner. If he does, you will all be assured of your places.'

This information was greeted with a murmur of approval. The prevailing gloom, despite the continued existence of the coffin in the drawing-room, lifted, though Pringle remained sunk in misery despite anything Thalia could say. His gentleman was dead and the new lord had his own man. This was a truth Thalia could not deny.

The ceremony they had intended to be a quiet affair turned into a village celebration. Thalia wore one of the new gowns she had brought from London, as yet unworn, a shimmering cream and oyster shot silk creation with a fashionable train at the back, over which was added, in deference to the weather, a short pelisse of amber velvet.

She trod up the aisle on Captain the Honourable Timothy Oldham's arm. The erstwhile lieutenant had profited from Varley's death, having been promoted in his place.

Word of Hamilton's identity had quickly spread to Sandwich and, in honour of his lordship's years as a major in the army, Colonel Pink attended the ceremony and Captain Oldham brought with him an escort of junior officers and men.

So it was that, after the simple service was over, they left the church beneath an archway of officers' drawn swords and walked from the churchyard between ranks of stiff-backed redcoats shouldering their muskets. The feared invasion had not come and the military had little to do.

She felt so proud and happy that she had to pinch herself to be certain she was not dreaming. Emily's honorific bob and murmured, 'I wish you every happiness, my lady,' finally convinced her of her new status.

But she had to protest. 'Emily, if you call me "my lady" once more I shall disown you! We have become friends, and you will continue to address me as Thalia, if you please!'

Fanny, subdued among so many strangers, awed by the occasion, was very quiet. Thalia hugged and kissed her, Jack lifted her to receive her kiss.

Fanny whispered, 'Goodbye, Mama.' And, shyly, 'Goodbye, Papa,' but so quietly that no one else heard.

And Sidney drove them back to Asham while the rest of the congregation repaired to the King's Arms.

Thalia explained to Mrs Gale that Miss Wright was the friend she visited so regularly, but no one enquired into the identity of the child. So even in Stonar, Fanny would eventually be known only as their adopted child. Thalia did not feel that this was denying Fanny her birthright. It was, rather, safeguarding her future prospects.

Any gentleman making a serious offer for her hand would have to be told the truth, but no one else need ever know who her natural parents were. Not only to Fanny but also to the world, Fanny would be their child. And, if people suspected the truth, they would scarcely risk Lord Eardley's displeasure by broadcasting it.

Actually, if Jack did not care if the truth emerged,

then neither did she. Both Fanny and Emily would simply continue as part of their family.

The yard of the King's Arms rang to the sound of cries and laughter as the ale flowed. In the parlour with the vicar, the officers and the cream of Stonar society, Thalia smiled up at her husband, admiring the cut of his black superfine coat, the pristine white lace at his throat and that frothing from beneath his lavishly embroidered waistcoat, the fit of his buff breeches, the shine on his high boots.

He carried a cocked hat under his arm, the very one, he informed her, that he had worn as an officer. It might be shabby, but he would not part with that particular article of headgear for the world.

In the early autumnal dusk, Treddle drove them back to Stonar Hall, as he had driven them out, the rest of the servants either walking or riding in Mr Tope's coach or one of the estate carts.

Jack had had his things carried to her rooms. Sidney had unpacked them and put them with hers in the bedroom. Several personal items—a book, an informal dressing-jacket, some writing materials—had been left ready for his use in her sitting-room. She noted the decanters and glasses set on a side table. The room had already acquired a more masculine air.

Thalia turned to him once the door had closed behind them and touched his lean cheek, smooth still after Pringle's ministrations. Sid had been too busy fetching Emily and Fanny to attend his master before the ceremony and it had given Pringle something to do. 'It seems strange to think that you now have every right to be here with me, that no more scandal can attach to our names!'

'We should be sleeping in the master suite,' he remarked as he moved away to remove his coat and poke new life into the fire.

'If you regain possession of Stonar, we shall. You would then have a dressing-room! But the suite would have to be refurbished first,' Thalia declared. She took off the cream velvet bonnet she had worn for the wedding and perched it on a stand, stroking the silken folds and smoothing the amber satin ribbons. 'I could not bear to sleep in it as it is. I would be too easily reminded of Mr Tope.'

Jack came up behind her and put his arms about her waist. His lips touched the nape of her neck in a butterfly caress. 'It shall be exactly as you wish, my wife.' He repeated the kiss. 'You would have stunned everyone today had we indulged in a Society wedding. You looked exquisite.'

Thalia leaned back into him, thrilled as ever by the feel of his body moulding to hers. 'Thank you, my lord! Do you regret our hurried wedding?'

'Who,' demanded Jack indignantly, 'obtained the special licence?'

Thalia laughed and turned in his arms to reach up to encircle his neck. 'You did! Oh, Jack, I do wish Mr Tope had lived to be there!'

'Do you not believe he was present, in spirit?'

Thalia hesitated slightly and then nodded. 'Yes, I think he was. He approved the match, you know.'

Jack grimaced. 'I believe he would have sold the estate to me had he lived.'

'He must have left it to someone. He did make a Will. I hope whoever it is will be amenable.'

Jack pressed her face into his shoulder and gazed into space over her head. Tension had entered his body.

'So do I.'

Thalia felt the tightening of his nerves, the stiffening of his sinews. He must want the estate very badly.

'Do not worry,' she advised softly. 'I know Stonar has family connections and I know you love it as much if not more than I do, but you could use the money to purchase another estate. There must be one somewhere to take its place. It would not be disastrous if you could not purchase this one.'

'Yes, it would,' said Jack.

Thalia could not understand his strange mood. He seemed to be anticipating some calamity and this was not in keeping with his normally cheerful disposition. His spirit of adventure appeared to have left him. Secretly, she worried that he was regretting his union with so unworthy a bride.

Yet his desire to possess her had, if anything, intensified. Sometimes, over the next days, there was almost a desperation in the way he took her. After one such wild, abandoned demonstration of his need, as he lay exhausted in her arms, she plucked up the courage to ask him what was wrong.

'What could be wrong?' he demanded gruffly.

'Something is troubling you, husband. Will you not tell me what it is?'

He heaved a great sigh and kissed her neck. 'There is nothing to tell, woman. It is just the thought of the funeral tomorrow, of all the formalities, the reading of the Will. . .'

His voice trailed off. So that was it! He was still anxious over the fate of Stonar Hall. She stroked his shoulder.

'Tomorrow it will all be over. We shall know exactly where we stand. Sleep now, my love. We are in for an arduous day and should try to gain our rest.'

He grunted. 'You are in the right as usual, dear wife.' He kissed her w:····ng mouth before turning on his side and pulling her against him. She felt the touch of his lips on her hair. 'Sleep well.'

'You too,' she murmured, loving the reassuring weight of her husband's arm across her waist.

They were close physically yet in other ways not quite as together as they had been before their marriage. She could not understand it. Worry over the fate of Stonar Hall must be the cause of his strange mood.

A carriage, swathed in black crêpe and drawn by four black horses, their harnesses dressed with black ostrich-feather plumes, bore Sebastian Tope to his last resting place in the churchyard at Stonar.

Monday had seen the arrival of an old business acquaintance from London and on the day several of his local friends descended on Stonar Hall to pay their last respects. But in essence Tope had been a private, even a lonely, man and the funeral cortège was short. Mr Wyndham conducted the service and subsequent interment with a dignity commensurate with the deceased's consequence as owner of Stonar Hall.

Back at the Hall, after refreshments had been served,

Mr Quiller, the lawyer, called the senior and most long-serving members of the staff to the library for the reading of the Will. They were accompanied by Mr Tope's former hunting crony and a friend with whom he had often played chess. Jack escorted Thalia.

'I will not prolong these proceedings,' began Mr Quiller, gazing at the company over the top of the small lenses perched on his nose. 'We executed this, the late Mr Sebastian Tope's Last Will and Testament, on the sixteenth day of April, in the year of Our Lord eighteen hundred and two.'

That had been her birthday. Thalia remembered noting that Mr Tope had chosen that day, on which he had made her a gift of a beautiful mahogany writing-box, to consult with his lawyers. She had not known that he was making a new Will.

The reading began with small bequests of money to many of the staff with larger, generous sums left to Shepherd, Pringle and Mrs Gale. His riding horses went to his hunting friend and his inlaid chess table and ivory pieces to his chess opponent. He had made minor bequests of either money or artifacts to other friends and set aside a sum of money for distribution to any servant not otherwise mentioned, who was in his service at his death.

Quiller paused for a moment. Thalia sat close to Jack, her shoulder touching his. She turned to look at him with raised brows, enjoying the joke despite the sombreness of the occasion. Jack would have been included in that distribution of funds had he not abandoned his disguise and acquainted Mr Tope with the truth before the old man died.

Her name had not been mentioned yet. She guessed Sebastian Tope had left her rather more than the rest of his servants, for she knew she had held a special place in his affections. Yet when Mr Quiller began to speak again and she took in the import of what he was saying, she sat in stunned disbelief.

Mr Tope had left her the residue of his estate, all his money and chattels not already distributed—and Stonar Hall itself.

She *owned* Stonar Hall.

She gazed wide-eyed at Jack. He returned her look with a wry smile and resumed his task of picking fluff from the black sleeve of his coat.

The buzz of astonishment almost drowned Mr Quiller's voice as he read Sebastian Tope's final words. Congratulations showered over her head. Mr Quiller assured her that she would be welcome to remain in residence until the Will was proved and she became the legal owner of the property.

Jack kissed her and congratulated her. But his manner lacked conviction.

He was wary of her good fortune. That was only to be expected, since he had intended to purchase the property back. But now, since she was his wife, it was as good as his already.

She realised what had been worrying her. He had shown no surprise at the contents of the Will.

Of course he had not! A copy of the Will had been among the papers in Sebastian Tope's desk! Jack had admitted rifling through those drawers. She had not thought about it much since for she had quickly come to trust him, but during the search he had most probably seen a copy of the Will.

Thoughts and speculations seethed in her mind until, at long last, they were able to retire to her rooms. She felt cold, detached. Jack, she could tell, was trying unsuccessfully to disguise his unease.

She blundered straight in, probing to the core of her hurt.

'You knew,' she accused. 'Small wonder that you sought to secure my hand as speedily as possible!'

Jack leaned his elbow on the mantelshelf and placed one foot on the fender. Flames licked up the chimney, casting changing shadows over his face. He did not look at her.

'Yes,' he admitted, staring into the heart of the fire. 'But how could I tell you? For all I knew it was an old Will, no longer valid. But knowing that you might inherit made it damnably difficult for me to approach you. You made it plain that you were completely unaware of Tope's intentions.

'The moment I realised just how much my happiness depended upon making you my wife, I also knew that I could not countenance marrying you until I had secured the property by other means. I guessed what you would think. And so Hamilton, the footman, refused to commit himself and departed for London in an endeavour to sort out his own affairs.'

Thalia eyed him intently, longing to believe him. 'Which involved threatening that London lawyer into providing the money with which to purchase Stonar Hall from Mr Tope?'

'Exactly. And into restoring the town house to my

ownership. Had I been able to carry out my plan, Tope would then, presumably, still have left you his fortune, but I would have regained possession of the Eardley properties by my own efforts, not by means of a fortunate marriage.'

Thalia sank down on the settee and plucked nervously at the black ribbons decorating her dress. 'You would control that fortune. You desperately need the money.'

'My dear love, do you sincerely believe that I married you for that? In the end, knowledge of your likely inheritance became the single most difficult aspect of our relationship. Once I had revealed my true identity I longed to make a clean breast of the entire affair, but that would have been to betray the secret of Tope's bequest. And his condition had deteriorated to the extent that I could no longer approach him regarding the purchase of the property. I was in a devilishly difficult position.'

So that was the cause of the sense of estrangement she had felt. 'And what do you now propose?' Thalia could not eradicate the chill from her voice, for it lingered in her heart.

Jack stirred, turned to face her fully. 'What I would like above everything is for you to sell Stonar Hall to me. I know the estates will be united by our marriage, but I shall not feel that I have recovered the family fortunes as I should without rectifying the losses over which my father took his life. For that to happen, the property must be restored to the Earldom of Eardley.'

Thalia drew a breath. What he was saying made glorious sense. 'I see.'

He nodded. 'Capital. I would suggest that the money I pay you for Stonar is put into a trust fund, on which you may draw for life but which, upon your death, goes to Fanny, though it would continue to be administered by trustees if, God forbid, you died before she reached the age of five and twenty.'

Thalia frowned. 'You wish Fanny to benefit upon my death?'

'Indeed.'

'But what if I live to a ripe old age?'

'The trust could allow for part of it to be released to her at any time you choose. Together with the dowry I shall provide, the prospect of such a fortune will assure her of the expectation of a good marriage.' He smiled suddenly and her heart lurched as the old, teasing Hamilton appeared. 'The only disadvantage is that when she makes her come-out we may have to beware of fortune-hunters!'

He moved swiftly to sit beside her and took her hands in his. 'Thalia, my dearest love, believe me—I have tried to behave honourably, despite the difficulties. I need not have suggested a rush marriage as I did, but I was desperate to secure the hand of the only woman with whom I wish to share my life. I love you, my darling. Tell me, would you have had me hang back?'

Tears had begun to glisten in Thalia's eyes. 'No,' she whispered. 'And you shall have Stonar Hall, my love. But although you had said you loved me, I could not help but wonder whether you truly wished to wed me for the fortune you knew I would inherit.'

'I had, at one point, in my desperation, contemplated making a marriage of convenience to restore my fortunes. But having fallen in love with you—although I would not admit it at that point, even to myself—I knew such a course would be impossible. I wanted to wed no one else, but could not marry you because you might inherit something I badly wanted. My motive had to be pure.'

'Oh, Jack,' whispered Thalia huskily.

Jack chuckled softly, discomfited by his own confession. But his next words held all the sincerity Thalia could wish. 'Any more than I could have taken you to bed and left you to suffer the consequences without offering you the protection of my name.'

Thalia gave a shaky laugh as the tears at last overflowed and trickled down her cheeks. 'You were the most honourable footman I had ever come across. But Lord Eardley would have been embarrassed beyond all bearing had he been compelled to wed a low-born female who already had an illegitimate daughter!'

'Lord Eardley,' said Jack earnestly, sipping the tears from her lids and then kissing them, 'had already decided that, whoever Mrs Thalia Marsh turned out to be, she possessed enough quality in herself to equip her admirably to be his wife.' He kissed her mouth. 'Truly, my love. I wanted to regain Stonar Hall, but not at the expense of losing you as my wife.'

Their next kiss was interrupted by a knock on the door.

'That will be Pringle, come to see me,' murmured Jack. 'I intend to retain his services as valet, if you agree. Sidney is happy to be my general factotum and companion. For years now he has been more of a friend than a servant.'

'Of course,' murmured Thalia, sitting up straight and smoothing down her dress. 'Come in,' she called.

After Pringle had been told of Jack's decision and left, effusive in his thanks, Jack returned to sit beside her on the settee.

'These rooms are not suitable if we are both to have personal servants,' he declared, 'and you must shortly engage a lady's maid. Should we not consider moving to the main guest suite until the master suite is refurbished?'

Thalia nodded, though reluctantly. 'I will order the move tomorrow. It is not in use at present. But Jack, I shall be sorry to leave these rooms.' She looked at him, all her love reflected in her eyes. 'I have found my greatest happiness here, in your arms.'

'Your greatest happiness so far, my love,' corrected Jack as he once again pulled her against him. 'I believe we shall enjoy even greater felicity in the future.'

All constraint between them had vanished. And Thalia, savouring the outpouring of tender, committed love lavished upon her by her husband, believed him.

Historical Romance™

Coming next month

LADY DECEIVER
Helen Dickson

Miss Cordelia Hamilton-King was tired of the frivolous life, and wanted—horrors!—to work. She refused her influential father's help, and became Miss Delia King, secretary, at Stanfield Hall in Norfolk. That one small deception caused havoc.

Captain Alexander Frankland, newly restored to his ancestral home after the war, had connections with the Hamilton-Kings that Delia, in her growing love for her employer, knew nothing about…

A COMFORTABLE WIFE
Stephanie Laurens

Miss Antonia Mannering had made plans, and Lord Philip Ruthven featured largely. They had been childhood friends, but had not seen each other for years. She knew Philip was popular with the ladies, but he had never married any of them. Wouldn't he now be ready to set up his nursery? If she could prove to him that she could run his home, not disgrace him in Society, and be a *comfortable* wife for him, surely he would be prompted to propose to her—that she might fall in love had never occurred to her!

ARE YOU A FAN
OF MILLS & BOON®
HISTORICAL ROMANCES™?

If YOU are a regular United Kingdom buyer of Mills & Boon Historical Romances you might like to tell us your opinion of the books we publish to help us in publishing the books *you* like.

Mills & Boon have a Reader Panel for their Historical Romances. Each person on the panel receives a questionnaire every third month asking her for *her* opinion of the books she has read in the past three months. All people who send in their replies will have a chance of winning ONE YEAR'S FREE Historicals, sent by post—48 books in all. If you would like to be considered for inclusion on the Panel please give us details about yourself below. All postage will be free. Younger readers are particularly welcome.

Year of birth.............................Month ....

Age at completion of full-time education...

Single ☐   Married ☐   Widowed ☐   Divorced ☐

Your name (print please) ....

Address...

....

.... Postcode ....

THANK YOU! PLEASE PUT IN ENVELOPE AND POST TO
MILLS & BOON READER PANEL, FREEPOST SF195
PO BOX 152, SHEFFIELD S11 8TE